CANOES&COFFEE

THE COTTAGE COMPANION

Volume 1 - Version 1.1

CANOES&COFFEE
THE COTTAGE COMPANION

Kenneth Roland
& Friends

Dorian Blackwood

Kyle Rogers

Steve Boose

Matt Thurston

Hallie Ranta

Stephen Young

Special thanks to the guest writers for their contributions.

Thanks to the advanced readers; Andy Heller and Chris Stavropoulos

To Cousin Mary for allowing me to experience a cottage.

To my wife Rebecca for encouraging me to bring this project to life.

To my father, who always tried to follow what I was up to.

To my mother for subtly encouraging me to try something "different".

To Harry Scanlan for inspiring the boat stories.

To my father-in-law John Dickinson for continuing to read my stories.

To the crew and patrons of Writing Battle for inspiring me to continue writing and trying new genres.

To Ed and Amanda for their insights into what makes a great short story.

To Rebaken Enterprises for letting me put as many dedications as I want

And especially to you, the reader that made it this far down the page. Thank you.

Foreword

There is a magic to reading at the cottage. Time moves slower and our brains allow the stories to take root in our minds as nature surrounds us. I have never owned a cottage, but have been lucky enough to be invited to friends and family's dwellings, as well as to rent a few. On bright, sunny mornings as the sun stretches across a dock, the pages of a book can feel like a blanket for your soul.

Stories are your companions during quiet rainy days and in the still, solitude of the evening. Don't get me wrong, cottage time is never just about relaxing with the view, it's the worn deck of cards, the half done puzzles splayed across the table and the laughter of family staying up too late talking. It can also be the squeals of excitement as someone stands for the first time on water skis, or the thrill of a motor boat bouncing across the lake. It's about that feeling of awe at spotting wildlife and the peace that overtakes you on a winding hike. Cottages and the ability to "get away from it all" inspire memories that live deep in our consciousness and nestle into our lives.

This anthology was built on those feelings, from tweaking the fear in all of us as thunder roars during the dark of night, to the joy of finding a new passion, the stories in this anthology flow from one emotion to another. The book is built in sections for your current mood. Creepy and spooky in Thunder Storms, adventure and mystery in Rain Showers, coziness and love in Cool Evenings, and humour and fun in Warm Days.

To make it truly the ultimate book for the Cottage, I've included puzzles, and games throughout, as well as a log for each story so you can leave behind a legacy for the next cottage dweller. If you feel anything is missing, include it in your review on Amazon and I'll be sure to look into it for the next anthology.

I really hope you enjoy it, it has been an adventure to create.

Kenneth Roland

How to Use This Book

This anthology is broken into four sections. Each section has loose genre attached to it. Thunder Storms - Horror and Thriller, Rain Showers - Adventures and Mystery, Cool Evenings - Family and Romance, Warm Days - Humour and Light Hearted. Each story should take less than 30 minutes to read, so you can pick the book up for short periods of time and read at random, or have at it and attempt to read them back to back.

After each story is a log page. Use that to track who has read the story, when and what their thoughts were. It's an interesting way to gather feedback from lots of cottage guests over a period of time and see the history of the book as different people flip through it and tuck it away again.

Scattered throughout the book are puzzles, feel free to photocopy, or otherwise reproduce the puzzles as you see fit. If you do them in pencil, you may be able to erase them a few times.

CANOES&COFFEE
THE COTTAGE COMPANION
Contents

Thunder Storms

Rain Showers

Cool Evenings

Warm Days

Thunder Storms

The Old Manse

Kenneth Roland

Rachel didn't believe she had ever witnessed a thunderstorm like this back home. Lightning licked the sky, criss-crossing from cloud to cloud, then spiking to the ground as peals of thunder would shake the old manse where she was curled up on a chaise lounge. When they first found this old church home on the vacation rental website it had seemed like a literal godsend. Her and Ben had called Lucas and Olivia right away, excited to book a couples weekend. Now she was beginning to wish they had found somewhere with a gas fireplace. Ben was currently bent at the old hearth attempting to start a fire from what logs had been left by the last tenants. Olivia and Lucas had gone to explore the small house. Rachel imagined they wouldn't be long. She heard Ben curse and went over to him, resting her hand on his back as she bent down to look at the situation.

"These are never going to light," Ben said, pushing at the charcoal logs with a metal poker. "I think they're burnt out. We're going to need some kindling." Rachel sighed. Ben pushed his shaggy hair out of his eyes and looked at her. "What are the odds we'll find anything inside? Anything outside is going to be drenched."

Rachel always liked Ben's eyes. It was the first thing that attracted her to him. They sparkled in a hazel brilliance. You could believe you were the only thing in the world when they looked at you. "Maybe the basement?" she said.

"Oh yeah!" he said excitedly, standing. "Lucas! Did you guys get to the basement yet?"

"Not yet," came the reply from one of the two interior doors. The living room was the first thing you walked into when you came into the house. There was a door to a large kitchen and dining area, and another to a hallway with two bedrooms, a bath, and an old study. Lucas and Olivia returned from the hallway. "Check out what we found," Lucas said as they entered. He was carrying an old leather bound book, cream colored pages showing at the edges. A large crack of thunder suddenly shook the room and Olivia jumped.

"Oh God!" she stammered, and they all began to laugh. "That scared the shit out of me!" she laughed.

"Check this out," Lucas handed the book to Ben.

"Do you want a glass of wine Rachel?" Olivia asked as she went towards the kitchen. "These two and a book could be the rest of the night, I mean, what if they decide to try and read it?" Rachel laughed and nodded.

"Har, har," moaned Lucas. "I read a lot until I met you. You're just too distracting." Olivia wiggled her butt as she went into the kitchen area. Rachel began to follow then turned back to the boys.

"Before you get too deep into your book, can you help Ben try and get a fire going, it's freezing in here."

"She's cold twenty-four-seven," Ben said.

"Olivia too!" laughed Lucas.

Ben put the book down on the old oak coffee table and headed towards the kitchen. "Let's check the basement for wood, then I'll take a look at your book."

Lucas followed him, "It's a diary. I think it's like the first minister that lived here or whatever." They passed the girls attempting to uncork a bottle and went to an old wooden door. The individual boards were visible and a lift latch kept it closed. Ben thumbed the black metal and pulled the door towards him. Plank wood steps led down into darkness. He twisted his lips, examining the cobwebs. A small ledge ran along the edge of the stairs containing rusty tools, jars, and bottles. Dirt was everywhere and a damp, musty smell wafted up from the lower level.

"Well, there's not going to be wood down there," Ben said. He started to push the door back shut.

"What are you talking about?" Lucas laughed. "Don't be a baby. Where's the light switch?"

"I'm not seeing one," Ben said. He stepped out of the way. If Lucas wanted to go down, he wasn't going to stop him. Lucas pulled his phone out of his pocket. He swiped it a few times until the flash lit up. He began to twist the phone holding it out into the stairwell. It shone on the worked stone of the main floor and then down into the stacked stones of the basement. The floor at the bottom appeared to only be about six feet down. He finally spied a hanging string in the center of the stairs and yanked on it. Soft warm light glowed into the stairwell. It appeared another light had come on in the basement as shadows of the stairs appeared on the wall. Neither light was very bright.

"There ya go!" Lucas shouted. "C'mon, let's burn something."

A screech suddenly filled the kitchen and the two boys jumped, startled. Lucas almost fell down the stairs. The girls began to laugh hysterically. They had to balance their wine glasses to stop them from sloshing out onto the floor. Ben collected himself and shook his finger at them. "Ok, that's not funny, Lucas could have died."

"And you could've shit your pants," Rachel laughed.

"We're going downstairs …" Lucas yelled as he put his foot on the next creaky step. "If you're lucky we'll come back." Ben turned to follow him.

"Maybe we'll be lucky and they won't come back," Olivia chuckled.

Lucas and Ben could hear running water. Likely the rain in the downspouts, or leaking into the basement somewhere. The basement led from the stairs out under the rest of the house. Thick posts held up large wood joists for the floor. The cavities between the joists were filled with things hung on nails, cobwebs, and dust. A single lightbulb hung just beside the staircase. It illuminated just under the stairs where there was a collection of logs and kindling for burning. "Ah hah!" rejoiced Lucas, quickly bending to pick some up.

Ben looked out into the basement. It was stacked floor to ceiling with antique furniture and tools. Bits of wood, metal, and glass seemed to be everywhere. There was only a small path left that appeared to turn and twist as it wandered through the piles. "Do you see this?" he said to Lucas.

"What?" Lucas stood and turned. He took the time to inspect the piles. An old doll carriage, some kind of drilling machine, and a wash tub were in the pile closest to him. "What the hell is all this?" he said, stepping towards it. He picked up a rusted metal tool with handles like scissors that expanded out into two huge hooks. "What the hell would you use this for?"

"Maybe for ice blocks or something?" Ben scratched his hair. He stuck his head slightly into the corridor formed by the junk. "It goes on forever, it's like a maze in there."

"Weird," said Lucas, tossing the (maybe) ice block holders back into the pile with a clang. He shook his head. "Ok," he said excitedly. "Let's go burn some stuff." Clapping his hands together, he turned back to the wood pile.

The boys' hands were too full to close the basement door. They trundled through the kitchen with their load of wood. Ben was first and could see the back of the girls' heads as they sat on the couch. They were close together and looking at something directly in front of them. "Guess who's got wood?" he laughed.

"Oh my God, Ben," Rachel sighed. The boys dropped their piles by the fireplace. Ben immediately began to stack the kindling around the old logs. "What made you pick up this book, Lucas?" Rachel asked.

"What do you mean?" asked Lucas. He was brushing his hands off on his khaki pants.

"It's a ratty old diary, why did you think to look at it?"

"I don't know. I like old stuff, you should see the basement, it's full of old stuff by the way. Anyway all the other books looked like text books or bibles or something, the diary stood out."

"Did you read any of it?"

"Just glanced in it and saw it was handwritten. Why? Did you guys find something juicy in there?" Lucas smiled and rubbed his hands together.

"Not really juicy, more like disturbing," Olivia said. "I think this guy was a psychopath."

"What? You guys are letting the storm get to you. He was a minister. Plus it was like a hundred years ago. Times were different."

"Listen to this," Rachel said, pulling the book closer and moving her feet off the couch onto the floor. "The children are sad, 'cause the children are bad, heathens to God, they go under the sod," she read.

Ben whistled from his position by the fire. "Jesus," spat Ben, "that's a bit harsh."

"Right?" said Olivia, she turned to Rachel. "Read him the one from November 11th."

"Oh yeah!" Rachel began to flip the pages of the book, "Listen to this, *'November 11th, 1924. Stephen Williams and his wife brought their son John to see me tonight. He had the devil in him as surely as I write. Moles of all colors across his back. The extraction was unpleasant yet necessary. May his soul return to the maker. May the devil be trapped in the child's body forever. I reckon the world is better off tonight'.* What the hell does that mean?"

"Geez," said Lucas.

"Fires going!" Ben said excitedly, standing to reveal a large blaze. They saw lightning out the window and then the room went black. The fire created shadows that danced around the room. It was only a few seconds until a huge crack of thunder made them all start.

"Just in time," Lucas sighed.

"What the hell," moaned Olivia. "Hopefully this doesn't last." They all waited, as though the power would come back if they just stayed quiet. The fire crackled and popped. Rain pinged against the windows. No power returned.

"Well I need a beer," said Ben. "Oh!" he exclaimed suddenly, "What the hell?" The girls turned to see what Ben was looking at. The kitchen was glowing with a dull light that dimly poured out from the basement onto the ceiling.

"Maybe it's on a battery," Lucas said. "We did leave the basement light on."

"That seems odd," Ben said over his shoulder as he walked into the kitchen. "But you know the beer won't stay cold with the power out. Better get into 'em."

"Yeah, grab me one!" Lucas shouted.

Ben opened the fridge and felt around in the dark for two cans. The door blocked the light from the basement. It slowly faded to a glow, then disappeared altogether leaving Ben in the dark. As he closed the fridge door with his foot, he shouted into the living room, "Guess it wasn't a *good* battery." There was a loud bang in the basement that echoed up the stairs. "What the hell was that?"

"Did you fall?" Rachel shouted from the other room.

"That wasn't me," Ben said as he passed a beer to Lucas over the heads of the girls. "Something fell in the basement."

"Should you go check it out?" Rachel asked.

"Hell no," said Ben, opening his beer. "That basement's a deathtrap. It's piled with junk."

"And he's scared," Lucas joked.

Rachel took the diary and went over to sit by the fire. She pulled her legs up into the chair and flipped towards the end of the book. Olivia brought their wine glasses and sat on the hearth. She placed a glass on each side of her.

"Listen to this one," said Rachel, " '*April 16th, 1925. Storms all day. The noises continue. I believe the demons are returning. I stayed at the church most of the day. They wouldn't dare enter the house of the Lord. Upon returning to the manse I discovered the place in shambles. Hung more crosses in the stairwell.'* I think he's starting to go crazy."

"Sounds like it," said Olivia, holding her glass. "Serves him right if he was hurting kids." She took a long drink.

"Oh look!" exclaimed Rachel flipping some more pages. "The writing gets super messy at the end. He's not even putting dates anymore." She flipped a few more pages then read, *"There's no stopping them. God has forsaken me truly now. Cursed be the demons! I've hidden my sins in the word of God where they can't get a hold of it. May they burn in hell for all eternity."*

"Holy crap," commented Ben, "Do you really want to keep reading that thing?"

"Was there a bible in the study?" Rachel asked, ignoring Ben.

"Oh!" exclaimed Olivia, jumping up. "We should totally check! What if there's something hidden in it!" She took long strides towards the hallway. Rachel quickly got up and followed.

Lucas looked over at Ben, "Well, they're having fun," he shrugged.

Olivia stopped when she hit the dark hallway. Rachel almost ran into her, diary in one hand and wine glass in the other. Olivia pulled her phone from her back pocket and swiped on it. Nothing happened. "It's dead," she said in disbelief.

"Figures," Lucas chuckled from the living room. "Use mine, I was just using it downstairs." He pulled out his phone and attempted to swipe it open as well. "Hmm," he muttered, "mine's dead too."

"What?" Ben questioned looking at his own dark cell phone. "The lightning strike must have caused an electromagnetic pulse or something. How can all the phones be dead?"

Lucas grabbed an old antique candle holder from the mantle. "Did you know they call these chambersticks?" He asked as he took the candle from it, sticking the wick in the fire. "Cause they used to use them to go to their chambers, it sounds …" he trailed off as he turned to see everyone glaring at him. "Ok, too much, I just found it interesting." He walked to the front of the group and led them down the hallway.

They entered the dark study. Bookshelves lined one wall from floor to ceiling. An antique desk was under the window with brochures for local attractions spread out on it. There was a guest book and a pen made to look like a quill. The third wall had two cozy chairs with a table between them. Lightning lit up the trees outside the window and for a moment the room was brightly lit. Lucas moved to the far corner and held the chamberstick up to the top shelf. The girls stood back and eyed the shelves keenly. Ben sat heavily into one of the chairs and drank his beer.

Lucas lowered the light to the second shelf, "This is where I found the diary," he stated, pointing to an empty spot on the shelf. There was slightly less dust on the shelf in a straight line to the edge where he had pulled it out. The other books looked old. Their spines all faded to the same rusty brown, moss green, and gray. They quickly scanned the shelf and moved to the next.

"What is that?" Olivia suddenly whispered and everyone stopped moving. There was a low, quiet thud. After a few seconds, it repeated. Again and again. Thud. Thud. Thud. It was coming from below them.

"That's weird," Ben said, sitting up. "I can feel it in my feet now." He looked down at his sandals.

"Somebody has to go down there," Rachel stated. "Something is making that noise." Everyone looked at each other but no one made a move.

"Let's find the bible first," Olivia finally stated. They began searching the shelves faster as the noises below them grew louder. Another flash lit the room temporarily and Rachel saw the embossed letters of B-I-B-L-E stand out from a large spine. "I got it!" she whispered excitedly.

"Why are you whispering?" Ben asked from his chair.

"I don't know," whispered Rachel. She pulled the book out from the shelf and Lucas held the candle over it. She opened it and they all gasped.

The book had been completely hollowed out. Only the edges of the pages remained and in the center was a wooden box with a hinged lid. Olivia grabbed the box and pulled it out of the book. Rachel quickly closed the book and placed sideways back on the shelf. Ben got up from his chair to see what they had found. The thudding in the basement grew louder. The speed was the same. Thud. Thud. Thud. Olivia was shaking as she turned the box in one hand until the clasp faced her. It felt like no one was breathing as she unhooked the small metal latch. She opened the box slowly like she expected a snake to pop out. In the flickering light of the candle they could make out small black and white photos with white scalloped borders. The one on top appeared to be a girl with two tight braids pulled over her shoulders. She was wearing a plain dress with a coat over it. Rachel reached into the box and picked it out. BAM. The house shook and the group jumped as one. All eyes turned to the door of the study as a muted light crept across the edge of the door in the hallway. The light didn't really illuminate anything, it was a pale iridescent fog that floated along the floor.

"Put it back!" Ben shouted.

"No!" Rachel said. "I think they want their photos. I don't think they knew where they were." She flicked the photo at the light, like throwing a playing card. It twirled and soared, landing just inside the door. A buzzing started and Rachel screamed. She reached into her back pocket and pulled out her phone. It was vibrating constantly. "It's warm," she said as it shook in her hands. The screen lit up with the same photo of the girl she had just thrown. Slowly it brightened, and became color. The phone screen was now brighter than the candle. All four couldn't look away, losing whatever night vision they had. Lightning flashed out the window and the screen broke, fragmenting the picture as it faded away into darkness.

The luminescent fog had drifted into the room, it floated to the edge of the photo and stopped. After a moment it surrounded the image and absorbed it. The light briefly turned a bluish color, before fading back to a soft yellow. Lightning flashed outside, but the group moved closer to the desk at the window. The fog appeared to grow, no longer just settling on the floor but raising up like a snake head towards them.

"It can have all the photos!" Olivia shouted and reaching out as far as she could, she dumped the box onto the fog. The photos caused the fog to separate and distort as they floated through it to land on the floor. A breeze came into the room from nowhere and the candle flickered out, its smoke trailing off in a circle around the room. The light began to grow again, twisting into a funnel.

The tail of the lit fog slithered into the room and was engulfed in the blowing funnel of light.

Ben's hair was now blowing across his face, "Let's go out of here!" He shouted and pulled on Rachel's arm, edging around the light tornado in the center of the room and heading for the door. Lucas and Olivia went around the other side of the light and ran through the door after them. No one stopped until they were standing outside the house, near the entrance to the church. All four just stared at the house as it glowed brightly, almost as though it was on fire, yet there were no flames.

"We passed a Holiday Inn about an hour before we got here …" Lucas whispered.

"Let's go." said Ben, his hair matted down onto his face with the rain.

"But I forgot," started Olivia, but she was cut off.

"We can get everything tomorrow, I'm not going back in there tonight," Lucas said.

The light in the house suddenly flared out and all was blackness. Ding. Ding. Lucas pulled out his phone. He turned it to the others. "Severe weather alert" was on the screen in white block letters on black. "That was messed up," he said.

The four quickly piled back into Ben's hatchback. "Am I crazy," said Rachel, "Or just before my phone smashed, did the picture smile?"

Ben steered the car out of the church parking lot and onto the paved road.

No one answered Rachel.

A small ball of light floated out of the old manse and followed the car as it drove away.

WHO	WHEN	RATING

Notes:

☆☆☆☆☆

Notes:

☆☆☆☆☆

Notes:

☆☆☆☆☆

Notes:

☆☆☆☆☆

Notes:

☆☆☆☆☆

Notes:

☆☆☆☆☆

Notes:

☆☆☆☆☆

Notes:

☆☆☆☆☆

Lefty Cottage Crossword

This is a duplicate of the puzzle on Page 13 for left handed people.

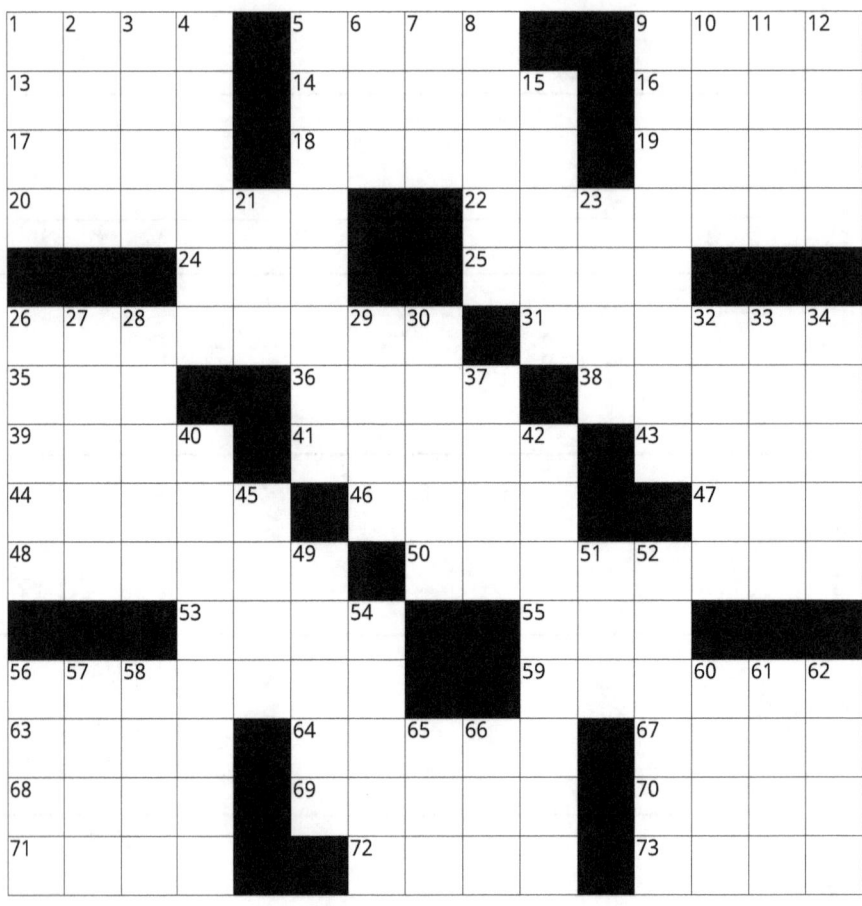

Across

1 Is in a play
5 Farm unit
9 Carol opener
13 Take it out on the lake
14 Shade of blue
16 Sheltered, at sea
17 A prom rental
18 You click it
19 "Understood"
20 Pep
22 Deep-fried appetizer
24 Seems like forever
25 Too colorful
26 Taxi waiting area
31 They come and go
35 Prefix meaning "three"
36 Turn sharply
38 Mail-order pioneer
39 Diana of "Game of
   Thrones"
41 Community rec. centers
43 Doctors "Now!"
44 Hawaiian pool house
46 A space cloud
47 Airport screen org.
48 Sun blockers
50 Prancer, for one
53 Tidy
55 Use oars
56 Vacation home
59 Changes chemically
63 Track shape
64 Green-skinned pear
67 " __, right!"
68 News article intro
69 Walk loudly
70 Supermodel Taylor
71 Med School subj.
72 Sailing the seven __
73 Grade Sch. Level

Righty Cottage Crossword

Solution on next page, be careful not to peek!

Down

1 Up to the task
2 Quarter, for one
3 Not wild
4 Mall makeup
5 Kind of surplus store
6 Dove's sound
7 Street Fighter protaganist
8 Painter's stand
9 Salon supply
10 In addition
11 Fishing rod attachment
12 Ship's backbone
15 Building blocks
21 Obtained

23 Your inner workings
26 PC key combo for "copy"
27 Helvetica look-alike
28 Firm refusal
29 Nautilus captain
30 Interior designer's concern
32 Starbucks order
33 Rub out
34 Astronomical red giant
37 Hard to find
40 Knight's glove
42 Saddle attachments
45 Thought
49 Epic tales
51 San Francisco's ___ Valley

52 ___ Johnson, a.k.a. The Rock
54 Camping shelters
56 Coke or Pepsi
57 Bakery fixture
58 I did it!
60 Put a roof on
61 Steal
62 Leveling wedge
65 Average guy
66 Granny, in Germany

Old Souls

Kenneth Roland

Watching the road drift by, Maeve was day-dreaming about how amazing this vacation would be. Linda had found them the perfect cabin to rent online. Two bedrooms, a view of the lake and a price that was almost too good to be true. They packed and began the ten hour drive by eight in the morning. Grabbing coffee and breakfast, they blasted tunes for the first few hours, chatted for a few hours more, and then slowly drifted off into their own worlds. Linda was driving, eyes focused on the road ahead. Maeve couldn't tell what she was thinking about, or even if she was thinking about anything. For herself, Maeve was just watching the scenery pass by; a huge variety of trees, rocks and vegetation. Not many cars now that they were in the north.

A large painted plywood sign for "Last Gas" was on the side of the road. Faded and chipped it advertised cola, firewood, and marshmallows. "Let's stop here," Maeve said, pushing herself up in her seat.

Linda blinked and looked around, "Oh yeah, good idea." She twisted her head to stretch her neck. "I was lost in my own world there."

"Same," Maeve stated, slipping her feet into flip flops.

The noise of the tires grew louder as they pulled off the main road into the gravel parking lot. Linda eased the car into a spot beside the gas island and stopped. "Put forty bucks in," Maeve said, "I'll go in and see what they have."

"For sure, I want to come in too, I love these old general stores," Linda replied.

The store was done in wood siding, with a house attached to it. The owners obviously lived here. Maeve smiled as she pulled open the door and a bell rang. So classic. The inside smelled of cut wood and pine needles. The floor creaked as she walked across it. She didn't see anyone and began looking through the few aisles that were there. Ramen noodles, canned food, bags of chips and other non-perishables. There was a section of souvenirs, mostly moose keychains with red maple leafs on them. The back of the store had birthday cards and rain suits, Maeve wondered if they ever sold anything besides gas and cigarettes. She picked up a dust covered book, "The Inconvenient Indian" by Thomas King. Someone had once tried to bring some culture to the little shop, but found the clientele uninterested. She put the book back down.

"Where are you girls headed?" came a woman's deep voice.

Maeve jumped, startled. She turned to see the woman behind the counter. A faded blue vest over a buffalo plaid shirt. Her blond hair was turning gray and pulled into a large ponytail that was pinned up to her head. Her square face was rugged and wrinkled. "You surprised me, sorry," Maeve said.

The woman laughed, "Well you're obviously Canadian, apologizing for me."

Maeve smiled and felt more at ease. "Yeah, we're just up from Toronto. Trying to get away for a week."

"I don't blame ya," the woman said. "I'd try to get away from Toronto too. Where are you staying then?"

"We got a vacation rental on Whitefish Bay, called The Shaws," Maeve continued to browse as she spoke, slowly moving towards the counter.

"The Shaws?" the woman clucked her tongue. "You'd have to pay me to stay there."

"Oh no," Maeve looked up at the woman, "why's that? The pictures looked great."

"Oh yeah, the place is nice enough, but nothing good ever happened at The Shaws. It's got too much history, if you know what I mean."

The bell on the door rang as Linda came in, she smiled at the woman behind the counter. "What do you mean 'too much history'? Is it a murder house?" Maeve asked.

Linda's smile faded and her eyes widened, "What are we talking about?"

The woman behind the counter held up her hands, "It's not a murder house."

"Thank God," Maeve said.

"The Shaws was built on bad land. No one wanted it when they built there, no one wants it now. It's been for sale since the 70's. Makes sense that they would try to rent it. Gotta make something out of it."

"Oh c'mon," Linda said. "Bad land?" She smirked. "Is this like a hazing you do?"

The woman shrugged. "Not me. I'm sure you'll all have a great time. Good that there's a group of you. I'm just glad I'm not the one going up there."

Maeve and Linda looked at each other. They'd never been referred to as a group before.

"Did you find anything?" Linda asked, and Maeve shook her head.

As she placed two bills on the counter Linda said "We'll stop by on the way back and let you know how it went."

"Sounds good, I hope you all enjoy it." The woman tucked the bills in the register, "Sincerely, I do."

It was quiet for the rest of the ride. It took about thirty minutes to get from the shop to The Shaws. Marked with a simple wood sign on a stake at the side of the road. A white "For sale by owner" placard was laying in the tall grass next to the sign. Linda turned into the narrow driveway, watching the ditches carefully on either side.

"Must be a storm coming or something," she said. "The car says it's only eighteen degrees out, but it was twenty-two when we left the shop."

"Weird," said Maeve, "It looks clear."

The driveway wound between tall pines that seemed to push in on either side. Once in a while a branch would rub against the side of the car, as if caressing it while it passed by. The branches were low and overgrown, reaching out into the laneway with scrubby limbs. Linda leaned forward to look through the windshield, hoping the bit of extra space would give her better vision.

"This isn't a good sign for the state of the cabin," Maeve said, watching the ragged trees slowly pass. The driveway suddenly opened into a clearing with a gravel circle around it that led to a covered front porch. There was a carport extending from the porch that provided shelter to unload the bags. Behind the cabin light streamed through an opening in the trees. Beyond the back of the house they could just glimpse gleaming water with gentle ripples in it.

"You were saying?" Linda quipped.

"Oh yes! It's beautiful!" Maeve was eager to get out of the car and see the inside. The second the car rolled to a stop under the awning, her door was open and she was trying the front door. "It's unlocked!" she shouted back at Linda.

Linda rubbed her arms. "It's chilly, I'm going to grab a sweater before I come in, want one?"

Maeve hadn't noticed the chill until it was brought up. "Yeah, I could use one. Probably the bay that causes the temperature difference."

"Makes sense," said Linda, popping the trunk.

Both women had their university hoodies on, Linda's in blue from North Carolina, Maeve's in red from McMaster. Linda pointed it out, "We couldn't be more different."

"Opposites attract," said Maeve. "You'd know that if you went to a real school." They both laughed as they walked through the main floor of the cabin. A great room spanned the entire back of the house with windows showing the gentle slope to Whitefish Bay. There was a large kitchen table at one end and a living room with a fireplace at the other. The kitchen was at the front of the house, but opened to the great room. A staircase and washroom completed the floor.

"This is amazing," Linda gushed. "We should totally buy this place!"

"Oh yeah," Maeve started sarcastically, "I'd love to drive ten hours every weekend to get away from it all."

"Please, we both work remotely. We could just move up here for the summer."

"Now that's an idea," Maeve agreed. She pulled open the sliders onto the deck and a chill hit her through her sweater, causing the hairs on her neck to bristle. "It's cold out here," she said as she stepped out. The water was beautiful, slow waves pushing up on a sandy beach. "It's gorgeous though."

Linda came up behind her and put her arm around her. "It's weird. I feel like someone's watching us. Like there's a security camera or something."

Maeve looked around. "There's no one around for miles. Just you and me." She smiled and leaned her head on Linda's shoulder.

"I don't know, it's creepy. Like someone is out there."

"Who could be out there?"

"I don't know. Hunters or something," Linda shrugged.

"Well now you're giving me the heebie-jeebies," Maeve said. "I'm starting to feel like someone is watching us too."

Linda shivered. "We're just creeping each other out now. There's nothing here." She took her arm away and stuffed both hands in her front pocket. "We're just too used to the noise. It's so quiet here."

Both listened for a while to the waves and the trees. Suddenly a snake appeared on the edge of the beach. It slithered across the sand and into the water. Both women shivered now. "Oh God, that's just gross." Linda said.

"I'm not going in the water now," Maeve added.

"Well it's not going to stay there forever." They watched as it skimmed the surface then disappeared under the ripples.

"Oh God." Maeve rubbed her hands together and grimaced.

"What is that in the water?" Linda asked, squinting her eyes to peer at the bay.

"It was a snake," Maeve said.

"Not the snake, the weird glowing bit, right there," Linda pointed her hand straight ahead.

"I don't see any glow," Maeve said. "I do see footprints, who would have been down there?"

"It's like a triangle, that's not a natural shape," Linda pointed repeatedly, as though that would help. "It's got like an eye in the middle."

"I don't see anything except the footprints, maybe it was hikers," Maeve stated. She tried to follow a line from Linda's outstretched finger to the bay, but only saw the gentle ripples as the wind pushed over the water.

"Forget the footprints. You don't see that?" Linda's voice was agitated. "It's coming up out of the water. The triangle of light."

"I don't see anything," Maeve replied. "It's just the bay."

"Seriously?" Linda questioned in anger. "It's going back down, you don't see that *giant* light?" She turned to Maeve and grabbed her by the shoulders. Pushing her round to face out to the water. "Right there! You don't see that?"

Maeve was getting perturbed now. "Linda, stop. There is nothing there. You're getting hysterical."

"Well it's gone now," Linda said from behind her. "I don't know how you didn't see it. It was just … floating there … some kind of shape with an eye."

Maeve turned to look at her. Linda was still staring out at the bay. "You know what," she said softly, "you've had a long day of driving. Probably some kind of eye strain or ghost image, staring at the road that long. Why don't we go inside, you can take a bath, I'll make us something to eat, and you'll feel better."

Linda stared for a moment longer, then shook herself. "Maybe you're right. I could've sworn though." She looked back at the bay, and then into the house. "It was a long drive." She sighed heavily. "Yeah, let's do that. What are you going to make?"

"I brought a caesar salad, and I've got chicken breasts," Maeve started.

"Yeah, you do!" Linda laughed, and began tickling Maeve.

"Okay," Maeve giggled, "Stop, stop. I'll go cook. You just relax."

The oven timer showed fifteen minutes when the vision started. Maeve was checking the stove and the digits of the clock began to twist. Slowly turning into a triangle with an unblinking eye in the middle. Maeve blinked and tried to clear her eyes. "God, I must be tired too," she thought. The vision remained, the eye staring endlessly into her. She tried to rub her eyes and realized she could see it even with her eyes closed. She blinked a few times to verify it wasn't going away. Wetting a cloth, she folded it and placed it over her eyes. Instead of fading away, the vision seemed to get brighter. Maeve began to panic, looking around the kitchen frantically. Everywhere was the triangle. She realized it was blazened onto her eyes, it moved with them, always in the center, never blurring, never changing. She had a dizzy spell and crouched down, scrunching her eyes shut as hard as she could. There was blackness everywhere except the glowing triangle and unnerving eye. "Linda!" she screamed. "Linda, I need your help!"

She could hear sloshing and that distinct squeaking sound wet skin makes as it rubs against the tub. She tried to calm her mind as bangs and thuds came from upstairs. "I'm coming!" Linda shouted.

Maeve rocked back and forth on her heels, elbows wrapped around her knees, hands over her face. The eye wouldn't go away. Instead of fading to blackness it began to pulse, like it was just under her eyelids, attempting to get in sync with the flow of her blood. She could feel every vein in her body as her heart pumped madly.

Linda bounded down the stairs and across the kitchen. Her bathrobe half tied as she skidded to a stop and wrapped Maeve in a tight hug. "What's the matter? What's going on?"

"Your triangle ... with the eye ... it's inside me, I can't get it out."

"What do you mean honey?" Linda grabbed Maeve by the shoulders and rocked her back attempting to look into her eyes. "Open your eyes sweetie, it's Ok."

"No," Maeve shook her head, "It's everywhere, it won't go away. It's like it's burnt into my retina."

"You can see it now?" Linda asked.

"I can *only* see it. Eyes open, eyes closed, it's always there."

"Here, here," Linda prodded, pulling gently at Maeve's hands. "Just take your hands away for a second, let me have a look."

As the hands came away, Linda gasped. "What is it!?" shouted Maeve, "What's wrong?"

"Your eyelids are glowing Maeve, it's like when you put a flashlight up to your hand or something ... it looks like your eyes are shining light through your eyelids."

"Oh my God, oh my God, oh my God," Maeve started repeating.

"It's ok, it's ok," Linda said, "Let's just get you to open them up and we can check. Maybe it's just something in the air, or something." She began to sit Maeve down on the floor, allowing her legs to stretch in front of her. "Just put your head down, breathe through your nose, you're going to be just fine."

Maeve tried to relax, her legs bent in front of her, hands on her thighs. She focused on breathing in through her nose and out through her mouth.

"Now slowly open your eyes," Linda prompted.

Maeve was still breathing purposefully. She slowly began to blink her eyes open. Each time a flicker appeared on the floor in front of her. The triangle with the eye. "I can still see it," she said.

Linda stared at the illumination on the floor. "That's the same thing I saw in the bay," she whispered.

"You can see it?"

"Hell yes I can see it, it's projecting from your eyes onto the floor!"

"Oh my God, what do we do?" Maeve cried. She began to look around the room, the projection following the movement of her head. It drifted across the floor, onto the cabinets and then onto Linda's face. Linda just stared at Maeve's eyes. Each orb only projected half the image, but wherever her eyes went the image stayed in focus and seamless. The rest of Maeve's face was etched with sadness and it broke Linda's heart.

"Come with me," she said suddenly, pulling on Maeve's arm. "Come to the deck."

"How is that going to help?" Maeve asked, struggling to stand, she let Linda guide her through the cabin.

"I don't know if it will, it's just an idea … maybe I watch too many movies."

It was twilight, the light fading on one side of the bay as the sun set on the other. "Look into the bay," Linda said, "Try and look where I saw the light earlier."

"I never saw that light," Maeve pleaded, "I don't know where it was."

Linda watched the triangle move over the bay as Maeve looked around, "I can guide you. It's further from the beach, and more to the west."

"Which way is west?"

"Towards the sun Maeve!" Linda yelled.

"You're not helping Linda!" Maeve yelled and the light shone back in her face. Linda had to blink away the spots that stuck to her.

"Sorry, sorry, just look in the bay."

The triangle moved across the beach again and out into the bay. Maeve slowly looked around in ever growing circles. After a few passes, Linda shouted "There!" A reflection of the triangle could be seen under the water. "That's it, something's happening!"

"I still can't see the other light," Maeve whispered. "What's it doing?"

"It's coming up to join your light, it's exactly the same shape and position, it's just coming up through the water."

"What happens when they meet?" Maeve asked.

"I don't know, but it's about to happen right now," Linda replied.

The two women shot into the air. Linda attempted to grab Maeve with one hand and her bathrobe with the other. Maeve discovered she couldn't move her head, always staring at the spot in the bay. They flew up past the roof of the house, past the trees and into the cloudless night.

Both women were screaming as they peered down at the house below them, then Linda stopped. She saw the circle of the driveway where they came in, the clearing in the shape of a triangle around the house. The entire landscape was the symbol of the triangle and the eye.

"Maeve!" she screamed, "Look at the driveway!"

Maeve was unable to turn her head or blink. A loud, deep, rumbling voice echoed in Linda's head, "Now you must donate. I demand a donation."

"What kind of donation?" Linda screamed into the wind.

"I wish for existence," the voice rumbled. "I require love. A couple who are joined by love, spanning across time, from body to body, the pure essence of being. I require the entire existence of this couple. Their beginning and their end, I want all of it."

"You can't have it!" Linda screamed, shaking her head.

"I can, I will, and I do," replied the voice, "my wish is fulfilled. The donation is complete."

The wind picked up and blew the women in wide circles, slowly lowering them until they landed on the beach, feet sinking into the wet sand.

"I can see!" Maeve exclaimed looking around, "I don't see the triangle anymore."

Linda sat on the sand, staring at the bay blankly. "What the hell was that?"

"I don't know," Maeve said as she sat down beside her. The couple stared out into the bay, afraid to touch each other. Afraid to move. "A shared hallucination?"

Linda shook her head, "What are we doing here?"

"We came up to get away from it all," Maeve answered.

"Get away from all of what?"

Maeve stared at her for a minute. "I don't know," she finally replied.

"Do we come alone?" Linda asked, her eyes desperate.

"Yes," Maeve bit her lip. "Yes, of course, it was a couples get away, I mean a romantic get away."

Linda just stared at her. They could hear a beeping sound emanating from the cabin.

"Oh my God the chicken," Maeve shouted and began to run towards the house.

Linda looked back out at the bay. Pink and orange crests falling across the white tops of the waves. She saw a snake on top of the water. It slithered across the beach, following footprints in the sand. The footprints ended abruptly, as the snake went into the woods.

Maeve was surprised to find the table set, she didn't remember doing that, and certainly wouldn't have set it for four.

WHO	WHEN	RATING

Notes:

☆☆☆☆☆

Notes:

☆☆☆☆☆

Notes:

☆☆☆☆☆

Notes:

☆☆☆☆☆

Notes:

☆☆☆☆☆

Notes:

☆☆☆☆☆

Notes:

☆☆☆☆☆

Notes:

☆☆☆☆☆

Old Souls

The Cottage Word Scramble

All of the following are cottage related words that have their letters scrambled. Attempt to unscramble them onto the blanks provided. Answers provided in teeney tiny type and upside down at the bottom of the page.

IABNC _____

OGUWBLNA _____

ODGLE _____

HAECTL _____

EHTRAH _____

HRCOP _____

DERGNA _____

USCTRI _____

PFALCRIEE _____

RNDCUSOTIEY _____

TRTEERA _____

OYZC _____

ETRBMI _____

DHTCHETA _____

CEKD _____

Answers: CABIN • BUNGALOW • LODGE • CHALET • HEARTH • PORCH • GARDEN • RUSTIC • FIREPLACE • COUNTRYSIDE • RETREAT • COZY • TIMBER • THATCHED • DECK

28

The Echoes of Windy Oaks

Kenneth Roland

Windy Oaks was an old village. It had never qualified as a town, but maps labelled it as one. Most residents believed it was upgraded out of pity. The town square was surrounded by streets named after trees. Pine, Willow, Maple, Spruce and of course Oak Street that ran through the center of town. It had two churches, a town hall, volunteer firefighter station, bar/eatery (The Lucky Logger), book store (Windy Wonders), and even a hardware store (Ralph's Hardware). The town had a population of almost one thousand that swelled to over five thousand in the summers as cottagers, campers, and RVs of all shapes and sizes swarmed into the woods, hills, and lakes surrounding the town on all sides. Winters could be hard in Windy Oaks, but the summer always brought tourists with deep pockets and many wants that helped the town through the rest of the year. They had survived before the highway was built, and they still survived after the highway was canceled. They didn't rely on thousands of cars going by every day needing gas, food, or beverages. They relied on the naturalists, the enthusiasts, and the woodsmen.

Each spring, before the tourist season started, Windy Oaks held a festival. The Storm Festival was like a harvest festival other towns held in the fall. Houses were cleaned, gardens were mulched, banners of green and yellow were strung along the streetlights. The Storm Festival was for the townies, a celebration of the influx of tourists and cash they were about to have.

Although the festival was a big deal, no one actually knew exactly when it would occur each year. The Storm Festival happened on the first thunderstorm of spring. It could be a random Tuesday when the skies would suddenly darken and everyone began closing their shops and gathering their families. Sometimes it was in the middle of the night; a flash of lightning rousing the townspeople out of their beds and into the streets. Everyone participated, there were no exceptions.

Gregor sat in the Lucky Logger at a table facing the window. The winds were lively, but not violent. The trees that lined the main street barely swayed as though they were slow dancing, not the flailing and heaving needed for a good storm. He had nursed his pint since three, almost an hour now. He swished the golden liquid around the bottom of the glass watching James quickly stride down the opposite sidewalk. He continued to watch as James skipped across the road, holding out a hand as though he could stop the car headed towards him via shear will. He yanked open the door to the bar and came inside. The entry was windowed as well and Gregor could see James checking his hair before pulling open the interior door.

James spun his head as his eyes adjusted to the interior. He saw Gregor by the window and headed towards him immediately. He gave a half-hearted wave to Brenda at the bar, but didn't order anything.

"Gregor, I saw Edna Wessel," he said excitedly.

"Good afternoon James," Gregor said coolly.

"Yeah, good afternoon," James pulled out a chair and sat down. He leaned on the table immediately, putting his face close to Gregor. "Did you hear me? I saw her."

"No you didn't, James," Gregor rolled his eyes behind his glasses before focusing them on James face.

"Oh, right, you don't believe me? Well, come with me then, I'm telling you I saw her."

"Just like you saw Roy last week?"

"Yes! Exactly like that. Well," he paused, "not in the same spot, but the same way you know? Like they were just standing there. Staring at me."

"What'd I tell you last week James?"

"Don't go spreading this around," James sighed. "But I'm not, I came to you right away. I mean, you're the mayor, you gotta do something." James placed his hands flat on the table and stared into Gregor's eyes. "I'm telling you, they're coming back."

Gregor slid his chair back and got up. He didn't like James this close. "No," he said slowly, "they're not coming back." He picked up his glass and headed towards the bar. "You know who did come back James?" Gregor placed the stale beer on the shining wood and Brenda immediately put a full one beside it. James stared at him expectantly. "You did James. You came back. How long were you gone at that fancy state school?"

"Eight months," James stammered, "What does that have to do with anything?"

"They teach you anything at that school? Or was it all just pot, parties, and women?"

"What?" James stammered.

"The council agreed to let you go to that school, remember?"

"Yes, I remember."

"You were supposed to be learning marketing and sales. You come back and suddenly you're seeing people that are gone. Sounds to me like you filled your head with magic beans if you catch my meaning." Gregor stood at the table, looking down on James.

"What? I didn't do any drugs if that's what you're saying. I'm telling you I saw Edna out in the woods, standing there in nothing but what God gave her, just staring at me. I'm totally sober and I'm not lying. She was there, right by the creek."

"Why would she come back?" Gregor was agitated now. His voice was starting to get rougher, "What purpose would it serve for her to come back?"

"I don't know," James fingers started to twitch on the table top as Gregor sat back down. He looked James in the eye until James couldn't take it anymore and looked out the window.

"Look," Gregor smiled, "You've been away for a while. You probably got home sick. Maybe, you started thinking about the people that are no longer with us. You come back to town and the memories come flooding back. Make you see things. That's probably what happened."

James flicked his gaze back to Gregor. They had known each other James' whole life. The smile on Gregor's face was warm and nostalgic. "Yeah," he sighed, "yeah, maybe that's it. Homesick. I've never been away from Windy Oaks before."

"None of us has," said Gregor gently. "Change is hard. You're doing things most of us only dreamed of. I'm sure it's putting a lot of stress on you."

"It has been different," James said thoughtfully. He wondered if it was possible it had all been in his head.

"Look," Gregor said, adjusting himself in his seat and sitting up straight, "Brad has been looking to talk to you about the book store. He thinks he's leaving money on the table. Why don't you go give him some of that education we paid for." Gregor smiled again before taking a drink. James could tell that was the sign the conversation was over. He got up from his chair and steadied himself.

"Can I buy you that beer?" he asked.

Gregor laughed. "I don't pay for beers."

Two days later, the sky was dark. Ominous clouds rolled in from the east. Darker points swirled into the gray's, spinning and churning back into the single body. The winds were constant but gusted and shimmied as they blew.

Windy Oaks began to prepare for the celebration. Gregor was leaning on the bed of his truck, talking to Will on the other side. He glanced up as the day darkened. "Looks like today's the day," he said, still looking at the sky.

Will pulled off his ball cap and looked up as well. After a while, he replied. "Yuup. This is it I imagine. Take care Gregor," he turned and walked off towards his own pickup.

"You too Will," said Gregor half-heartedly as he pulled the driver's door open. He sat in the seat a bit before starting the truck. Staring out the windshield at the dark clouds. Winter was over. Spring was about to burst and then the tourists would arrive. Cabins full, trailer parks busy and the streets lined with people, all thinking everyone else they saw lived there. The money would flow again and everyone would get fat for the long winter. He smiled and started the engine. His wife would be looking for him to make sure he was dressed appropriately for the events to come.

James was helping Brad rearrange the books on display at Windy Wonders, the town books store. James had spent all of his time since coming back showing different shops how to effectively showcase their wares. He shared his eight months of schooling with everyone, spreading the knowledge to the whole town. He noticed the shadows disappearing as the sky darkened out the front window of the shop. "Looks like StormFest will be tonight," he said as he placed a book face out.

"Likely," said Brad. He didn't talk much. James had tried to explain that customers liked a chatty proprietor, but Brad wasn't quite catching on.

"Who do you think will be Storm Catcher this year?" James asked.

"Dunno," replied Brad, carrying more books towards the front.

James sighed. "It's usually someone older," he said, hoping to eke out more of a response.

"Uh huh," said Brad. He placed the books on the checkout counter and went to the window.

"Alright," said James, standing from the display and admiring his work. "Guess I better get ready. See you there."

"Yep," replied Brad.

The storm started slowly, lightning bouncing across the clouds in the distance. Then you could hear the rain coming across the woods. It started as a low rumble, no way to distinguish individual drops. As it approached, different sounds began to fight each other in a bout of noise. Rain on the rooftops competed with water running into the sewers for the right to be the most glorious sound in the storm. Then a crack of thunder would shake the ground and everything seemed quieter for a moment afterwards.

James huddled under the large canopy tent with the rest of the town. He began to button up his raincoat as he watched the small stage set up at the front of the tent. Gregor was standing to the right of the stage talking to the council. Brenda saw James and came over to stand with him. "You ready for your first festival since coming home?" she asked.

"I think so," he said, "I'm not sure I'm ever ready for these things."

"Yeah, they weird me out too," she said. "But it's only once a year and you have to admit it works."

"Does it?" James asked, turning towards her as he pulled his hood up. "You think the tourists wouldn't come if we didn't do this?"

She looked up at him thoughtfully. "I don't know," she shrugged. "I try not to think about it too much."

Gregor was ascending the stairs. When he got to the middle of the stage, the crowd began to clap. James wasn't sure why, and didn't bother. Gregor tapped on the microphone once causing a thump to echo through the tent. It was louder than the thrum of the rain on the canvas. "Thank you everyone for coming to this, our one hundred and seventy-third annual Storm Festival," he shouted into the microphone and the crowd roared. He waited for a few seconds before holding up his hands to silence the crowd. "Thank you, thank you," he said. There was a clear plastic rectangle in the canvas above his head, and he looked up into it now. He watched as the lightning bounced from cloud to cloud illuminating him on the stage. "Let's not waste any time," he said, lowering his head back to the crowd. "If everyone could position themselves properly. Hands outstretched, make sure your fingertips can't reach the person next to you. C'mon everyone, quickly now." The crowd began to shuffle and move until everyone was approximately six feet apart. "Ashley and Brandon,"

Gregor shouted, "I can see you holding hands, c'mon now." The crowd laughed. Ashley and Brandon separated, looking into each other's eyes as they reached out, fingertips just barely separated.

"Thank you everyone," Gregor continued. "I'd like to say a few words before the festival begins. Everyone knows the importance of this festival to Windy Oaks," he began. James tuned out the speech coming through the loudspeakers and looked around. Everyone looked tense, but excited. All faces were looking up at the stage, burning Gregor's words into their brains. He caught a shimmer out of the corner of his eye and thought it might be the first strike. He turned and looked down his row past Brenda and the rest to the edge of the enormous tent. There was Roy. Standing at the end of his row. Not looking at Gregor but staring directly at James. Roy was completely naked and shining with an electric energy. James frowned, this wasn't possible. Roy had been gone for over five years. He turned back to Gregor and tried to focus on his words.

Another flash caught James' eye and he looked to the other end of the row. There was Edna, her belly hanging in a curve over her privates. Her eyes were just two balls of light staring directly at him. He shook his head. This wasn't happening. No one else was reacting. It was impossible.

He squeezed his eyes shut and wished he could touch someone. He couldn't, he was isolated in his six foot square like the rest of the town. He tried to look at Gregor and focus. Standing on the stage, he could see Martin, Linda, and others, all previous Storm Catchers, all glowing and naked.

Gregor was still talking "Let's haul back that tent boys!" he shouted. With his words the dome of the tent separated as if by magic falling aside on long poles, pulling the fabric out into the street. Rain fell on James and he began to freak out. He pushed through the crowd, shoving Brenda out of the way as he made his way to the edges. Everyone was shocked. This had never happened. "Don't you see them!" he screamed as he ran. "They're back! The echoes of Windy Oaks!" He cleared the edge of his row and began to run for the sidewalk. Gregor frowned on the stage. Others were gasping and turning to look as James ran.

James made it to the door handle of Windy Wonders when the lightning struck. It plowed through his scalp and exited his left leg. He fell as a burning husk to the ground, smoke trying to escape the rain slowly drifting up.

"To another great year!" Gregor yelled into the microphone and the town erupted in applause.

WHO	WHEN	RATING

Notes:

☆☆☆☆☆

Notes:

☆☆☆☆☆

Notes:

☆☆☆☆☆

Notes:

☆☆☆☆☆

Notes:

☆☆☆☆☆

Notes:

☆☆☆☆☆

Notes:

☆☆☆☆☆

Notes:

☆☆☆☆☆

Flytrap

Stephen Young

I set the trap. It was Matthew's idea, the flytrap. If there really was some kind of big bug under the bed, you needed a big bug trap. That was his little-kid logic anyway; he was only five. He'd made it, but was too afraid to set it. So, I offered to help.

There were more bugs in the family's lakeside cabin than back home. I'm not afraid of bugs. I'm a little afraid of spiders but I pretend to like them. Our dad tells us they're more afraid of us than we are of them. I pushed the glue-covered sheet of cardboard deeper under the bed. Up close its chemical stink had burned my nostrils. Big brother mission accomplished. I started to crawl out from under the bed and my hand got stuck in the glue. Disgusted, I pulled to free myself but was stuck fast. I lay flat, trying to see what the flytrap was caught on. I couldn't see much, but I could see the trap there, several inches away from my hand. I felt whatever was stuck to my hand tug a few times, I tugged back and it went still.

With my free hand, I fumbled my phone from my pocket and flicked on the light. A thread caught in the light, stuck to my hand. There were dozens of the threads, I saw. A scream caught in my throat as I looked further back. Tugging at the threads were slender legs, each longer than I was tall. Eight giant eyes glittered darkly as the flattened thing crept forward.

It was not afraid of me.

Matthew eventually came to look for me. I'd dropped my phone when the thing got me, light still on, so the results were well lit. His horrified face was reflected eight times in the light as the thing's fangs were sunk deep into my mummified body. My corpse shrank in front of my little brother as the thing sucked out my liquified insides. Matthew's mouth opened in a silent scream—it must run in the family.

Matt ran away as one of the thing's long legs lazily reached out to grab him. The monster's movements drunk and slowed with the ecstasy of its feed. It wasn't long though—Matt came back. In his tiny little hand, he held a blue Bic lighter. It was the one mom used for lighting the wood stove. She'd kept it hidden so we wouldn't play with it. I didn't know where, but apparently Matthew did.

At my little brother's return, the monster began reaching towards him again, movements still drunk and slow. Matthew spun the flint…and nothing happened. He tried again but his hands were small—not strong enough to spark the lighter. A clawed leg reached out from under the bed and Matthew scrambled back, openly sobbing in fear. Tears and snot ran down his face, a face contorted in fear…but also anger.

Out of reach, Matt tried again to get the lighter to work. I wish I was able to tell him how it worked, but he was a smart kid. After all, he'd made the flytrap on his own. Matt used both thumbs, one on top of the other and pushed for all he was worth.

The lighter sparked.

Snik

There was no flame.

He made a frustrated sound. Guttural and full of rage. Terrifying coming from a child so young.

The thing was done feeding; my body was little more than a husk wrapped in web. Its movements were becoming more lively, more aware. My little brother's attention was rapt on the lighter.

Snik snik

He didn't notice the thing creeping forward.

Matthew gave a gasp of surprise as he sparked the lighter once more and a little flame sprung to life. His eyes were trapped to the flame for a moment, staring at his tiny triumph. He did not see the thing reach out and grab his leg.

Matt screamed and kicked as he was pulled under the bed. His flailing caused him to get caught up in some of the webs. His legs stuck together and he was slowly pulled under, closer and closer to my desiccated husk. All the while though, he kept both hands on the lighter, both thumbs pressed down painfully hard on the tab. The little flame hadn't been shaken out by his struggles.

Fully under the bed now, Matthew looked over…and saw his flytrap. Despite the fear, and the sticky threads, Matt reached out and touched the little flame to his trap.

The results were immediate. Whatever solvents made up the glue ate the flames hungrily. In mere seconds the entire trap was engulfed. Threads of fire raced everywhere under the bed, leaping from the trap.

The monster let go of Matthew's leg in surprise. My little brother grabbed the edge of the bedframe and hauled himself out. The fast-spreading flames caught his pants on fire and he kicked them off. Burned, but free of both the fire and the webs, Matthew ran out of the room once more.

Run Matthew, run.

Mom and dad ran back to the cabin when they saw the smoke. The neighbours came too. They weren't far by lake standards, just next door, but they don't build the cabins close together at our lake. A quick visit that Matthew hadn't wanted to attend, so I'd been told to watch him. They found Matthew out front, curled in a ball, sobbing. All the more sad and pathetic looking for the lack of shoes and pants. In the few minutes it took mom, dad, and the neighbours to run over, our family cabin had become the biggest bonfire the lake had ever seen.

It took half an hour for the fire department to show up. Thankfully our cabin being so far from its neighbours meant there wasn't anything convenient nearby to catch fire. Matthew tried to explain what had happened, but he was cursed with a five-year old's vocabulary and imagination. Would you believe a five-year-old that told you he found a spider as big as a person? There was no burned spider corpse to be found, just my charred bones, scrubbed clean of any evidence to verify Matthew's claims.

His big brother had been killed and eaten by a monster; it had almost got him too.

Sadly, no one believed him.

Flytrap

WHO	WHEN	RATING

Notes:

☆☆☆☆☆

Notes:

☆☆☆☆☆

Notes:

☆☆☆☆☆

Notes:

☆☆☆☆☆

Notes:

☆☆☆☆☆

Notes:

☆☆☆☆☆

Notes:

☆☆☆☆☆

Notes:

☆☆☆☆☆

Cottage Crypto

Nothing says fun like a little cryptography at the cottage! Seriously, if this isn't your thing, just skip it. But if you like these little challenges, give it a go. Every letter has been swapped with a different letter, with some deduction you'll be able to figure out the secret message.

Encoded Letter

A	B	C	D	E	F	G	H	I	J	K	L	M	N	O	P	Q	R	S	T	U	V	W	X	Y	Z

Real Letter

The Secret Note

UXY ACUUJVY KL UXY

____ _____ __ ____

NYLU EDJAY

_____ _____

JHQ UKTY CP QYJO

___ ____ __ ____

DKPY KL NYUUYO JU

____ __ _____ __

UXY AJNKH

___ _____

Lighthouse Keepers Secret

Kenneth Roland

"Somebody should do something", Janis said. She was standing on the rocky peninsula staring at the old black and white striped lighthouse. "It's beautiful," she sighed. The lighthouse was built in the 1920's. Its wood siding was starting to look dank and stained. The keeper had died many years ago and a government agent came out once a month to check if it was working. Otherwise no one ever thought about it. The stripes wrapped around the tower like a scarf, protecting it from the cold of the ocean waves. The scarf came down and wrapped around the attached house. The upper floor was done all in black clad wood and the first floor in white.

Peter looked up at the towering wood. "Yeah, if you had millions of dollars you could do something."

"What?!" Janis exclaimed. "It wouldn't take millions, just a little tender loving care."

"Oh yeah, TLC would definitely get rid of the rot," he nodded. "I forgot how tender loving care removes decades of decay," he mocked.

Janis gently punched his shoulder. "Don't joke. You'd be amazed at what some love can do." She smiled up at him. He looked back at her and had to smile as well.

"It certainly changed me," he said and leaned in for a kiss.

"It did," she said after a moment. "Let's buy it."

"What!?" he exclaimed. "It's a piece of crap about to crumble into the ocean."

"No, it's a piece of history about to give us purpose," she replied.

They both watched the waves come in against the rocks around the lighthouse, smashing white spray into the air. The ocean was slowly remodelling the rock, making it smoother, more beautiful.

"Didn't someone die there?" Peter asked.

Janis smiled, "Now look who's into the history."

Peter sighed. "So the government gives us a subsidy right? For running the lighthouse?"

"Yes," she knew they were about to start an adventure. "Plus, the historical society has some money they are willing to give for the restoration. It's still considered habitable, so we can live there while we work." She was feeling giddy.

"Well, we might as well go look at it, I guess," Peter said. Janis wrapped him in a bear hug and pressed her head against his chest.

"This is a great idea you had," she said, smiling deeply. Peter just laughed.

The purchase of the old lighthouse went pretty smooth. By June of that year, after reams of paperwork and meetings that seemed to go on forever, they were handed a ring of keys and the deed to the property. The keyring was loaded with a mix of new and antique keys of all shapes and sizes. Janis couldn't wait to find out what they all opened. It felt like it was going to be one surprise after another. The keys jostled and clinked hanging from hand now as she and Peter walked up the stairs to the old building. Peter held her other hand. He had become just as excited as her as the months had passed. He was smiling broadly as they reached the door. He stared up at the tower as Janis sorted through the keys attempting to find the one for the front door.

"I think we need to go straight to the top and get a picture," he said, grinning.

"For sure!" Janis replied excitedly. Finally a key turned in the lock and the door opened. Her red hood bobbed as she bounded up the stairs after Peter. His prescription safety glasses knocked against his nose as he ran up the stairs. His gray t-shirt hugged his back as he bounded up the stairs towards the ultimate level. They burst out onto the top level balcony and stared at the ocean around them.

"This is amazing," Peter said looking around.

Janis took a moment to take it all in. She zipped up her red hoodie to the top. It was chilly on the top deck. "Ready for a selfie?" she said.

Peter leaned in close, his arm around her waist. "Totally," he replied.

She held her phone out over the balcony, the phone pointing towards them. "Here we go," she said.

Three. Two, "Why do you have a timer on your phone?" Peter asked, reaching towards the screen just as the camera triggered, capturing them forever.

Janis laughed, "Oh my God, that's perfect," she smiled. "That's going on our new Instagram account 'LighthouseRenovate'." She posted the photo with a large grin across her face.

"I like that," Peter said, "Starting a new account for our new life." He placed his hands on the railing and looked out over the ocean. "This truly is amazing," he said.

Janis took a moment to take in the full view. The lighthouse was on what now appeared as a small outcrop of rock into the ocean. Waves battered three sides as she stared down. She began to feel noxious looking straight down and had to adjust her gaze to the horizon.

"It is beautiful, looking out," she said.

"Less so, looking in," Peter replied, turning to lean his back against the railing. The paint on the old wooden lighthouse was peeling badly. The house at the bottom was built of old brick and stone and didn't have the same issues, it looked rustic and almost charming. "I'm going to get the mower and trimmer and at least get the yard looking good," he said, pushing off the railing and heading inside.

"I'm going to find out what all these keys open," Janis spoke to his back.

The key ring given to her by the real estate agent was a mess. There were no markings on any of the keys, and Janis basically went by the look of the lock to determine which type of key would fit. She managed to find the basement key, the bathroom key (why was there a lock on the bathroom), the shed key, and the key to the light room. That was the most important, as their government subsidy depended on them keeping the light shining brightly.

In the end, there was one door in the basement that she didn't know what lay beyond. Otherwise, she had opened everything in the lighthouse. A pile of keys were now labeled on the large oak kitchen table. The ring was down to two unknown keys. Not too bad Janis thought. She could hear Peter's truck pulling into the driveway. She looked out and saw it was loaded with drywall and lumber. She watched him exit the truck, excited to show the progress she'd made. He had a Tim Horton's bag and two coffees as he came across the yard. Now Janis was really excited.

She took the coffees as he came through the door and placed them by her labeled keys. "Look at this!" she said in a sing-song way, dragging her hand along in front of the keys..

"Ooooohh, that's amazing," Peter said, placing the bag of breakfast sandwiches down and pushing the keys around to look at them. "The guy at the hardware store said something interesting," he started to talk as he opened the bag and pulled out two paper wrapped english muffins. "He was saying that just before the old lighthouse keeper died, he started doing some restorations of his own. He bought some sheets of drywall, mud and paint. Not much, the guy said, and he never came back for more. Weird eh?"

"Why is that weird, surely he tried to maintain the place?" Janis asked around a mouthful of muffin and sausage.

"Weird that I haven't found anything that was done recently, and haven't found any drywall laying around. What did he do with it?"

"Oh," Janis was thoughtful, "Ok, that is weird."

"Right?" Peter said, enjoying his own sandwich.

"Well," Sarah said, putting her sandwich down and spinning around to head to the study, "I also found something weird." She returned with a manilla folder that she placed on the kitchen island and opened, pushing keys out of the way. The folder was full of old newspaper clippings. None of the old faded clippings had photos, but some had wood cut drawings. Each one was about a ship-wreck. The lighthouse keeper must have collected them over decades.

"Wow," whistled Peter. "These are cool." He pulled one over to him and read as he finished his sandwich. Janis slid one out of the pile with her finger and examined it.

After a few minutes Peter stood up straight. "This article is a hundred years old," he said, pointing at the dateline, "1924". He whistled. "How old was that lighthouse keeper?"

Janis looked thoughtful. "We should check that out when we can. Just another mystery I guess."

Peter pushed his article back into the pile. "Did you find the basement key? I wanted to check it for water damage. It looked pretty rough when we did our walk-through."

"I did!" Janis exclaimed, sorting quickly through the keys to find the one labeled 'basement'. Peter took the key, gave her a peck on the lips and went out of the kitchen.

Janis collected the garbage and grabbed her coffee. She went over and flipped open the garbage can and chucked in the wrappers. She went to the sink and peered out at Peter's truck as she sipped her coffee. She was wondering what the cost of all that material was when she heard a shout. She noticed the clock on the stove wink out. "Oh no," she said and ran to the basement stairs, "Are you alright?" she shouted.

"Yes, damnit," came a cursed response out of the darkness in the basement. After a few seconds she saw a light appear and shift around the tiny basement. The stone wall along the edge of the stairs eventually lit up with a circle of light that grew bigger as Peter came towards the stairs. Peter appeared, slightly bent over in the six foot basement. "I was looking at the fuse panel and obviously touched something," he shrugged. "Grab a flashlight though, I did find something." His own light turned and headed back into the darkness.

Janis went back to the kitchen and opened their newly appointed junk drawer. She grabbed a flashlight and clicked it a few times to see if it worked. She headed over to the stairs and shone it down the wooden steps. They had been painted white at one point, but the centers were all worn to the wood. "What did you want me to see?" she asked. She had her coffee in her other hand and took a sip as she came down.

"Remember I hadn't seen where the keeper would have used the drywall?"

"Yep," she said as she hit the bottom. She wasn't tall enough that she had to duck, but she stooped over a bit anyway, not used to the short height of the ceiling beams.

"I hadn't noticed this in the inspection," Peter was saying, shining his own light over to a small area where the stone basement protruded out of the house. "I think I believed it was the outdoor entrance for bringing wood or coal in. But it's not." He went into the cubby and played his flashlight over a smooth wall that was surprisingly clean. He knocked on the wall with his other hand and got a sharp knock.

"What is it?" Janis asked.

"There's something solid behind it," Peter explained. "The drywall must be right on top of another wall or something. Weird eh?"

Janis was picturing all the work that had to be done upstairs. New flooring, plaster, electrical, and plumbing. "Why would he re-drywall a wall in the basement, when there's all that work to do on the rest of the lighthouse?"

Peter leaned on the wall, pointing his flashlight at the floor. "I have no idea," he finally said.

"Should we see what he walled up?" Janis asked.

"Sure," hummed Peter. "But first I gotta get the electrical working again and I'm going to start demo on the second bedroom so we have a nicer room to sleep in. Maybe I'll look into this tonight."

"Do you need me?" Janis asked.

"Nope," he replied quickly, heading back to the fuse panel.

"Awesome. I'm going to keep cleaning for now, the place is filthy."

"Sounds good!" Peter chirped.

The couple spent the day working hard. Peter had the power back on quickly and then tore into the second bedroom. Janis had three large garbage bags by the end of the day and wide plank flooring in the kitchen shined. The musty smell they had originally walked into was gone. The lighthouse smelled like vinegar and lavender. It smelled clean. They sat out at the picnic table to eat dinner. They lingered there sipping wine and watching the sunset until the breeze picked up and Janis got chilled.

As she opened the door to the house she saw the basement door and turned back to Peter, "Do you want to open that wall now and see what's in it?"

"Sure," he replied. His hands were full of plates and cutlery and he took them over to the sink.

"I can do those tomorrow," Janis said and grabbed a hammer out of Peter's tool bag on the floor, "I'm excited to know what he was covering up."

"You're hoping it's a safe, eh?" Peter laughed.

Janis chuckled. "I wouldn't complain," she said. "But I was looking at those newspaper articles again and looked up some of the boats. There's an oddity. When I look on Wikipedia, the number of deaths in each wreck was one more than what the newspaper reported."

"What?" asked Peter from behind her on the stairs, "Every one?"

"Yeah, every article is off by one. Or Wikipedia is wrong, I don't know. Wikipedia had a footnote that the numbers were based on the passenger list, not the bodies found."

"Interesting," said Peter.

They had reached the smooth wall. A bare bulb hung in front of it. "What do I do?" Janis asked, tapping the wall with the hammer, "Just smash it?"

Peter laughed. "You could. We don't know what's behind it, you may want to hit it with the claw on the back and pull off a piece first so we can see."

Janis flipped the hammer around and raised it up. She took a deep breath and smashed the claw into the drywall. The metal pushed through easily and hit stone. It slid down, hooking itself onto the wallboard. Janis gave it a yank and it pulled a large portion of the drywall with it. "Woo!" she yelled. "That was fun!" She began smashing and pulling until they could see a large portion of the stone wall behind it. On the edge of the hole, in the center of the wall they could see wood. Janis moved towards the center to expose more. After about 10 minutes there was a large opening in the drywall. They could see an old wooden door behind it.

"Why would he drywall over a door?" Peter wondered aloud.

"Perhaps, it's the door to hell!" Janis giggled.

"I've heard about those," Peter laughed, "I'd drywall over it too. Maybe we should leave it alone?"

"What?!" Janis smiled, "I don't think so!" She returned to her demo, sweat beginning to drip down her face, mixing with the plaster dust. Peter began to pull off sections and toss them on the ground behind them. It wasn't long before the entire wall was exposed. The same stone as the rest of the basement with a large solid wood door in the middle. Thick black metal hinges held the door to its frame. A large metal plate was on one side with a keyhole and handle.

Peter grabbed the handle and jiggled it. "It's locked," he said. "This is really weird."

Janis stepped back and got out her phone. "We need to post this!" she said.

"Nah, let's wait until we clean it up a bit," Peter said. "This could definitely get us some followers though."

"Damn right it will, everyone is going to want to know what's inside," Janis said as she clicked a few photos.

"You said you had two keys left, right?" Peter said, "Let's get 'em and see if they fit."

Janis didn't wait for him to finish and was half-way up the stairs already. She was back quickly with two big thick old keys. She wiped a spot clean on the cement floor and took a picture of the two keys. "I'm still going to post a teaser," she said as her thumbs typed quickly, "We may have just found what one of these opens ... more to come #mystery" she wrote. She picked up the keys and handed them to Peter.

He looked at the first one and immediately gave it back, "That's definitely not going to fit," he said. He pushed the second one into the lock and twisted it. There was a satisfying click as the lock sprung open. "Ok, here we go," he said.

Janis looked on with excitement. She started taking video of the opening with her phone. Peter pulled the door open to reveal darkness. He reached along the wall inside until he found a light switch. The room burst into light and both of them gasped.

The room was set up like a dining room. A large rectangular table filled the center, with a crystal chandelier lighting everything. Chairs surrounded the table and in each one sat a person. Their clothes were from different times, some in suits and dresses, some in Bermuda shorts and tank tops. One woman wore a muted orange, butterfly collar blouse and bell bottom pants. None of them moved. Their eyes stared blankly at each other across the table, their shadows stretched onto the floor and slightly up the wall. All hands were placed on the table around place settings as though they were about to eat and had frozen in time. "What the f…," Peter let the words trail off. Janis moved closer to him. She had forgotten she was recording on her phone and the screen slowly dropped until it was taking a video of the floor.

"What is this?" she whispered.

"I have no idea," Peter whispered back. They almost felt like they were interrupting something. The room was dusty and dank, turning all the colors to gray. A thick layer of dust ringed a fedora on one man's head. Peter slowly stepped into the room, being careful not to touch anything until he could peer at one of the people. "Are they mannequins?" he asked aloud.

Janis stayed close. "No, look at their skin, it's all stretched and leathery, not plastic."

Peter realized the eyes were bright and too shiny. "These are glass eyes," he whispered in shock. "I think they were stuffed."

"What?!" exclaimed Janis, "Like an animal?"

"Yeah, like taxidermy or whatever."

They moved a little further down the table.

Peter reached out to touch the woman in the orange shirt. "Don't touch it!" Janis hissed.

Suddenly the door slammed behind them and they both jumped, turning to see a bearded man in a cable knit sweater standing with his back against the door.

"You don't live as long as I have without borrowing some spare parts," he groaned. His voice was like rocks rubbing together. "People were starting to notice my … longevity. I had to disappear for a while."

Peter stepped in front of Janis. "Who are you?" he said, attempting to sound more in control then he felt.

The man lifted a large spear gun and pointed it at them. "Ships don't wreck like they used to," he growled, "had to get creative."

Janis felt Peter's body slam into her as she tripped stepping backwards. Her head bashed against the concrete floor. Blackness began to come into her vision from all sides. The last thing she saw was two empty chairs at the table.

WHO	WHEN	RATING

Notes:

☆ ☆ ☆ ☆ ☆

Notes:

☆ ☆ ☆ ☆ ☆

Notes:

☆ ☆ ☆ ☆ ☆

Notes:

☆ ☆ ☆ ☆ ☆

Notes:

☆ ☆ ☆ ☆ ☆

Notes:

☆ ☆ ☆ ☆ ☆

Notes:

☆ ☆ ☆ ☆ ☆

Notes:

☆ ☆ ☆ ☆ ☆

Get Outta The Woods!

Start in the middle of the maze and find your way out. Good luck! (If you are one of those rebels that just can't help themselves, go from the bottom to the middle, just remember that makes you a bad person)

Voice of the Abyss

Kenneth Roland

With a wet, sucking sound Vincent pulled his boot out of the muck on the edge of the lake. He loved field work. So many biologists got stuck at a desk, studying fish sounds, or updating databases of plant nomenclature. He pulled on the rope leading into the murky water, watching the surface split around the cord as it came towards him. This was exactly where he always planned to be. Standing on the shores of a lake, surrounded by cabins, testing the water, sampling fish populations, and then relaxing in his own cabin every evening. There was no other work he could see himself doing.

"Careful with the device!" Monica shouted from the shore, waking Vincent from his reverie.

Right, Monica was here as well. She was the engineer that had designed and built the device. It had a little bit of everything; sonar, microphones, cameras, sample collectors. If there was any bit of information a biologist could want, the device would collect it. The only issue was that the engineer came with it.

"I'm being careful," Vincent replied.

"If the device hits the rocks by the shore, it could damage it."

"There are no rocks here, that's why we chose this spot, remember?" Vincent rolled his eyes. "The whole reason I'm standing in the mud?"

"Well," Monica said with resignation, "still be careful. There are years of work in that device."

Vincent saw the white plastic edge of the device appear above the water. It was like a large pill capsule. Only about three inches around, but two feet long. "I got it," he called, thinking about a few minutes ago, when he was alone with his thoughts.

He hefted the capsule out of the water. It was heavier now, loaded with water samples automatically taken at different depths as it sank into the lake. "Tomorrow we should take the boat out and run tests closer to that island," he pointed with his free hand at the rocks and trees jutting out of the lake a few hundred yards from the shore. He slipped a bit as he got further onto shore, and the device slammed into the muck as he scrambled for his footing.

"What did I just tell you?!" Monica yelled.

Vincent put his head down and swore. "I'm trying to be careful, it's hard with all this mud. If we take the boat tomorrow you won't have to worry about mud and rocks."

Monica sighed. "Fine." She didn't like boats. She didn't really like the water at all. She didn't swim, and would even avoid a bath, if the shower was available. She actually liked working with Vincent, and admired his ability to get right into the dirt and grime. She just enjoyed her clean workshop more than wriggly things and the incredibly hard to predict ways of nature. "Do I have to go in the boat?"

"You'll love it," Vincent said as he approached her.

The small aluminum boat with outboard motor was exactly what Vincent was hoping for. It was exactly what Monica was dreading. It chugged through the water, banging and bouncing with every wave and then sending reverberations through Monica's bones. "I really thought we'd have a research boat," she said.

Vincent laughed, "On this lake? Who would pay for that?"

"I don't know. I've watched Shark Week. They seem to have nicer boats than this."

"Oh yeah, if we had Shark Week money, we'd be doing this on the ocean, not on a tiny lake in cottage country," Vincent quipped.

Monica sighed. "Well, what's the plan for today?"

"We go out by that island, drop in your device and check out if there's any difference between the island shoreline and the mainland."

"Interesting. Why would there be, you think fish know they are near an island compared to a larger landmass."

"They might. And we're going to find out."

Monica clutched the sides of the boat as it rocked its way out to the island. They stopped a good distance from the island. Vincent was checking the depth of the lake on a screen in his hand. "Hmm."

"Don't do that. If you have something interesting to say, just say it," Monica said. "Don't just 'hmm' and make me ask you what it is."

"Sorry," Vincent said, "The depth-finder is showing that it's forty-five feet deep here."

"That seems high," Monica said.

"Yeah," said Vincent. "We're only like fifty feet off shore … it shouldn't be that deep."

"Unless it's a forty-five degree incline," Monica mused, "That's pretty steep for a glacier formed lake."

"Exactly," Vincent said. "Will your device give us an idea of the topology of the bottom?"

"It will," Monica was getting excited. "That would be interesting to see."

"Already getting it set," Vincent said as he started prepping the device to be lowered into the water.

The two watched the tablet Monica held as Vincent lowered the device into the water. Data began to appear immediately. Water temperature, depth to the bottom, clarity, and more all showed immediately. One window showed a live feed from the 360 degree camera mounted on the device, but it was mostly just bubbles and dark water. The camera had sound and the tablet was playing gurgles and swooshing sounds. Monica tapped on the screen until it showed a chart mapping out the bottom as the device sent out sonar and listened for the echoes to judge where the ground was. The edge of the island dropped off naturally for about fifty feet and then suddenly rounded in on itself. It was like a shelf in the water that suddenly ended leaving a void underneath. "We're at fifteen feet," Vincent said as he lowered the device hand over hand into the water.

"I've never seen anything like that," Monica squinted at the screen. "It's almost like erosion from a waterfall, but there would never have been a fall here."

"Agreed," Vincent nodded. "These are glacier lakes, erosion fifteen feet down doesn't make any sense."

The chart filled in more and they could see that after the shelf, the ground came back out quickly, almost to the edge of the shelf and then began to head straight down.

"Glaciers also don't leave straight lines," Vincent murmured.

"No," Monica agreed. "This island shouldn't be here. It's almost like it was added after the fact."

"Look at that!" Vincent said excitedly pointing at the window with the live video feed. The edge of the island appeared in the murky water. It looked like elephant leather, pock marked and rough.

"That doesn't look like rock," Monica pondered. She was intensely intrigued now. This was not normal data collection. Something was off here.

Vincent took a moment to look over the edge of their boat. The line disappeared into the void after only a foot. "I can't see anything down there by eye."

"No, I'm surprised at the clarity we're getting at depth," Monica said.

"We're at thirty feet," Vincent voiced.

"Almost to the bottom," Monica was saying when suddenly they both gasped. Vincent stopped lowering the line. On the video screen was what appeared to be a large eye.

"What the f ...," Vincent started to get out when the pupil of the giant eye slid across to stare directly into the camera. It was surrounded by a luminescent, green iris that swirled and bloomed, like milk added to coffee.

Monica couldn't speak. She just stared mesmerized. The video was just murky water around the eye, no way to see what it was attached to, or how. It didn't blink and just gazed straight at the camera, like it was seeing her watching it. She knew this was impossible and shook her head. "This is recording," she told Vincent.

This caused Vincent to shake his head. "Good, cause no one's going to believe this. That's one hell of a fish." He continued to stare at the screen in Monica's hands.

"If that's a fish, it has to be over three hundred feet long," Monica whispered.

"What?" Vincent asked, "But, it has to be a fish, what else would be down there?"

The aluminum boat rocked back and forth as it was hit by a wave. Monica used her free hand to grab the edge. Vincent rode it out, holding the line steady to the device.

"Ok, well that was wrong," he said.

"Seriously, stop doing that," Monica turned to him. "You're just wasting words to comment that something was wrong instead of telling me what was wrong. Am I supposed to guess?" she looked directly into his eyes.

"Sorry," he said. "It's just that that wave came from the shore, not the lake. That shouldn't be possible."

"Waves coming from the shore … no that shouldn't happen."

"Right?" Vincent used a hand to scratch his curly hair.

"Oh my God!" Monica said as the video showed what appeared to be a tentacle come directly at the camera. It wrapped around it and pulled the device directly to the eye. The tablet speakers emitted a squishy noise and then the sound of water flowing rapidly around the device. The glow of the iris faded as only the pupil was now on the screen.

"What the hell is that?!" Vincent shouted, jabbing a finger at the tablet. He quickly brought the hand back to stop the line from sliding as it edged out of the boat.

"I have no idea," Monica breathed. "Pull it up."

Vincent attempted to pull on the rope, but it was tight against the edge of the boat with no slack. He stood carefully and pulled, causing the boat to lean.

"Ok, stop!" Monica yelled, grabbing onto the side again. "You're going to tip us over."

"What am I supposed to do?" Vincent asked. "That thing has your device, do I just let it have it?"

"Maybe if we give it a little slack, we can jerk it back," Monica said, staring at the screen.

Suddenly out of the tablet speakers emitted a deep rumbling sound and the two scientists' eyes went wide. "Huuuoooo".

"Did it just speak?" Vincent yelled.

"I don't know!" Monica yelled back. "Why are we calling it an it? It just has to be a trick of the light." She looked around. They were the only boat visible. No one was on the shore of the island or the mainland. "Maybe we're being pranked."

Vicent looked around as well. "I don't think we are. There's nobody around and we literally made the plan to check this island yesterday. Unless you're pranking me?" He stared at her.

Monica's eyes were wide and full of fear. Vincent knew immediately that this was not her doing.

"Huuuoooo arrrrrrr yuuuuu," thrummed across the lake.

"Ok, that was a sentence," Monica gasped.

Vincent's head was on a swivel, looking everywhere. "What the hell was that?"

The pupil on the screen twitched and bubbles escaped around it. The boat started to rock again, waves coming from the shore and rippling out. "I don't think that's an island," Vincent said.

"Don't be ridiculous," Monica said, attempting to determine if the beach was moving or it was just the boat rocking. She gripped the side of the small boat so hard her knuckles were turning white.

Something hit the bottom of the boat with a thunk, causing Monica to jump.

"This is freaking me out," Vincent said, hanging onto the line.

"I am not Ok," Monica cried.

More thumps as things smacked into the small boat.

"What do you want?" Vincent screamed.

"Waaaat dooooo yuuuuu waaaant," came the voice.

"We're just scientists!" yelled Vincent. His face was pale and his eyes shook. Monica stared at him, sucking in breaths.

"I am," said the voice.

The crazy stopped. The boat sat silent in the water. After a few seconds, Vincent tugged on the rope. The device came up easily and he began to reel it in quickly. He looked back at the screen. The eye was still there staring at him as he pulled the device up as fast as he could.

Suddenly the eye blinked, "I am ... fishing," came the voice.

The water split to the sides as the boat was sucked under. Monica felt the water pushing her down as the boat quickly disappeared into the murk. It was filling the void as the boat plunged downwards. She kicked towards the surface, fighting the currents. She struggled against the water flow, until she felt Vincent's head under her hand. She shoved it down and pushed off, fighting for the surface. Her head cleared the water and she gasped. She immediately began swimming away from the island, towards the mainland.

After fifty yards she looked back. There was no sign of Vincent. There was no sign of anything. She started to cry. She felt guilty. As she reached the shore and could stand, she pushed her legs to carry her out of the water. As she finally fell onto the shore, she heard it. "Come back, it's ok, I forgive you."

Never. She would never go into the water again.

WHO	WHEN	RATING

Notes:

☆☆☆☆☆

Notes:

☆☆☆☆☆

Notes:

☆☆☆☆☆

Notes:

☆☆☆☆☆

Notes:

☆☆☆☆☆

Notes:

☆☆☆☆☆

Notes:

☆☆☆☆☆

Notes:

☆☆☆☆☆

Rain Showers

The Cabin Party

Kenneth Roland

"Why do we have to go to this reunion?" Mike whined as he and his wife Kathy sat in congested traffic along the highway.

"Because Uncle Harold invited us, " Kathy said, "What more reason do we need?"

Mike rolled his eyes. "He's not going to leave the cottage to us babe, we don't need to be there."

"You never know," Kathy said in a sing-song voice, "From what I've heard, Uncle Harold is upset about Peter leaving his job at the firm."

"Oh! Peter's leaving the firm?" Mike sat up in his seat, his seatbelt attempting to hold him back. "So you think the cottage may be up for grabs?"

"Don't say it like that Mike," Kathy said. "The man is a human being. It's not all about his cottage. But, yes, since the reunion is *at* the cottage, I really thought we should go."

Mike was beaming as he watched the road edge pass by his window. "It is a beautiful cottage."

"For sure," Kathy replied, "but it's also four hours from home. Six on weekends."

Mike stared out at the sea of cars. "Yeah, I'm noticing that."

When they finally arrived at the cottage they saw Tom and Lisa's small Ford Fiesta was already there. Lisa was Kathy's cousin. Her and Tom lived in downtown Toronto. Kathy felt Lisa looked down on the suburbs surrounding the huge city, as though it was a prison sentence for second class citizens. The Fiesta was parked on the front lawn, and Kathy pulled their minivan up beside it. Trees had been trimmed behind the cottage and Kathy could see the burn pile still smoldering in the side yard. This is why we aren't going to inherit the cottage, she thought, we don't come up and do the work.

Mike threw open his door and got out to stretch. "God, it feels good to get out of the car," he said. "Maybe people don't even need cottages. They should just drive for four hours to feel the relief of getting out of the car."

Kathy smiled. "Maybe."

"It's like taking your skates off after a game, it feels so good."

The cottage was a large A-frame, sitting on the rocks above the lake. Kathy turned and took in the view. It was stunning. Water gently lapping up against a rocky shore. A large wood dock stretched out into the lake. A palette of vibrant greens and subdued browns touching the dark blue of the lake and cloudless cyan of the sky. "You don't get this view when you take your skates off," Kathy said, "You just see stinky feet."

Mike went to the trunk and started to get their bags out as Kathy wandered down to the water. Someone had taken down a tree and there was a pile of wood chips where the stump had been. Tracks of a vehicle had sunk into the soft grass and she followed these to the pile of logs and sawdust. She didn't know what type of tree it was by the logs, she never was very good at recognizing the different species. As she looked at the mud and sawdust sticking to her shoes, she really wasn't sure why she came to look at the mess at all. She attempted to shake off the dirt and started around to the back of the cabin. Mike caught up to her with the luggage, breathing heavily. "Thanks for the help," he said. Kathy smiled.

There was a door to the cabin from the driveway, but no one used it. Everyone went around the back, heading down the slope to see the lake and come into the large glass doors that crossed the entire back of the walkout bottom floor. As soon as Kathy looked back at the cabin, she knew something was wrong.

Just inside the glass doors Lisa was kneeling down and violently shaking, her hair pulled back in a ponytail. Tom was rubbing her back with one stocky arm, his other hand held a cell phone to his ear. Kathy began to walk faster towards the doors, pulling her own phone out. Had she missed a message? Nothing. No signal either. How was Tom getting a signal?

Kathy slid open the door and stared at the two with wide eyes. She said nothing, just waited. Tom glanced at her and motioned to Lisa, then he walked away, still holding the phone to his ear. Kathy ran to Lisa's side and knelt down beside her. "What's going on?" she asked quietly.

"Uncle Harold's dead!" Lisa sobbed.

Kathy was stunned. She couldn't speak. She turned her head to see Mike awkwardly trying to drag the luggage through the door. He seemed completely oblivious. Turning back to Lisa, she began to sob as well, "Oh honey, oh my God."

It was a while before Lisa was able to talk for long periods without breaking into tears. She led Kathy and Mike upstairs to the main floor. At the point where the stairs turned to head up to the loft was a sheet covering Uncle Harold. Tom had taken care of covering the body and calling the rest of the family. He was able to head them off before they arrived, most were now booking rooms at a hotel thirty minutes away.

"How does Tom have a signal?" Kathy asked, perplexed by his ability to use his phone reliably.

"You probably missed it, I did too," Lisa said, "but Tom noticed the big square dish on the roof. Apparently it's StarLink or *something*. The cottage apparently has Wi-Fi now. He said he's using some kind of voice over IT thing, I don't know," she sobbed again, "you'd have to ask him."

"Uncle Harold got the Internet?" Kathy asked, shaking her head. "That doesn't sound like him."

She took Mike's hand and they went over to the body. Squatting down together, they took a moment. Mike reached out and slowly uncovered Harold's head. It was pretty bad. Kathy put her hand up to her mouth and began to sob. It was definitely Uncle Harold. Even in this state, she could recognize that it was him. As Mike covered Harold up with the sheet, the reality of the situation hit Kathy. She began to cry in sobbing heaves.

"Hey!" a booming voice echoed through the cottage, "Look who caught up with the times!" Peter came around the corner from the front entrance. His black hair was shiny and slicked back to his head. He strode with all the confidence his six foot four frame allowed him. His hands were out and open as he came into the great room. "I didn't think you'd ever …" he stopped and stared at the faces all around him. His eyes flicked to the sheet, "What's going on?" he said.

"Oh Peter!" Lisa began to cry again, hurrying to hug her cousin.

"Whoa. I'm Ok," Peter said, hugging Lisa close.

"The police will be here in about thirty minutes, and the coroner is coming right behind," Tom said as he walked into the room. He looked tired. "Oh, hey Peter."

"The coroner?" Peter asked.

Lisa began to explain. She told about her and Tom arriving to find the tree cut down and the satellite dish on the roof.

"That tree always overhung the roof," Tom explained, "He probably could've just taken down some branches, but I guess he got over zealous."

"Sure," said Peter with a shortness that surprised Kathy.

"We came in the back, like everybody does," Lisa continued, "We didn't see anyone so we unpacked. Then Tom went up to the kitchen to get a beer and that's when he found …" she couldn't continue.

"It looks like he fell down the stairs from the loft," Tom added. "He's pretty broken up. I checked for a pulse or any signs of life," he shrugged. "He's gone."

"Wow," whispered Peter, looking over at the sheet.

The room was quiet for a moment. "Where's the rest of the family?" Peter asked.

"I managed to get a hold of them," Tom said. "They've stopped at the hotel off the highway."

"Ahh, good," said Peter. It seemed like he was in charge now. "Well I guess we just wait for the police. We'll definitely have to plan something for Uncle Harold back home. I think he would've wanted a celebration. I guess that's what he was hoping for this weekend." Peter frowned for a moment.

"Actually," Kathy interjected, "Do you know why he was having this little reunion at the cottage?"

"Probably just to announce the new Wi-Fi," Peter shrugged.

Lisa looked up. "It is weird that he got Internet at the cottage," she said.

"Why?" Peter asked. "I mean, I'm up here more than he is these days. He probably wanted to help out, he was considerate like that."

"Yeah," Tom said, "But he was also against technology at the cottage. I mean, the cottage doesn't even have a landline."

Peter just shrugged again.

"I don't understand how this could've happened," Mike said suddenly. Everyone turned to look at him. He was standing at the body, looking up the stairs. "I mean, he has nothing in his hands or near him. There's railings all the way up and it's a pretty narrow staircase. Surely he could've caught himself unless he was holding something."

The group moved over to the stairs and looked up again. The stairs were open backed and led straight up to the loft. The towering windows of the a-frame backed the loft. There was a desk and chair at the top. Kathy noted that the chair was rotated so that it faced across the loft, not towards the stairs. "Hmm," she said out loud. "It's like he was talking to someone up there." She carefully stepped over the body. She noted both feet were laying on the bottom stair. She began to climb the stairs.

"Don't touch anything," Peter said, "The police are going to want a clean scene."

"I've watched enough crime shows to know that," Kathy said.

Lisa left Tom and followed Kathy up the stairs. Kathy attempted to take note of everything in the loft. The entire loft had a rustic wooden railing around the edge that became the handrail of the stairs. There was a loveseat at the far side and the desk and chair at the top. Nothing blocked the view out the windows. A large area rug covered most of the floor and this drew her attention. There were wood particles stuck in the fibers of the carpet by the loveseat. Someone had been sitting there. Someone that had also been out at the shredded tree stump.

There were papers on the desk. The view out the window caught her eye and held it there for a while. The lake was gorgeous. The property sloped down to it with a path winding down to a large dock that lurched out into the water. An old metal boat and larger sport boat were tied to it at the end.

"Did you find anything?" Lisa said. She was right beside Kathy and the voice startled her.

"Well someone was up here," Kathy said.

"How do you figure?" Lisa looked intense.

Kathy wasn't paying attention. She spotted a business card. It had fallen beside the desk, but its glossy coating was reflecting the light as it poked out from the back of the desk. She knelt down and crawled under the desk.

"What are you doing?" Lisa asked.

"Are you girls alright?" Michael called up the stairs.

Kathy ignored him, she was focused on that card. She pulled the corner and it slid out into her hand. A smiling face greeted her as she held it up. The card was for a real estate agent specializing in vacation homes. She grimaced and stuck it in her pocket before backing out from under the desk.

"What was it?" Lisa asked.

"Just a business card," Kathy replied. Her head was full and she had to shake her it before she could pay attention to the conversation currently happening. Mike had come up the stairs as well and the loft was starting to feel crowded.

"Find anything interesting?" Mike asked.

"Not really," Kathy mumbled. She leaned over the edge of the loft and called down to Tom as she pulled out her phone. "Hey Tom, what's the Wi-Fi password?"

"Oh, hang on, it's in my phone," Tom said, looking up. He began to tap on his device and soon recited a random list of letters, numbers, and symbols.

Kathy frowned as she attempted to enter the characters.

She held the railing as she descended the stairs. "Peter, do you know what Uncle Harold's plans were for the cottage?"

"Geez, Kathy, a bit soon for that isn't it?" Peter said.

"I'm just wondering," she said. "I'd always assumed it was going to you, since you were here so much."

Peter laughed, "I wish. Uncle Harold wasn't my biggest fan. He let me use it because I kept it up. Opened it, closed it, put the dock in, that sort of thing. We were rarely here at the same time."

"I didn't even know you were up here that much," Lisa said.

"I'm surprised," Peter said, "When I did see Uncle Harold, he was always talking about you guys being here."

Kathy's head spun, "What? Tom and Lisa come up?"

"Almost every weekend, from what I heard," Peter shrugged.

The real estate website came up on Kathy's phone and there it was. "Beautiful A-Frame cottage in sought after area."

"Oh my god!" Kathy said. She turned on Lisa. "You killed him!"

"What!?" Lisa exclaimed.

"Uncle Harold was going to sell the cottage. That's why he put the Wi-Fi in. Prepping it for the sale."

"That's crazy!" Lisa was agitated. "What's wrong with you?"

"Oh please," Kathy said, "There were wood chips from the tree on the carpet upstairs. You two were up there with him. He probably told you he was planning on selling and that's why he was having a get together. So everyone would have one last visit. When you found out you wouldn't be inheriting the cottage you pushed him down the stairs!"

"That's absurd!" Tom said.

"You were definitely here while Uncle Harold was still alive," Kathy pointed at them.

"You have no proof of that," Lisa said.

"Then where did Tom get the Wi-Fi password?"

There was a knock at the front door. The police had arrived. Just in time.

WHO	WHEN	RATING

Notes:

☆☆☆☆☆

Notes:

☆☆☆☆☆

Notes:

☆☆☆☆☆

Notes:

☆☆☆☆☆

Notes:

☆☆☆☆☆

Notes:

☆☆☆☆☆

Notes:

☆☆☆☆☆

Notes:

☆☆☆☆☆

The Cottage Word Search

All of the following are cottage related words have been hidden in the grid below. They may be forwards, backwards, vertical, horizontal or diagonal. Some letters may be used more than once. Try to find them all.

```
S M O O S E C A M P F I R E D
L U R F O R E S T S T A R S S
A J N E C M V C O T T A G E C
K T P S A A M K R C B R F P A
E Z R A H D N F A E O I I E B
M G R A N I C O I Y G A R G I
O F I S I C N M E S A G K D N
O R V C A L A E U I H K S F S
N I E P O U E K W S T I T U L
P E R S A O S R E A C R N N O
I N O M S D K A R R T R A G S
N D A O B G D O G O E E A I T
E S R R M A P L U E P L R T L
H I K E S W I M E T E E A V P
R O W S T E N T O T T E R X N
```

BIRDS	LAKE	RELAX
CABIN	LOST	RIVER
CAMPFIRE	MAP	ROPE
CANOE	MOON	ROW
COOKOUT	MOOSE	SAUSAGE
COTTAGE	MUSCRAT	SMORES
EGGS	OAK	STARS
FIR	OAR	SUNSHINE
FISHING	OTTER	SWIM
FOREST	PADDLE	TENT
FRIENDS	PANCAKE	TRAILER
FUN	PEG	WATER
HIKE	PINE	
KAYAK	READ	

Lost Treasure of Spruce Hollow

Kenneth Roland

Uncle Russel was dead. I'd only met him at funerals, and now I was at his. There weren't many people to meet at this funeral. The funeral home itself had the largest contingent. Uncle Russel's lawyer hovered by the door, his neighbour stood by the casket. The latter looked twitchy and eager to leave. I bounced between lawyer and neighbour, sorry that I had ordered a buffet for twenty. You have to do something right? He's family. Sort of. He was my grandpa's brother. No kids of his own. My grandfather's only son was my dad. Luckily my mom's side of the family was huge. I briefly thought about calling some of them to see if they would want leftovers.

Russel had left me everything. Which after the cost of the funeral and the lawyer had left me a thousand dollars in the hole and a crappy house out in the woods. I hoped selling the house would at least put me back in the black.

When I would bounce to the lawyer, he would offer me the *same great service* that he had given to my uncle. As I rebounded to the neighbour, he would ask when I would be selling Uncle Russel's property. Neither one seemed to be too cut up about Russel being dead.

"Looks like the neighbour is interested in buying the cabin," I said to the lawyer. "Will you be able to help with that?"

"Of course he is," the man snorted. "You may have a lot of offers with the Legend of Spruce Hollow and all."

"What legend is that?" I asked, attempting to delicately eat a triangle of egg salad sandwich.

"I'm surprised you haven't heard of it, your Uncle was all in on the lost treasure."

I swallowed hard. "I'm interested now. What treasure?"

The lawyer changed his stance, apparently settling in. "During the revolutionary war, the settlers in Reedsville became worried that the British would confiscate anything they had of value to fund the war effort. So they gathered everything together, made an inventory of it and sealed it in a cave in what we now call Jack's Mountain. When the war was over, they went back to get their stuff and it was gone."

"That sucks," I said.

"Exactly. But then someone found another entrance into the cave. It led to a property owned by Jacob Lancaster. A property he called Spruce Hollow. Jacob went into the war late and was killed. No one ever found the valuables and since then the property has been subdivided and sold off. Your uncle owned the location of the original house. A lot of people believe that Jacob went in through his separate entrance, took the valuables, assuming the British would be blamed and hid them on his own property. They've never been found."

"Interesting," I said, "And people are willing to pay more for the house because they think there's treasure there."

"That's what they think."

"And how come nobody's found it?"

"Maybe they have," the lawyer mused. "But I've never heard of anyone giving up the place and moving to Fiji. They all seem to hunt until they die. It's very hard to prove that something isn't hidden."

I thought about that for a moment. Once someone says there's a treasure, it was difficult to guarantee that there wasn't. Maybe you just didn't find it. Maybe it was somewhere you haven't looked. "So this Jacob could've put the valuables anywhere?"

"Or maybe he wasn't even the one that took them," the lawyer shrugged. "Robbers may have found it and went south, who knows?"

"And now I own the property?"

"You will, once the paperwork is done." He smiled politely. I had a feeling he was over the treasure business and relied on paperwork to make his wealth.

The house, such as it was, sat in a square of spruce trees. Someone had purposely planted them all around the perimeter of the property, likely trying to hide what was happening on the property. A gravel driveway cut through the tree line and slowly curved up to the house. It was creepy passing through to the inner property. I felt like I was in the middle of nowhere yet crammed into a small space, caged from the rest of the world.

The yard had obviously been neglected for a long time. Tall grasses, thistles, and wildflowers grew everywhere except for a path to the side porch. Sidewalk blocks were barely visible as the edges of the yard grew over them. The house itself was sided with wood that was once red. The paint was peeling and falling off in places and made the entire place look brown, except for the window frames that were a faded creamy colour. As much as I thought the outside looked pretty bad, it didn't prepare me for the inside. I had to use my shoulder to get the door to move and it opened to an unlivable space. Boxes, papers and junk were piled everywhere. Only a small path of discarded papers led deeper into the house. I flicked the light on and stared. Why was I here? I could just sell it as is, and forget I ever saw it. But I owned a house, it was mine, how could I not see it.

I followed the path through the piles of junk to a kitchen in the back. It was slightly cleaner than the living room and dining room I passed through. You could get to a small table that was piled with notes on auctions in the area. Uncle Russell must've been tracking items that were sold that could be part of the treasure. The chair was clean and I could almost picture him just getting up from it and heading out to dig in the yard. I opened the back door and pushed on the screen door to survey the rear of the property. Shovels, pick axe's and other garden tools leaned against the house, and the small back deck sagged a bit as I stepped out onto it.

I could see the cave entrance where the treasure supposedly resided. Someone had put up a sign, "Abandon hope, all ye who enter here". Probably thought they were funny. I rubbed my hand along the worn wood of the railing. Treasure hunting was not for me. Mucking about the dirt and dark. It sounded dreadful.

Maybe my treasure could come from the house. Clean it up, make it look nice and sell it. Looking back into the house I realized it was almost as cramped and dark as the cave. Maybe my treasure was insuring it and burning it to the ground. That thought brought a smile to my face as I headed back in.

After hours of piling research papers into stacks based on their contents I unearthed a filing cabinet. It was only half full and the documents pre-dated my Uncle Russel, previous searchers that had failed to find anything. As I filed Russel's research, I was fascinated with the details of all the digging that had been done. I wondered if there was much of the mountain left, or if it was almost all hollowed out and waiting to collapse. I found multiple maps and drawings that led me to believe there was no part of the cave that hadn't been investigated. The only interesting one was tucked into a faded manilla folder. The mapped looked old and the writing appeared to be original. Not from a fountain pen, but from a quill or similar with drops and stains. All it showed was circles with rough distances between them, presumably in feet or paces. The beginning of the map was torn off, along with half the compass, so north could be in one of two directions. Unfortunately it was only half there. It had been torn roughly across the middle. A note written in sloppy cursive was tucked into the folder with it. "Joseph Lancaster's half of the map. His brother didn't trust him with the entirety. Found on Joseph's body in Virginia. Purchased from James Kahn, 1932." The writer didn't leave their own name.

I tucked the folder into the front of the cabinet. It may be worth something.

Eventually I created a hill of black garbage bags in the front yard and could see most of the floor in the living room. I had been surprised to find furniture tucked up against the walls that was buried beneath papers and artifacts. I had no idea what some of the tools and bits were, or why anyone had kept rocks and dirt in their investigation of the treasure. The furniture was in pretty good shape. I wondered how long it had been covered and protected by the trash from the various treasure hunters that had owned and lived in the house. I wondered what the value of a 1940's living room set was. Could be more money in the bank.

I was about to roll out my sleeping bag for the night, then thought the floor may actually be cleaner than the rug that was covering it. I lifted the front of the sofa and pulled the carpet from underneath it. I rolled the carpet across the floor and then yanked the far end from under the chairs. The floor underneath looked like it was just laid. Obviously no one had moved the carpet in a long time. Of course they hadn't, it was buried under junk. I felt better about rolling out my sleeping bag and actually placing my pillow on the floor. I put some white noise on my phone in hopes it would lull me to sleep.

After all the lifting, I slept like a babe. I dreamt of families packing away their most precious items, wondering if the British would take them, or thieves, or if they would even live long enough to find out.

Upon waking, I stretched myself out, attempting to rid myself of the crick in my back and felt the floor move with me. Not all of it, just under my rump, like a piece of the hardwood was loose. My mind lept to the possibilities!

I was out of my sleeping bag in no time and shoved it heavily out of the way. I had to turn on the lights in the dim morning light, but there it was; a thin crack between two boards. I placed my palms on it and shifted it around. It moved slightly from side to side. This board was definitely not nailed down. I could see a dent in the board next to it like someone had used a screwdriver or butter knife to pry it up.

I literally ran for the assorted tools I had collected on the kitchen table and grabbed a slot screwdriver. I jammed it into the same spot where the marks were and pried. The board popped up and over with a bang. There it was, an opening in the floor. A tin cookie box was nestled into a wooden chest mounted to the joists. I couldn't believe my eyes. The tin had an old castle printed on it with the name Gray & Dunn; not a company I was familiar with.

As I was studying it, the screwdriver rolled into the hole and there was a bang as a violent arc of electricity shot between the lid, the screwdriver and a nail in the chest. The lights went out in the house and my eyes had to adjust to the dimness. The castle was now blackened and the lid had popped off. I was shocked, but luckily not literally. I had been just about to reach in and lift out the tin, I can't imagine what would have happened.

I was too scared to reach in now and returned to the kitchen for another screwdriver, ensuring it had a fat plastic handle. I used it to poke at the lid. It moved easily, no shower of sparks, or explosions. Still I used the screwdriver to catch the edge and lift it out. Inside the box was a bunch of papers and coins. I poked at them timidly. Nothing. Still scared, I carefully reached in and snatched at the papers, yanking my hand back quickly. I wasn't killed instantly, and let out a breath I hadn't realized I'd been holding.

The first thing I looked at was an envelope. It was labelled "Original manifest of items stored. Acquired 1923." Completely different handwriting from the other note, and inside was a document with a list of items and family names. I quickly glanced over the list: two candlesticks, plated silver, McDonald; $2.15 coinage, Rubel; the list went on and on. Gold plated collection plates from the First Baptist church, pearl inlay cigarette case from the Johnson family, I could almost feel the loss for each of the families and for the community as a whole.

There were more notes and hand drawn maps, but then I saw the torn edge of the next page. It had to be the other half of the map. The cave entrance was obvious the second I saw it, and the other half of the compass rose, but to my surprise there was still no North marked in any way. I quickly returned to the filing cabinet leaving the rest of the papers in my hand on top of it, I pulled open the top drawer and fetched the first half of the map. It was possible no one before me had ever held both halves even though they were so close together this whole time. I placed the two pieces on the kitchen table and carefully fit them together. The cave, the circles, the rose, all lined up. I turned the map so the cave mouth was at the bottom, envisioning how you would have to move in the cave to get to each circle that would lead you to the next one. Did the circles represent forks in a system of tunnels, or some kind of stalagmite or similar.

The map obviously started at the cave mouth, which opened to the west, so I tried to orient the map so that at least one line of the compass rose made sense. It didn't work. There was no way that the cave entrance and the compass rose made sense together. I stared at the two pieces, flipping one over and then the other. After about five minutes of spinning the pages and looking at it from every angle I let out a deep sigh. I wasn't a treasure hunter. The only thing I knew was that X marked the spot. Suddenly I realized it wasn't a compass rose at all. It was an X through a circle. It was literally X marks the spot. The cave entrance WAS the start, but the map didn't lead into the cave, it led AWAY from it. My heart was pounding in my throat. This changed everything. The treasure wasn't in the cave, of course it wasn't! Jacob wouldn't hide the treasure in the cave. That's the first place people would look!

The sunlight was starting to stream through the dirt on the windows. I rushed to get socks and pants on, almost falling over as I struggled to stuff my leg down the narrow jeans. I left my boots untied as I stormed out to the cave entrance. I smiled at the sign. "Abandon hope, all ye who enter here" was more valid than they knew. You needed to go the other way!

The first circle had forty-five written between it and the cave entrance. I started to pace in long strides. They all used paces back then right? Soon I had entered the back door of the house, traversed the entire thing and exited out the front. I was standing on the driveway, almost on the road. It didn't feel right. But would the road have been here? So much could've changed in a few hundred years. I looked at the next note. Fifteen paces, or maybe feet to the south. I paced along, just inside the spruce trees that loaned their name to this place. I could feel my face drop in awe as I looked ahead. I was approaching a large boulder. It sat alone, without any other rocks or landscape to attend to it. This was the circle! Obviously, the first boulder had been removed to create the driveway. Someone would be very upset if they had lived to see it removed. Here was me, without any experience or knowledge of the Legend of Spruce Hollow, solving it by myself, because I actually bothered to clean up!

The circles quickly passed by as expected and I came to the large mound of stones where the treasure was apparently buried. My hand shook, holding the map in front of me and staring at those stones. I realised I was starting to sweat, a bead of water running down my side from my armpit. Could this really be it? Had I found the treasure others had searched for for hundreds of years?

It's been fourteen years since that moment. The house has been consumed again, by papers, rocks, and small trinkets I've dug out of the yard. Ha! The yard. I call it that, but it's mostly just a wasteland of holes and piles. Some of the spruce trees have died. Apparently I've dug out too much of their root system. I feel like it's out there somewhere, but how do you prove that it isn't? I could be off by only a foot or two on any given dig. Uncle Russel, why did you do this to me?

WHO	WHEN	RATING

Notes:

☆☆☆☆☆

Notes:

☆☆☆☆☆

Notes:

☆☆☆☆☆

Notes:

☆☆☆☆☆

Notes:

☆☆☆☆☆

Notes:

☆☆☆☆☆

Notes:

☆☆☆☆☆

Notes:

☆☆☆☆☆

Are We There Yet?

Try to find your way through the maze of traffic to get to the cottage

Into The Woods

Dorian Blackwood

Harriet sat in the driver's seat with her hands tight around the steering wheel; although the car had been idling there for the past two minutes. Augustine glanced at her mother from the front passenger seat and bit her lip. She turned to look out the window at the old, thatched-roof cottage, with its mud walls and overgrown garden. "Wow!" she enthused. "It looks so much smaller than I remember!"

Harriet stirred. She forced a smile and switched off the engine. "I'm not surprised, bobbin," she reached over to pat her daughter's leg. "You weren't even as tall as the gate over there when we last visited."

Augustine grabbed her mother's hand and held it for as long as she could. Until Harriet gave her another forced smile and the two of them climbed out of the car.

The heat tasted of dust, aged wood, and dried grass. Augustine could hear the buzzing of insects and the rustle of the wind through the leaves as she looked towards the ancient woods towering over the cottage. Like a verdant wave, waiting to come crashing down and swallow them whole.

It stirred something at the back of her mind. A faint recollection of squinting into bright, morning light, and her mother undoing her seatbelt. How her mother's faded T-shirt and tumble-down hair had still smelled of the hospital.

Shouldering her rucksack like a soldier preparing for a final march, Harriet walked up to the wooden gate. It hung on an angle from the low stone wall, overgrown with moss and vines. Pushing it open, she called out. "Nagrona! We're here!"

No one answered.

The front door was unlocked, so the two of them stepped inside. Augustine was startled at how the interior was so dark and cold. A single, small window provided meager light from the far end of the room. She had the sudden impression that she'd clambered up onto the counter and looked out through that exact window a long time ago.

Even as Augustine squinted and tried to acclimatise, her mother followed the unseen paths of her childhood and moved on ahead, still calling out for Nagrona. Because God forbid, she ever be allowed to call her own mother something other than her name.

Augustine shook her head, attempting to dislodge the bitter thought. Stepping forward, she ran face-first into something hanging from the low ceiling, which had all the whisper-softness of a thick spider's web. She panicked and swatted at it, until she realised it was a bundle of plants, not quite dried. She was grateful her mother didn't pop back out until she'd navigated around it.

Harriet returned to her daughter's side. "She must have gone into the woods. It is the season for collecting elder flowers."

Augustine was aghast. "She's supposed to be resting! She almost died, like – last week!"

"I know," Harriet's voice was soft and concerned.

Augustine could have pinched herself for her thoughtlessness. "I'm sure she's fine, mum. Nagrona's one of the hardiest people we know! She must have lost track of the time, that's all. I'll go and see if I can find her."

Harriet seized her arm. "No!" she gasped.

Augustine stopped, taken aback at the edge of fear in her mother's voice.

"I – what I meant was I should go," her mother's grip relaxed, and she stroked Augustine's arm with her thumb. "Thank you for offering, bobbin. But the woods are…well, the woods are old, and tangled, and people get lost there all the time. I'm more familiar with the area, and I know all the places Nagrona might be. It'll be quicker if I go and look for her."

Augustine knew her mother wasn't thinking of other people, or even of what was more sensible and convenient. She was thinking of the time that Augustine herself had gone missing in those woods as a child for almost a full week.

"You're right, mum," Augustine reassured her. "I think it might be better if I get us set up here for the night, before it gets too late. Which room is ours?"

"That would be lovely, thank you. The first room there is Nagrona's, so don't go in there," she pointed at one of the dark spaces in the wall, and then at the similar blackness beside it. "Ours is the last room there. It's going to be a squeeze for both of us to fit in the bed. But perhaps this is how I can make up for all the cuddles I've been missing."

Augustine wriggled her hands under her mother's arms and pulled her in for a hug. "Mum, we've been over this! You and dad need to retire, and come and move in with me. We'll go for walks on the beach! We'll get ice-creams and matching sunburns. You'll listen to me give the same three speeches about whales, pelicans and marine life to tourists all summer. It'll be great!"

Harriet managed a soft chuckle and kissed the side of Augustine's head.

When her mother left, Augustine roused at herself. "Get it together, Augustine St. Lewis," she addressed herself in a stern voice. "Mum needs us! And I ... I need to be able to see once I shut the front door." Taking her phone out of her pocket, Augustine turned on the flashlight, shut the door and took a proper look around.

All of them knew Nagrona was a witch, and that she still made a living selling herbal teas and remedies. In fact, it was one of her customers who'd come across her when she was in the midst of a heart attack and phoned for help. Although her big brother now claimed that he was far too old to believe in things like magic, she was sure even Samson would have his doubts if he saw her cottage now.

Mismatched glass containers rested on crooked shelves, some of which did seem to contain dried lizards and dead spiders. There was a fireplace against the wall, large enough to cook two hapless children in, bundles of plants hanging from the ceiling, and trinkets and candles nestled into all the crooks and crannies.

It was a surprise then, to discover their room was so plain. Nothing was in there except for a single, narrow bed with a wrought iron frame, a stand and washbasin, and a single wardrobe. At least the sheets were clean, and the mattress wasn't the horrid kind with creaking, pointed springs. Although it did have the distinct smell of all old, unmoved things. Where the dust hadn't so much as settled on it, as permeated into the fabric itself.

Sitting on the edge of the bed, the oppressive stillness of the cottage weighed down on Augustine. Although she would swallow her mother's entire collection of pins and needles before she ever admitted it, she wished her brother was there. Almost as if she'd summoned him, her phone rang in her hand and Samson's name flashed up on the screen. "Speak of the devil! What's up, big bro?"

"Don't call me that, we're not in a nineties sitcom."

Augustine almost gave herself a cramp from how hard she rolled her eyes. "Are you calling me for a reason, or…?"

"You didn't call to say you've arrived," he tutted. *"We agreed that was the plan."*

"Don't be such a fusspot. We're here, we've arrived! But Nagrona's stepped out."

"Stepped out? She was in the hospital barely a week ago. She should be at home resting."

"That's what I said! Mum thinks she might have gone into the woods to collect more ingredients for her teas and things. She's gone to look for her."

"You're not thinking of going in there as well?"

"Ugh, Sam!" Augustine groaned. "I'm not five! It's not like I'm going to wander off again!"

"Don't snap at me!" he retorted, doing the exact thing he was ordering her not to. *"You don't know how hard things were for us back then. Our parents were worried sick! You at least have the luxury of not remembering anything."*

Augustine rankled, preparing to launch an all-out counterattack. However, something he said gave her pause. "Wait," she said, "us?"

"Forget it. How long ago did mum head out?"

"On no, don't even think about weaselling out of this one," Augustine gloated. "You said 'us', not 'mum and dad'. You were worried about me too, Sam? I'm touched!"

"Don't be stupid, Augustine," Samson muttered. *"You wouldn't have been there at all, if not for me. I was terrified I'd never see you again."*

Augustine's smile plummeted. "That wasn't your fault, Sam," she insisted, softening her tone. "If the doctors had listened to what mum and dad were telling them, it would never have gotten so bad! You would never have needed to go to hospital at all."

Samson made one of his usual noises where he didn't agree with her, but wasn't going to dignify her words with a proper response.

"I know it was awful, and me being here brings up bad memories," she continued. "But I'm here to help mum, not to give her more things to be worried about. You know I'd never hurt her like that."

He exhaled. *"I know. I suppose I'm still bothered that I can't be there too, that's all."*

"Listen Sam, even if she did have some way you and dad could keep your support devices charged, Nagrona doesn't have running water, or indoor plumbing. I don't even know how we're going to use the bathroom."

"You're kidding."

"I wish I was kidding!" Augustine twisted around so she could sit cross-legged on the bed and look out the window. "How's dad, anyway? He must be glad to have you home again for a longer visit."

As he talked, Augustine kept her gaze fixed on the woods outside. She was aware of the slow progression of the afternoon sun, and the deepening of the shadows between the trees. She was relieved when her mother emerged, until she saw how her head was down, and her arms folded.

Augustine scrambled to her feet. A moment later she saw her grandmother appear as well. "She's here! Nagrona I mean," she interrupted her brother. "I can see them coming back to the cottage now."

He hesitated. *"How does she look?"*

Augustine could see her grandmother was thinner than she remembered, although she still had that hard, unfeeling sort of look about her. And as Harriet passed close enough for Augustine to see her pained expression, what little compassion she'd scraped together for Nagrona withered. "She looks alive at least," she said, her voice tight. "I have to go."

Harriet made an effort to seem cheerful as she entered the cottage. Nagrona, on the other hand, gave her a quick, curt look and said nothing as she swept past.

"I'm glad to see you're so well, Nagrona," Augustine kept her voice light. "We were all worried when the hospital called."

Nagrona snorted as she picked up a box of matches from the mantlepiece and struck one. "Worried I'd pull through, more like."

"Please don't talk like that," Harriet murmured. "We were worried. We are worried."

Nagrona acted as if she hadn't heard a word her daughter said. She set about lightning a few of the lanterns strung from the ceiling, and some candles.

Augustine moved to her mother's side, putting an arm around her waist. "I've set up our room, mum. It's nice and cool inside the cottage, so we should be quite comfy tonight."

Harriet gave her a grateful look and kissed the side of her head again.

As she laid in bed that night, Augustine was struck at how familiar and yet unfamiliar it all seemed. Coarse linen, scraping against her bare knees, her mother's warmth against her back, and the constant, overwhelming scents of different plants. All of which followed her down into fragmented dreams. She was in the woods, the trees towering over her. She could hear music and laughter.

Someone held her hand, and the two of them danced through the dappled sunlight. She was drawn towards a ring of people in strange clothes, all dancing around the protruding roots of a great oak tree. She broke free when she heard her mother's voice, calling out her name–

"Augustine," her mother's hands were warm against her bare arms. "Come with me, bobbin. Come back to bed."

Augustine stumbled a little as her mother turned her around. She could still see the oak tree; its trunk so wide it would take her an entire lifetime to walk around it even once.

"That's it," Harriet guided her across the floor. "Come with me."

"Mum?"

"I'm here, bobbin," her mother paused to give her a gentle squeeze, a grounding touch which painted over her dreams in great black streaks of wakefulness. "We're going back to bed so we can get our rest for tomorrow."

"We'll miss the dance," Augustine protested. "It's almost over."

Her mother's grip tightened around her.

Augustine was disoriented, unable to tell where she was. Although now she was aware her feet were cold and aching, as if she had been standing on the hard floor for some time. "Mum, where am I? Where has the oak tree gone?"

"All the trees are outside," Harriet murmured, leading her to the bedroom. "We're safe in Nagrona's cottage right now. We came here to help look after her, remember?"

Augustine did remember, and still she felt confused as her mother helped her into bed and laid down beside her. "I was in the woods," she mumbled. "I thought we were having fun. But now I don't know. I think – I think I was scared."

"There's nothing to be afraid of now," Harriet soothed, holding her tight. "You don't belong to the woods. You'll never be taken back there again, I promise."

At breakfast the next morning, Augustine dug into a generous helping of her mother's porridge. She wanted to ask Harriet about her sleepwalking incident, but couldn't now be certain if it had even happened or whether she had dreamt it all.

Harriet kept insisting it wasn't their fault, and that neither Augustine nor Samson could help their random bouts of sleepwalking. Augustine had hoped it wouldn't happen while her mother had so much else to be concerned about.

Harriet, meanwhile, puttered around the cottage. To Augustine, it looked like all her mother was doing was moving things from one container to another, or shifting them left or right. Yet it somehow made the whole place look a lot tidier and more organised. She had also propped the front door open to let the fresh air in, despite Nagrona's obvious disdain.

Augustine felt vindicated that even the insects couldn't contend with the stifling smell of the place, and didn't venture inside.

"She must be quite tired," Harriet murmured to herself as she stood before a rather cluttered corner.

Augustine refrained from pointing out if Nagrona was so tired, she shouldn't have refused to eat breakfast with them and gone straight out into the woods. "We'll take care of her while we're here, mum," she promised. She scarfed the rest of her porridge and shooed her mother off when Harriet came to collect the dishes.

Nagrona didn't like being looked after, of course. She did whatever she could over the week to make that point as clear as possible. Augustine despaired that where her mother had been hoping for some sort of reconciliation before the end, Nagrona had decided to unleash all her remaining vitriol upon them. It didn't even seem to matter to her if she did it in front of her customers either.

Augustine had been prepared for this. She'd learned from a lifetime of arguing with her brother that the best offence, at times, was to be so positive, so cheerful, and so tooth-achingly sweet, the other person simply gave up in disgust.

It worked quite well on Nagrona for a while too.

Nagrona was seated in her armchair next to the fireplace when Augustine emerged from the bedroom that morning, leaving her mother to get dressed. Which was odd, since her grandmother made every effort to avoid them as much as possible.

"Good morning Nagrona," Augustine chirped. "What a good night's sleep I had! There's something so glorious about being out here, in nature. Isn't there?"

Nagrona gave a snort. "You're a spoiled brat, all right. Although not half the fool your mother is. You have a backbone at least. I'll give you that much."

Augustine had intended to start the fire for breakfast. She paused and looked over her shoulder at the bedroom door, then turned to face the old woman. Nagrona lifted her chin. "Am I wrong? She was too meek to face me herself, so she's brought one of her whelps to use as a crutch. For all the good it's done her, she still cowers like a mouse."

Augustine breathed in. She understood how snakes must have felt in the moment before striking, as the venom gathered in their mouths. But then she looked at Nagrona's gnarled, arthritic hands and her hollow cheeks. She thought of her living out in this old cottage, having to draw water from a well if she so much as wanted a drink. She thought of how, if no customers had come past that morning, she might have died right there – all alone.

And she still would, when the two of them left.

Augustine breathed out. "I'll never understand what it's like to be so miserable and hateful," she said softly. "You know we didn't have to come here. Mum could have told the hospital we're estranged, and gone on with her life like nothing ever happened. You could have been kept there under observation, or even forced into care. But mum didn't want that to happen because she's a good person. You didn't teach her that Nagrona. You neglected her, and neglected me too."

Nagrona's fingers dug into the arms of her chair. Something dark twisted in her expression, a bitterness which she had been nursing for so long it had become a part of her being. "I did, did I?"

"You were supposed to be watching me when I went missing. Am I wrong?"

Nagrona rose from her seat, drawing the folds of her shawl around her. "Your fool of a mother has secrets of her own. Go and ask her, brat. Go and ask her what she wished for in those woods, and what gifts she squandered."

Augustine refused to rise to the bait. "Whatever mum did or didn't do, I know for a fact it was the right choice."

Nagrona bared her crooked teeth. She swept out of the cottage, slamming the door behind her.

As much as Augustine didn't want to let her grandmother get under her skin, Nagrona's accusations weighed on her mind. It didn't help that her sleepwalking continued, and she kept dreaming of the woods. Each time she did, the dreams became a little more distinct, a little more peculiar and frightening.

She had the feeling she'd been taken further in than she'd wanted to go. That she'd been frightened and cried for her parents. Yet the details all seemed so unreal; so implausible. Nothing but the imagination of a lost child at work.

As their last few days at the cottage drew to a close, Augustine finished cleaning out the fireplace and turned to her mother. "Mum?"

Harriet looked around from the last set of shelves she was organising. "Mm?"

"Nagrona said something to me the other morning. I know I shouldn't take it to heart but…"

Her mother came straight over and knelt beside her. "If she said something cruel or hurtful, it's not true Augustine," she said, rubbing her daughter's back. "She should never have spoken to you in that way."

"It wasn't like that. It was about the time I went missing." Harriet tensed.

Augustine hesitated for a split second and then dove in. "She said there was a promise you made in the woods, and acted like it had something to do with what happened to me."

Harriet exhaled as if she'd been holding her breath since that fateful summer. Her shoulders lowered and there was almost a look of relief tangled together with her resignation. "It's a beautiful morning," she said, holding her hand out to Augustine to help her to her feet. "Let's go outside."

Augustine expected her mother to take her along the lane and put the woods further behind them. But instead, she drew Augustine towards them, to a narrow trail that had been worn into the grass and the dirt which skirted the edge of the tree line.

Harriet was quiet for a while, and Augustine let her mother gather her thoughts uninterrupted. Insects flitted around them while birds swooped in and out of cover, taking their fill. A sense of anticipation and potential hung in the air.

"I know there's a lot of things I haven't spoken about," her mother began. "But the truth is, there are a lot of things I still don't understand, and things I'm still coming to terms with myself."

Augustine held and squeezed her mother's hand.

"You know Nagrona believes in magic and witchcraft," Harriet said. "But she also believes that when she gave birth to me, she lost her power."

"What?"

Harriet gave her a soft, sad smile. "She never speaks about my father, but I believe he left her when she was still pregnant with me. So, this was her way of coping. She tried a lot of things to regain that power. Things I understand now were harmful, and that I should never have been exposed to. But back then I would have done whatever it took to make her look at me and love me. Except…"

"Except?"

Harriet stopped walking. She breathed in and out in small, shuddering breaths.

"It's all right mum," Augustine soothed. "We don't have to talk about it if it's that horrible."

Harriet pushed on. "You deserve to know," she said, drawing Augustine closer to her. "It wasn't long after things were becoming more serious between your father and I that Nagrona thought she found the solution. A spell, a wish that had to be made over the oldest oak tree in these woods. But I couldn't go through with it, even after we'd hiked for hours to find the tree."

Despite the heat, a chill trickled down Augustine's spine. She thought of her dreams, of the figures that she'd seen dancing around the old oak tree. Except last night, she'd dreamed the people were all sobbing and pleading for the dance to end.

Harriet drew in a shuddering breath. "Nagrona told me the spell required me to make a promise. To give up something of myself to the tree that I treasured. So, she wanted me to swear that I would never have children, knowing how much I wanted to be a mother."

Augustine stared at her. Her mouth open and closed, but she was too stunned to think of a response.

"Yet when I stood at that oak tree, all I wished for was to have children," Harriet swallowed. "Children I could love, like Nagrona could never love me. And I did, despite the doctors being so certain your father and I would never conceive, we were blessed with two, beautiful children."

Augustine looked into her mother's face. She saw all her pain, and all the scars from her own mother's absence of love laid bare. Her entire being ached as she suddenly understood this was what made Harriet so desperate for her and Samson to never feel that way. "Mum," she murmured. "I – oh, mum."

Harriet reached out to stroke her cheek. Her fingers were warm and calloused.

"Nagrona believes because I made that wish, the woods demanded some sort of payment in return. That they tried to take you from me."

"She really thinks that's why I went missing?"

Harriet nodded. She lowered her hand and turned to look at the woods, and into their past. "Samson needed to be moved to a cardiac unit at another hospital. It was too far for us to commute from home, and all we could find was a single-bed room at a motel. Your father kept insisting he would sleep in the car, even knowing how it could hurt his health. So, after we talked it through, we made the choice for him to take the motel room and us two to come here. Nagrona's cottage was less than six hours from the hospital. You were going to stay with her until Samson's operation was over, that was all."

"But she left me alone."

"For hours," her mother's voice twisted with the first real anger Augustine had ever seen Harriet show towards Nagrona. "We had to find out from the police that our daughter had gone missing, because she didn't think it was important enough to call us herself. I can't even describe how we felt, bobbin. How I felt, for trusting her. If I hadn't of been so weak and so stupid–"

"No mum!" Augustine interrupted, pulling on her mother's hand until Harriet looked at her. "You had no other choice! Sam was in hospital and there was no one else who could help out. I was a child, and Nagrona should have known better than to leave me alone with the door unlocked."

"Bobbin, the door was locked, and all the windows were still shut when the police searched the cottage," Harriet told her gently. "That's why we asked you so many times how you got out."

Augustine blinked. "It had to have been unlocked!"

Her mother shook her head. "Nagrona locked it before she left, and I know from experience a child can't open that lock without help. The police said it hadn't been forced from the outside either."

Augustine's brow furrowed. Yet all she could remember was the faintest sound of music and moving towards the door through the gloom of the cottage.

"We searched high and low for almost a week before the police called off their search," Harriet continued. "People kept telling us that our chances of finding you were so low. But we wouldn't give up. Something in me kept pushing me deeper and deeper into the woods. I'm not ashamed to admit I was in a state when I was the last one left searching that night. I screamed and I shouted, and I cried. I think I even threatened to set fire to the woods if I didn't get my daughter back."

Augustine watched the hurricane of emotions pass through her mother, and imagined her kneeling amongst the undergrowth to look for clues as the twilight stole between the trees. Alone, desperate – determined. She couldn't help but think that if her mother did have some sort of power, it was the strength of her love.

Harriet exhaled. "It was ridiculous, of course. So, when I was calm, I picked up the search again. Not ten minutes later I stumbled across the old oak tree where I'd made that wish. You were right there, my lost little bobbin; fast asleep among the roots."

Nagrona had no intention of seeing them off. She was glad for them to be out of her life and what little she had left of it. She passed them while Augustine and Harriet were packing the car as she headed towards the woods, a basket slung over her arm.

Augustine chased after her. "Nagrona - wait!"

The old woman stopped and turned to her with a scowl. "Your time here is done, child. Get gone with your mother and stop bothering me."

Augustine stood her ground. "Mum told me what happened. About the wish she made and where she found me after I went missing."

"And?"

"I don't know if magic is real or whether the wish mum made came true. I don't even know if the dreams I have about these woods are real," Augustine said. "All I know is that it doesn't matter. You don't have to love mum or care about me. Because we love her and she loves us. If I'm ever lost in the woods, she'll find me. If she ever gets lost, we'll find her. No matter what."

Nagrona shook her head in disgust. She turned and walked off into the woods.

Augustine stood for a while longer, breathing in the stifling summer air and thinking of all the sorrows and secrets the old trees had seen. Here was the place her mother's past had festered and turned to grief. Here was the place the old witch had cast aside her own child, and all the happiness the two of them could've shared, chasing after a power that might never have existed. Here, the impossible seemed all too possible; and all too frightening. She would be glad to leave it behind her.

"Bobbin," Harriet walked up beside her. "Is everything all right?"

"Just saying goodbye," Augustine replied with a smile. She gave her mother a gentle nudge.

"I'll take the first half of the drive, mum. You should get some rest."

"You're too good to me."

"I learned from the best," Augustine grinned.

Harriet put an arm around her as the two of them walked back to the car.

WHO	WHEN	RATING

Notes:

☆☆☆☆☆

Notes:

☆☆☆☆☆

Notes:

☆☆☆☆☆

Notes:

☆☆☆☆☆

Notes:

☆☆☆☆☆

Notes:

☆☆☆☆☆

Notes:

☆☆☆☆☆

Notes:

☆☆☆☆☆

Cabin in the Pines

Kenneth Roland

It was perfect. No one around. No Internet. No cell service. Buying this cabin felt like the best thing Meredith had done in a long time. Her lawyer had said the divorce was an "easy" one. No kids, even split, easy. So why did Meredith feel like something in her had died. Trust was harder, she felt like she had lost friends and was lonelier than she'd ever been. She worried she may be feeding the loneliness by moving to the middle of nowhere for the summer, but this was also her chance. She was sick of writing blog posts about the latest technology innovations. What has technology done for her? It allowed her husband to hook up with his highschool sweetheart and leave her all alone.

The cabin was a good size. Tucked in among sugar maples, white pines, and balsam firs in northern Quebec. It was isolated and compared to the houses in her hometown of Ottawa, it was inexpensive. This was where she was going to write the next great Canadian novel. She could almost hear Margaret

Atwood quaking in her crocheted shoes. First she just had to empty the rental van and return it. There was always something between her and her dreams.

Meredith had purposely bought a lot of flat packed furniture that she could move by herself and build in the room where it would go. The van was full of heavy cardboard boxes, then her clothes, laptop, and kitchenware. She dragged the box with a future desk in it to the future study in the back corner of the cabin. The room was wrapped on two sides with windows looking out to a creek that fed a small lake. Inspiration was there, if she could just coax it to let her take advantage of it. Laying the box on its side, she reached into her pocket for her box cutter. Then she shook her head. No, first things first. Unload and get the van back. She thought she caught movement in the trees on the far side of the creek and watched the woods for a while. Likely a deer. It would be nice if the deer used her small stream to drink. Natural inspiration, undistilled.

She drove the empty van back into town and picked up some poutine takeout. She checked her phone while she was in town and had a clear signal. No messages. The smell of the gravy made her stomach rumble the entire drive back. Approaching the cabin, she wished she had left some lights on. She pulled up close to the front door and left the headlights on while she unlocked the door and flicked on the hall light. She thought about moving the car beside the house, but realized there was no need. Whatever she did was right. This was her house. Her castle. Her fortress of solitude.

She turned on the lights in the study and saw her reflection appear in the windows. She leaned against the wall and slid down to a seated position. Her cardboard container of poutine in front of her. She slowly ate with the provided plastic fork, staring at the unbuilt desk. She realized she should have downloaded a few podcasts while she had a connection in town, but nothing to be done about that now.

The wooden floor creaked a bit as she pushed and shoved the parts of the desk into position. Inserting the little dowels and screws to turn it into furniture. She thought of Pinnochio, "*I wish I was a real desk*", and laughed to herself. There was a clink as if something hit the window and she looked up. Her own face stared back at her, but she continued to look at the window. She hadn't thought of curtains. Why did she need them if there was no one around?

Now suddenly she felt exposed. She dismissed that feeling quickly. Starting down a path of fear would leave her in a bad place. The sound was probably just the wind, or an animal, nature could be noisy sometimes.

Meredith pulled out her phone to check the time. Damn, she probably should have put the bed together first. She shoved the desk up against the window, once again peering out the window attempting to see past her reflection. She put her laptop, a notebook, and a mug of assorted writing utensils on the desk. As she flicked off the light in the study, she thought she saw something out the window. No. She told herself. Just no.

She slept fitfully. She was tired, but the noises kept distracting her brain. She wondered how anyone ever slept alone in the woods. The wind made noise, the trees made noise, the animals made noise, and none of it was consistent. Meredith slowly went downstairs in her oversized t-shirt and sweatpants. She pushed some boxes around until she found the coffee maker, set it up, and started a brew. Looking out the windows she felt better as the grey cleared to colour. The water reflected the sun in bright yellow on blue. She smiled inwardly, this is what she had come for. She was chilled and returned to the bedroom for a housecoat and some slippers. In the study she flipped open her laptop and brought up a new blank document. *"The Cabin in the Pines"* she typed. Write what you know; the first rule of writing. Save; the most important rule of writing. There would be no Cloud backups here.

Meredith got her coffee and went out on the deck. She thought about the noises from last night, the movement out the window. Her fear and loneliness. Write what you know? All she knew was loneliness, and now she knew fear.

She would have to own it. She smiled at the thought. It was the perfect story. Topping up her coffee from the pot on the way back to the study she began to type furiously.

Caitlin was alone in her cabin. Her fingers twitched over the laptop. She had written two chapters already that day. Light moved across the floor as the day progressed but Caitlin never moved, too deep into the book now to let herself out of the zone.

Meredith continued to write with a passion that surprised her. Sentences becoming paragraphs, becoming pages, and chapters.

Caitlin stood and stretched. The encounter with the old man had left her mind flailing. The were was a scratch at the window and she turned

What was that? Meredith stopped writing to look out the window. It was dark both outside and inside the room. The laptop screen was the only light and she could see her own ghostly face floating in the window. When did it get dark? She stood and stretched. Reaching down to the laptop she clicked "Save". She thought about turning on the light then remembered the night before. She moved to the window to peer out, cupping her hands to block the remaining light. Some moonlight revealed the edges of trees and reflected off the water. Meredith shook her head. She needed to eat something.

She toasted a bagel and smeared it with cream cheese. She found herself ruminating as she ate. The loneliness was ebbing. Putting it into the story, placing the burden on her poor Caitlin was allowing it to leave her. She smiled. No fear now. Caitlin gets the fear, she'll have to deal with it. She brushed the crumbs from her hands over the sink, then washed them, hurrying back to the study.

Caitlin could only see her own reflection in the windows. The dark outside was absolute, trapping the light in the room, the way Caitlin was trapped in her cabin. She could hear a twig snap outside and the leaves rustling as though someone or something was stepping through them.

Meredith had to stop again. Had she heard leaves, or was it just in her head? She listened quietly for a moment. No. The world was trying to scare her, and she didn't have time for it. If the world wanted fear, she'd give it to them.

Rain began to pelt the old metal roof and Caitlin shivered at the damp. She started to go to the stairs to fetch a sweater when she heard wood creaking above her. Something was moving around on the second floor. She turned on the light and peered out the door. She felt safer in the study, but knew she had to leave or she'd be trapped there with her fear. The creak came again but further away. Something must be up there. The constant noise of the rain began to bother her. She strained her ears to pick out other noises.

When did it start raining? Meredith wondered. Droplets of rain ran down the windows and pelted the glass with soft clinks. The wind had picked up and she could just make out branches swaying and shuddering outside the windows. She must have subconsciously worked the noise into her story. Like incorporating sounds into dreams. Deep in the zone, her brain was just filtering everything from her senses, mixing it with her emotions and sending it to her story. It felt like true power. She heard a creak above her. She smiled and exhaled through her nose. "Bring it." she thought.

A light flickered on from upstairs, shining down the walls and spilling out into the kitchen. "H-Hello?," Caitlin managed to call out. She was surprised by how hard it was to get her voice to work. It was as though she'd forgotten how to talk, or had never known at all. Only the sound of the rain returned her call.

Meredith definitely heard something moving around upstairs now. It shuffled back and forth across the floor above her. The laptop glow illuminating only the keyboard, she continued to type, pouring out all her fear into her story. She was only a vessel, she didn't experience the emotions, just carried them forward. The shuffling became steps. Clear, harsh, steps.

Something caught her eye and she turned to see a soft light sweep into the kitchen. It wasn't artificial, but an organic glow that poured down out of the stairwell. She returned to her work, typing frantically.

The foot falls above began to move down the stairs. No!

Meredith jumped up from her laptop as the treads of the stairs creaked. She rushed out of the study and turned the corner to come face to face with the thing.

It was there. It was a man. Just a man. He was wearing a plaid jacket and a baseball cap. His face scruffy and worn and his eyes dark under the rim of the hat. "Well, look what I found," he said. Meredith wasn't listening, it was just a man, she charged up the stairs.

"You broke into the wrong house," she said calmly as she jumped onto him. He fell backwards, arms flailing as he attempted to stop his fall. He splayed out on the stairs and she climbed up his body until she straddled him. She grabbed his head with both hands and bashed it hard into the edge of the stair. The man immediately went limp. Meredith shouted at him, "No!"

She went to the bottom of the stairs and grabbed onto his boots. She pulled him down to the floor, his head bouncing off each tread. She raised her leg and jammed her foot into his chest. "No!" Blood began to creep out from head, but she could see his chest moving.

She went back to the study and checked her phone, no signal. She glanced at her laptop, then sat down.

Caitlin cowered as the man came down the stairs. He appeared to be a hunter, dressed in a thick camouflage jacket and pants. His beard was left unattended for weeks, wrinkles wound from under it to his eyes. She screamed.

Meredith sat back. She'd never smoked, but she thought if she had some, she would start right now. She breathed deeply, the adrenaline leaving her. She remembered her friend had given her an old phone that she could plug into the landline. She'd be able to call the police. For a moment she wondered how long it would take to find the phone, and then how long for the police to get out this far, then she brushed that off. No rush, she wasn't scared.

WHO	WHEN	RATING

Notes:

☆☆☆☆☆

Notes:

☆☆☆☆☆

Notes:

☆☆☆☆☆

Notes:

☆☆☆☆☆

Notes:

☆☆☆☆☆

Notes:

☆☆☆☆☆

Notes:

☆☆☆☆☆

Notes:

☆☆☆☆☆

The Bottom Fell Out

All of the letters fell out of the grid! We got them in the right column, but you need to put them back in the correct cell. As you enter a letter from the column below the cell, cross it out, so you can keep track of what letters are left for that column. With some work, you'll have the whole secret phrase. We've given you a few hints, and a few columns only have one letter ... those should be easy!

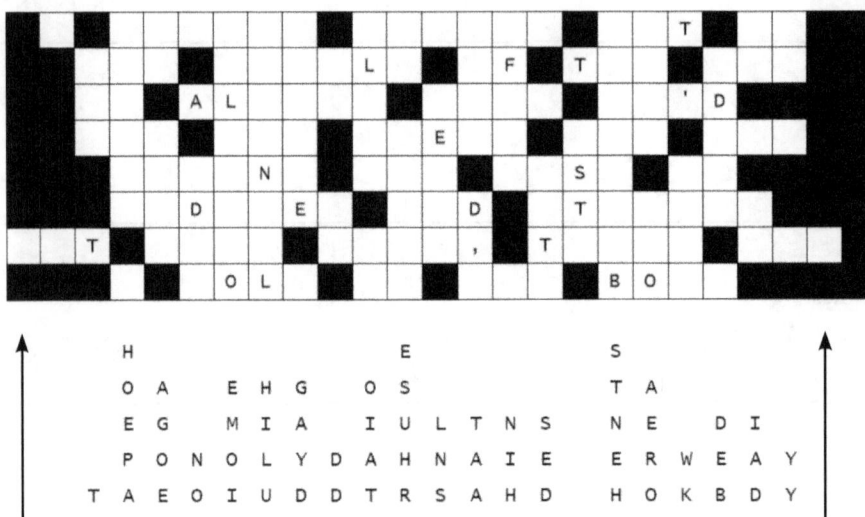

Heat Lightning

Steve Boose

Lightning, a single bolt of it, glittered in the sky, seemingly striking the road where it met the horizon directly ahead of us. Despite the day having been clear and swelteringly hot all through North Dakota and into Montana, a thick gray wall mounted up before us, having swallowed the sun as it descended into the late-afternoon sky.

"Dad..." I said nervously from my vantage point in the front seat of the family station wagon, a vehicle made conspicuously larger with the tent trailer being pulled behind and the large wing mirrors mounted above the front wheel wells to help my father see behind us.

"Maybe it's just heat lightning," said Dad. His voice was a mix of emotions – fatigue, irritation and annoyance, and perhaps just a little bit of fear. "Yeah, just heat lighting..." he said again, as if to himself this time, as if to try to reassure himself that all was well and that his plan for this trip was still working.

I wasn't necessarily convinced, and neither was my mother. I was only nine years old, and had to admit that I didn't really know any better. My baby sister, in the back seat, didn't have an opinion either way, as she was more concerned with the fact that she'd been in her car-seat for far too long, that her bottle was empty, her diaper was sweaty, and she wanted to work on this new (to her) thing called "walking" instead of just sitting, as she had been for so much of the past three days.

Mom had moved to the back to be with her two hours earlier, when we had pulled over at a campground in eastern Montana that proved to be full of Americans trying to get in one last camping week before their schools went back in August. Dad had planned on stopping there for the night, and shifting his mental gears back to "keep going" led him through a space of deep frustration, but he did so without using any of his "bad words" (which is to say, the ones that I got in trouble for if I used them in front of my grandmother!). Mom gave him a kiss and said, "Just find us a spot!" before heading off to watch Sis toddle around the edge of the parking lot.

Dad and I went through the camp guide and the map book together, trying to find somewhere that would let us stay. The staff had even let him use their phone to call campgrounds that would ordinarily have been their competition. Unfortunately, the first two places he tried were also full, so Dad looked a little further down the road. When he asked about one particular campground and how far away it was, the fellow behind the counter had drawled, "About a hunnerd mahls..."

I thought I heard Dad say a bad word under his breath, but out loud he said, "About two hours, then." The fellow nodded and Dad reached for the phone again. It was good to see him smile when he asked about reserving a site; when he hung up, he let out a long breath before saying, "All we have to do is get there...!" I checked the entry in the camp guide and found myself also smiling when I saw the symbol for a swimming pool.

After a day like today, the idea of a swim sounded really good!

Mom had said I could sit in the front seat and navigate, and I eagerly took my spot. The vinyl seat covering had soaked in the sun's glaring rays while we had been figuring out our little problems, and though the sizzle was only audible in my mind, my shorts-clad legs felt the way I imagined sausages must feel when they are first placed in the frying pan! The pain faded in a few moments, though, and we got on our way with me holding the camp guidebook open with one finger and the map book flipped to the appropriate section of the state.

Two hours later, despite the renewed energy he'd shown at the end of the last stop, Dad was done. Just done. The lowering sun had been shining through the windshield since mid-afternoon, and the air rushing through the windows was a lovely eighty-seven degrees – despite being Canadian, growing up across from Detroit meant that weather was always measured in Fahrenheit when it was hot and Celsius when it was cold. There was also something about saying that we had driven a thousand kilometers, as opposed to six hundred miles. We'd done a touch over a thousand kilometers that day, and Dad was just at the end of what he could do.

The true destination of our journey was a little corner of the world northeast of Regina, in Saskatchewan, although we were going a ways further west than that, all the way to Banff, Alberta, "just because we were in the neighbourhood", as Dad had put it.

Almost a year after the Second World War had ended, Dad had been born in said little corner of the world, as my Nana had been before him, but Papa had moved them to southern Ontario to be with his family so that he could work a factory job – the rural life in Saskatchewan had been a nice place to visit, but he had found that he simply couldn't live there full-time. He, his sons, and now his grandchildren, were very happy in Ontario, and intended to stay there to live out their lives.

However, this year, 1981, Nana's mother would be celebrating her ninetieth birthday, and she wanted everyone to "come home" for the party! For our family, Dad had come up with this plan to camp all the way out, rather than use hotels, or fly. We would go the American route, he said, and we'd actually go to see the mountains in Alberta, maybe even stick our noses into British Columbia a little ways! As he considered every thought and nuance, his eyes would seem to glow a bit as The Plan (as it came to be known) took shape.

Mom had tried to object, based mostly around the fact that Sis had just had her first birthday and would need to stop a lot, and that might create a bit of friction – heck, she had said at one point, by the time we get to Saskatchewan, we may not even like each other very much!

But Dad would not be deflected from The Plan.

It would work.

It would be great!

The first day, we had crossed the Ambassador Bridge and had headed across Michigan and into Illinois, where we stopped not far past the great metropolis of Chicago.

For our second day, we climbed north through Wisconsin and Minnesota before stopping for the night at Fargo, on the North Dakota border. I thought Mom and Dad were saying that we would be stopping at the house of my favourite character from The Electric Company television show – "Fargo North, Decoder" – but no, it was just another city. As we went through a K-Mart to get food for tonight and perhaps tomorrow, I kept asking if the city was named for the character, but Mom and Dad just rolled their eyes and bought me a puzzle book to 'decode' to go with all the comic books I'd brought to read in the car.

This third day of travel had been mostly straight west, which was fine when the sun was behind us, and even straight overhead, but as the afternoon had gone on, the sun had started to come straight through the windshield, and Dad's eyes had gotten tired quickly. Sis needed relatively frequent stretches and diaper changes, and I didn't mind the stops myself. The travel had just seemed endless on this day. But now, the hiccup with the camping spot for the night seemed to be on the verge of resolving itself, and as the campground's sign appeared on the left side of the road, I found myself imagining splashing down in the swimming pool's cool embrace...

But the lightning...

There was no thunder audible, and in my experience where we lived, by the time we saw the lightning over the trees, we'd been hearing thunder for a while, which meant that the storm was close. "Heat lighting", which Dad had suggested, was apparently something that happened on very hot days as the cool air of the evening came in – like the static that built up if you wore wool socks on a carpet, the cool and warm air sometimes sparked as they came together. Not a storm. Not with rain. Or wind. Just "harmless" lightning...!

The clerk greeted my father with a sweaty smile and checked him in expeditiously. He showed us on the map of the campground where our site was, where washrooms were located, and so on. When Dad mentioned the pool, the clerk's smile drooped just a hair, before he said, "Oh, yessir, we do have a pool..." The long day of travel was going to be worth every sweaty mile, as once we set up, Dad promised that we could fling ourselves into the pool and cool ourselves off before supper.

New energy was infused into our actions. We found the site easily enough, and Dad backed in onto a level gravel pad. We began what had become a well-choreographed dance, with Mom, Dad, and myself moving around the trailer – detaching the couplings to the car, swinging down the stabilizer legs, cranking up the roof, pulling out the beds, and so on. We'd done it a few times now, and once we got to the point that the interior was all that needed to be set up, Mom took Sis inside and shooed me and Dad towards the pool!

Dad and I grabbed our suits and headed towards the Office; the pool was behind it, as far as we could tell, and a little tuck shop was also open just off the patio around it. We quickly found the bathrooms, shucked our sweaty travel clothes, and pulled on our suits. I wanted to be the first one in the pool, so I wrapped everything into my towel and bolted for the door. The smile on my face threatened to turn into a giggle as I heard my father call after me to be careful! I tossed my bundle into a beach chair that was by the pool and turned to find...

Um...

That there was water in a purpose-built hole in the ground, surrounded by a concrete pad, itself sporting deck chairs and umbrellas so as to give the impression that the water in the hole was indeed for swimming, was undeniable.

And yet...

What was in the hole was green.

I could not have said for certain if it was the water itself that was green, or the liner was green, or both, as from the perspective of standing above it, nothing was clear. To be honest, at this point in my life, I knew very little about pools, except that they were generally blue, and that one could usually see light shimmering on the water, or on the liner that was holding the water.

This "pool" did not seem to have anything like that. On reflection in later years, I guess that it was lacking in chlorine to kill the biological bits that would have blown into it, and that the pump was failing to filter out any undesirable bits growing in the water. Thus, it had been left to become much like a pond, full of life instead of sterile and clean.

At that point in my life, I swam anywhere and everywhere – not well, mind you, but if it had water in it, I would most likely jump in, especially if I was hot and bothered as I was on that day. But this... this gave me pause.

"You going in?"

This was from Dad, behind me. I reflexively replied, "Yep!" and leapt as far as I could out over the nominal deep end and landed with a large splash.

The water was warm, like bathwater, having absorbed the heat of the day. I went down a few feet and did not hit the bottom, which was a good thing at that moment. Opening my eyes, I realized that I could indeed see the light coming from above, but it was murky – a pond was an appropriate comparison! I put my feet down to try to find the bottom so as to push to the surface, and felt a slight tickle on the bottom of my foot; whatever was growing on the bottom liner had extended tendrils upwards, not quite solid like grass, but more ephemeral.

Then my foot sank into it, down to the concrete bottom; it was like stepping into a mud puddle, slimy and deep, and I felt like it squish and close over my toes. A thrill of panic went through my chest, a worry that whatever-it-was was going to close around my foot and not let me get to the surface, that I would be stuck here, unable to sink, unable to rise, that I would open my mouth to cry out but suck in nothing but sickly green water... but before the thought fully formed, I pushed off hard; my foot slurped out of the muck and I shot to the surface. I did not feel clean. Despite being immersed in water, I felt dirty. I was not "refreshed" in any way, shape, or form.

I broke the surface and, on clearing my eyes, saw Dad's feet. He was standing at the side of the pool, not yet committed to leaping in. There was a curl to his lip and a rise in the eyebrow on the same side, with an unspoken question on his lips as to whether or not he actually wanted to join me in the water.

"Don't!" I blurted with my first breath after surfacing. "Just... don't." I swam to the ladder and clambered out. Each rung was covered with the same slimy whatever-it-was that had coated the bottom of the pool, and with each step, my disgust grew. I wiped my eyes and shook my head as I finally stood on the concrete pad. I waved Dad over so that I could keep my voice low, not wanting to offend anybody by blurting out my true feelings, but my father must have heard an echo of himself in me as I said, "It's not very refreshing... and it's actually pretty gross!"

"So I see," he said, with a slight chuckle. He pointed at my feet with his chin, and I glanced down to see muddy brown stuff on them, with pale green bits on the ankles.

"Ewwww...!" I hissed, which made him laugh even more. He then cocked his head at the pool, and as I looked into it, I could see my footprints marked out from where I had touched the bottom (the blue liner was now clearly visible), plus where I had stepped up the ladder. As it registered in my mind what exactly I'd been swimming in, my eyes grew wide in horror. I turned to Dad, and said, in a bit of a quavering voice, what I'd been thinking a few moments ago: "I don't feel clean."

"I don't doubt it," he said, still chortling. "Let's get a cool shower instead before we head back to the trailer."

The outside shower was refreshing, and I managed to get as much of the green and brown bits off my feet (and whatever other parts of me it had clung to) as was apparently possible. I slipped on my "comfy shoes", which were the ones I'd gotten last year and had now burst out both sides as my feet continued to grow; I used them for rough play or pool wear, loving how they snugged up with Velcro instead of laces. Dad stuck his head under the shower's stream, gasped once, and then just kind of sagged against the wall, visibly cooling on the spot. He smiled – a big, genuine smile, the first I'd seen in hours, and I hoped that the stress of the day would now be over and done. After a few moments, though, he turned off the water and reached for his towel.

It was somewhere around that point that we heard the first rumble of thunder. We glanced up at the sound, and realized that everything had gotten ominously dark. That wall of dark gray that had been to the west had now started to move over us, and the clear blue sky that had been above us all day was quickly disappearing. Camp staff came rushing out of the office to grab any furniture by the pool and throw it into either a shed or the open door of the tuck shop, which was then closed and latched.

Windows that had been open all day to let in even the slightest lick of a breeze were being slammed shut. Dad watched this as he finished toweling off, and then gave a wordless nod in the direction of the trailer. We started moving, with purpose and intent, but as we cleared the visible obstruction of the office building itself, as well as the few short trees around it, we turned around and got a better view of the sky, and I felt my adrenaline turn my previous nervousness into outright fear. The best, simplest word for what we saw was "scary". We couldn't even see the tops of the clouds, just a monstrous dark gray wall... but it was a wall filled with flickering, and the odd visible spark of lightning. And it was getting closer all the time. Dad *definitely* said another bad word, then turned to me and said, "Let's move!"

We broke into a trot, although with the next boom of thunder, I confess I put my head down and ran as fast as my little legs could carry me. Dad, not known for his speed, was nevertheless right behind me. Everyone else, it seemed, had already entered their trailers, buttoned up tight against whatever it was that was coming.

I threw open the door with a yelp, but Mom had heard the thump of approaching footsteps and was not surprised. Sis was asleep on the bed, which was a blessing for her. Dad clambered in behind me and pulled the door shut with a click. "This could be a bad one," he said to Mom, as he reached for open zippers to close the windows and try to seal out the coming rain. I could only agree. I climbed up on my bed to get changed into actual clothes, but Dad told me not to bother, just to stay there and be out of the way.

Lightning flashed again, illuminating the whole trailer with its intensity. Dad started mumbling under his breath, "A thousand one, a thousand two, a thousand three, a thousand..." and the thunder clapped with a sound like a breaking board before rumbling off into the gathering darkness. He turned to me. "What's that mean?"

I thought about what he had taught me when we were watching the thunderstorms at home, safe under the shelter of the garage, each sitting in a lawn chair, sipping from a can of Coke, and him slowly puffing on a cigarette, just marvelling at the power of the storm rolling down our street.

"Three means it's a kilometer away. Five is a mile."

He smiled. "I got to three, so...?"

"So it's close?"

"Right, it's close."

Another flash, another blast, much closer together.

"Dad?"

"Yeah"?

"It's not heat lightning, is it..."

Dad gave me a look that I had come to know quite well - a pursing of the lips, with the corners of his mouth going down, and both eyebrows going up towards his hairline. "No, no it's not."

There was a sharp patter on the canvas and on the tin roof of the camper as the first drops of rain began to fall. Mom began pulling things away from the canvas walls, as she and Dad had been told by the salesman that anything touching them would draw the water through via a wicking action. I went around my mattress and made sure everything was pulled in, which earned me a word of thanks. Mom was a little shaky, and I found myself asking her if she was all right; she replied, "There aren't any trees."

When I didn't understand, she said, "Trees offer shelter from rain and wind. But here, we're all exposed, out in the open!" Dad tried to say that we would be fine, but I could tell it wasn't registering with her, and possibly not even with himself. The rain started to gain in intensity; what had sounded like handfuls of gravel being bounced off the roof was becoming a near-constant rattle. But more disconcerting was the wind. When Dad and I had arrived at the trailer, the wind had died to almost nothing, leaving an eerie calm across the whole campground. As the rain got stronger, the wind arrived, gusting fiercely as it surged and abated, then surged and abated again. At the peak of a gust, the entire side of the trailer would roar with a lash of wind and water. The trailer itself flexed, just a couple of inches at a time, but enough to make Mom seem to turn a little green in the light glowing from the fixture on the ceiling.

Sis woke up and sat up on her bed. She'd never heard or felt anything like this before, but rather than break into tears of fear, she just looked around trying to figure out what was happening. Mom pulled up on the mattress beside her, and Sis moved over to cuddle with her. It happened to be on the windward side of the trailer, and as the structure again shifted in the wind, Mom put out her hand to hold one of the uprights, which extended up from each corner of the trailer box. As the wind continued to gust and swirl, the uprights shook and flexed, and I could see that Mom was trying to reinforce them, if not by her strength, then by sheer force of will. Her eyes were wide with terror, teeth gritted to keep them from chattering. Unfortunately if something actually broke, even her force of will wouldn't be enough to keep it all from crashing down.

After a few moments of watching her, Dad realized that he needed to make a decision. If the trailer was destroyed, all the way up here, twenty-four hours' drive from home, we'd be in a mess... but nothing like the mess we'd be in if one of us were to get hurt. I couldn't hear what he actually said to Mom over the roar of the rain and the howling of the wind, but I saw her turn woodenly, raise her eyes to meet his, and then nod.

Dad turned to me and said that we were going to the car, that I was going to lead the way and he was going to bring up the rear. Mom scooped up Sis and held her close as I jumped down from my bed, still in my shoes, and put my hand on the door latch. Dad said to me, "You just get to your seat; don't try to open any other doors!" I started rocking back and forth, like a racer eager to hear the gun. I saw Dad pick up a few things and stuff them in the pockets of his shorts, and then he said, "Okay, ready? One... two... THREE!"

I popped the latch handle with my palm and burst out of the doorway, not even bothering with the step, just leaping to the ground. Bolting to the car, I threw open the door behind the driver's seat, flung myself through it, and slammed it shut behind me.

In the less-than-ten seconds that I'd been outside, I got soaked to the skin. Mom had gone around the station wagon's front grill to the door behind the passenger seat, a bit more awkwardly due to Sis' weight in her arms, although Sis was clinging on tight and Mom probably didn't need to hold her at all. She, too, slid into her seat and slammed the heavy door shut behind her, the two of them now dripping onto the vinyl as she placed Sis once more into her car seat. I looked back at the trailer, and saw that Dad was struggling to get the door shut – the wind kept trying to rip it out of his hand and flatten it against the outer wall of the trailer. It took a few moments, but it finally closed and stayed shut. He turned towards the car and made his way rather carefully to the driver's door, opening it and yanking it shut with much less force than Mom and I had used.

"Why'd you come so slow, Dad! You were getting wet!"

Dad turned and I could see, in profile, the water streaming off his hair, down his cheeks, even down his nose, and dribbling all over everything. "Nope," he said. "After two seconds, I *was* wet. Then it was just a case of getting wetter... but trust me, I was already 'wet'!"

I laughed.

Mom laughed; softly, but definitely a laugh.

Sis had expressed her discomfort with some wails of dissatisfaction, but once we started laughing, she joined in with little baby giggles. It felt good. We knew that, whatever happened, we would all be safe together. When the laughter stopped, I actually gave myself permission to watch the storm. The station wagon was low to the ground, wide of wheelbase, and very stable, so although it shook and swayed a bit in the wind, it just felt safer than the high-sided trailer had when we were in it. And unlike the garage at home, if I stuck my face close to the window to try to see better I didn't get wet.

The campground had been a patch of flat land surrounded by an assemblage of low hills – whether they were humped up by something natural or were simply forgotten piles of dirt upon which grass and trees now chanced to grow was impossible to say.

By the time we got into the car, I would have said that it was as dark as I'd ever seen, between the sun having set, the heavy clouds, and the falling rain. But when the lightning flashed, it was momentarily so bright that I could have counted the trees on the tops of each hill! And the thunder was like explosions, blasts of sound that rumbled deep in our chests and caused us to twitch instinctively. There was no counting to see how far away the storm was; flash-to-blast was near-instantaneous, and with all of the rest of the lightning flickering through the clouds above, the rumble of the thunder was constant, sometimes overwhelming the sound of the falling rain. Fear melted, to be replaced by amazement and wonder. It truly was awesome to behold, in the purest sense of that word.

I have no idea how long the storm lasted. Could have been an hour, could have been only a few minutes, but for the time that it lasted, it was one of the most breathtaking experiences of my life.

Eventually, though, the time between the most vivid flashes of lightning and the loudest peals of thunder began to extend. When it got to several seconds, we noticed that the rain had begun to abate. At some point, I noticed that Mom had tucked in Sis with her bunny blanket, and she was fast asleep, damp blonde hair sticking to her forehead, but breathing peacefully.

Dad eventually announced, "Well, I don't know about the rest of you, but suddenly I'm starving!" He sent me over the back seat into the trunk to see if there was anything to eat in the cooler that hadn't made it into the trailer. Inside the brown plastic box were day-old submarine sandwiches that we had picked up in Fargo the night before – thin-sliced bologna with mustard and mayo, lettuce and tomato. They were, on one hand, slimy and gross, but on the other hand, given the fear we had just been feeling so recently, they were the most delicious things any of us had eaten in days.

By the time we had finished eating, the rain had stopped. Everything was dripping, and the puddles on the ground below were still a bit deep, but the storm had passed. I opened my door and looked up – the sky above was now clear of clouds, and in the darkness that remained, the stars had become visible.

Mom and Dad went and checked the trailer. Other than a few things getting a bit damp, everything was still strong and in-place, with nothing broken. Mom gave Dad a hug and cried a bit – tears of relief, she said – and he just held her and let her get it out. There was no way to get anything like a fire going, and with the adrenaline crash, we were all utterly exhausted. Mom fetched Sis, we all climbed into our beds, and Dad was snoring long before I got to sleep myself.

In all my years of camping, and of travelling while using campgrounds as my rest stops, that one stands out as the worst "camping day" of my life.

But I will also remember it as a day that ended with wonder and beauty, both in the midst of the storm and in its aftermath.

The next day, we set out for Banff... but that's another story altogether.

Canoes & Coffee

WHO	WHEN	RATING

Notes:

☆☆☆☆☆

Notes:

☆☆☆☆☆

Notes:

☆☆☆☆☆

Notes:

☆☆☆☆☆

Notes:

☆☆☆☆☆

Notes:

☆☆☆☆☆

Notes:

☆☆☆☆☆

Notes:

☆☆☆☆☆

Cool Evenings

Fireside Concerto

Kenneth Roland

Valerie glanced around at the assembled group. They looked tired. Exhausted really. She could understand. If it wasn't for deadlines, she certainly wouldn't be here either. She tapped her baton on the music stand in front of her to gather their attention. The room immediately got quiet and all eyes were on her. "Look," she started, "this is definitely a slog, but we are almost there." The chamber orchestra nodded and some murmured agreement.

Valerie had composed all the music in the last ten weeks, and now had only a week to record it. The director of the movie, "Letters From the Soul" had used temporary music in their rough cut, which happened a lot. This director had used music by John Williams, Hans Zimmer, and John Barry, arguably the greatest composers of the twentieth century. He then asked Valerie to "jazz it up, bring some emotion". No pressure there. She was burnt out, changing arrangements on the fly, and the poor group of twenty-four musicians in front of her were suffering for it.

Over the last ten hours she had taken no breaks. The musicians got them because it was mandatory, and Valerie used that time to edit and re-write more music. The entire week had been like that. Constant changes, task switching, and decision making. She couldn't even remember what she had put on this morning and looked down quickly to verify that she was indeed dressed.

"I'd like to try a take with Rebecca's flute alone for the first four bars, then the bass section for four more before the rest. I'll signal and count it in." She tapped the baton a few times and nodded to the sound engineer.

It started beautifully. Soft. Slow. A breeze in a meadow, rising slowly as it crested a hill. She pointed the baton to the right, just over the cellos. It was beautiful. A low continuous thrum under the wind of the flute. She nodded to the group and the full sound of the orchestra hit her, and then terribly broke her. By the sixteenth bar her chin was quivering, and by the twenty-fourth she was sobbing loudly.

"No! It's not going to be done," Valerie yelled aloud in her car. She was speaking hands-free to the producer of "Letters From the Soul", Monica Rose. "Tell Mr. Bring-some-emotion that not only did I bring the emotion, not only did I jazz it up," she spit the word jazz, "tell him I brought so much emotion I emptied my soul and lost everything. Maybe he can write a letter about that."

"Valerie," Monica's voice seemed to come from everywhere in the car, "where are you exactly? I can come and meet with you. Let's talk."

"I don't want to talk," Valerie replied, staring out at the highway in front of her, "I need rest. I need a break." She noticed a Grateful Dead sticker on the back of a Cadillac in front of her and almost cracked again. Monica was speaking again, but she could only think of that old Don Henley song. It reverberated in her head. You can't go back.

"Valerie!" Monica shouted.

"Sorry, I didn't catch that, some kind of incident on the highway,"

Valerie covered.

"I was saying, if you need a break, that's fine. We have what you recorded so far. We'll use that to begin test screenings. That gives you some time. Do your thing, get away, do a bunch of drugs, trash a hotel room, or whatever it is musicians do."

"Thank you," Valerie replied, ignoring the rock star references.

"But we still need to talk, I'm calling you in a week. I expect you to answer." Monica was using her producer voice.

"Sure, sure. One week." Valerie punched the big red phone button on her dashboard.

After embarrassing herself in front of the entire orchestra, some of whom she considered friends, some colleagues, and some she had just hired, she went home, packed a huge suitcase, her violin, and booked a bed and breakfast in Oregon. She had thought about going further, but decided that no one was chasing her. That was at ten o'clock last night. She'd been driving for twelve hours straight since then, only stopping for gas, and coffee.

She was just north of Medford when the woods separated briefly into the small town of Bella, Oregon; population two-thousand-five-hundred. It didn't take long to find her bed and breakfast on Main St. The Book and Nook with Cook was a two storey Victorian home situated on a tight lot right in the middle of town.

She pulled into the alley that served as a driveway and wedged her car into the empty space marked "Reserved for Guests of the Book and Nook with Cook". She had booked thinking the name was quirky and it was the right distance from Los Angeles, but was growing concerned with the repeated use.

She had her violin case in one hand and the other dragged the oversized suitcase behind her. She had worn a long jacket assuming the weather would be cool, but it was surprisingly mild. A summer breeze pulled at the scarf around her neck as she mounted the front steps, her suitcase thudding into each riser behind her.

An old bell on a spring rang as she pushed open the large front door. She looked around and was surprised to find an actual wood fire burning in the fireplace. There was a couch and chairs with a coffee table at their center surrounding the old stone hearth. She had expected to find a house converted into a bookstore, but realized it was more a bookstore converted into a house. Large hand-made bookshelves rimmed the room, taking almost every ounce of wallspace, but the floor layout still resembled a normal home. The staircase in front of her held framed advertisements and author photos along the wall, but the hallway past them was again filled with shelves. There was a dining room to her left, complete with table and place settings, yet again, every wall was lined with shelves from floor to ceiling.

She let out a breath. This was exactly what she was looking for. She had been worried at times, driving along the interstate, that she was about to be crammed into an apartment above a strip mall. She took a moment to stand her suitcase upright and place her violin case gently on the wide plank flooring.

A man's head appeared at the end of the hallway, jutting out from behind the staircase.

"Valerie?" he asked.

"Yes," she said, happy that the online booking had obviously gone through.

The man stepped fully into the opening and wiped his hands on a dish towel he tossed somewhere to his left. His dark hair was loose on top and cropped close at the sides. His smile was genuine and exposed glistening teeth. His eyes were bright and his whole demeanor seemed welcoming.

He stretched out a slim hand as he approached, "I'm Noah."

She took the hand and was surprised at the extremely light grip, barely touching and soft.

"You're Noah?" she said. "But you're Asian?"

Noah smiled broadly and looked down at himself, "Now when did that happen?" he mocked.

"Oh my God, I'm so sorry," Valerie immediately interjected. "It's just when I heard of a bookstore in a small town, owned by Noah, I assumed it'd be a Christian place."

"Wow!" said Noah, his eyes seemed to grow huge

"Oh my God!" Valerie moaned. She put her face in her hand and let her hair hang over her face.

"Look," said Noah graciously, "we can start again. I'm Noah. I was born in the USA like Bruce Springsteen. I go to the Presbyterian Church in town, which is Christian admittedly, but I've hosted Muslims, Sikhs, Buddists and even a few atheists believe it or not. And you are Valerie, who I know nothing about, but can't wait to learn more." He held out a hand.

Valerie looked up through her hair and saw no mockery in Noah's eyes. She smiled. "I'm so sorry Noah, I'm not in a great headspace, and just drove all night. I appreciate you giving me a second chance to make a first impression here."

"You're welcome Valerie. It's great to meet you. Your room is on the second floor, let me help you with your bags," he reached for the violin case.

"Oh!" she cried, "I'd appreciate carrying that one on my own."

"No worries," he said, and she believed it.

Her room was beautiful if spartan. It had a window at both the front and rear of the old house with giant redwoods in the back and a cozy street scene out of a Hallmark movie in the front. She glanced at her phone, saw the number of messages and decided to put it in a drawer. For a while she just stood, looking out at the enormous forest surrounding the town, letting her mind tune out completely. Then she sighed and spun, flipping open her violin case on the bed. She always felt better when she played. It was like the instrument was an outlet. "You only get out of the violin, what you put in," she remembered an old instructor telling her. "If you push anger through it, anger comes out. If you let your joy flow into it, joy will flow out. Put into it what you want to get out of it." She looked at the instrument snuggled into its red plush bed. It appeared so elegant and soft. She didn't think she wanted to put it through her current emotional state. She decided she would check out the bookstore, snapping the lid closed.

There were a few customers in the store when she came down the stairs. An older couple were browsing in the dining room, a younger child was in what she guessed would have been the study. She believed it was the mother of that child that was in the living room, sitting on the couch pulling apart a muffin from the coffee table with one hand and holding a paperback aloft with the other. A steaming coffee sat beside the muffin and Valerie felt immediately jealous. She paid more attention to the living room than she had this morning as she strode through it. There was a violin above the fireplace, very worn and old, but not expensive. She noted the steel strings. Probably played as a fiddle more than as a violin. A banjo hung on the wall beside the fireplace on one side and a guitar on the other. Obviously music was important to whoever decorated the shop.

She knocked on the old swinging door to the kitchen before pushing it open. She stopped halfway through the door. This wasn't a kitchen. Sitting in the center of the room was a Bechstein grand piano. It was positioned so when you sat on the bench, you could see directly through a picture window to the redwoods beyond. The walls had old tapestries hung everywhere, or were they carpets? The piano was beautiful, but she was pretty sure nobody was bringing coffee in here. She went back through the living room and down the hallway that ran beside the stairs.

Noah was in the kitchen, doing something at the island. Valerie had never really got into cooking, she was always too busy. She thought she might like to try it once she retired, whenever that was. As she entered she immediately looked at the wall that separated her from the piano.

"I'm guessing this wall isn't original," she said, catching Noah's attention.

He looked up from his bowl, "Good eye!" he said. "I actually have a piano room on the other side of that now. Couldn't have it absorbing all the cooking smells and moisture." He began to wipe his hands on a towel and walked towards her.

"Do you play?" she asked.

"Play is the appropriate word," he smiled. "I saw your violin when you came in, I assume you play as well?"

"I do. Not as much as I'd like, but I do."

"Do you want to play here?" he asked. "You can certainly play in the living room, the customers will love it."

"Really?" she said, "I'm not sure they want to hear what I have to put out."

"For sure, sometimes I play. They love it. I'll play with you if you like."

"Really?" Valerie said saltily. She felt that Noah was being brazen. "You think you could keep up?" she smiled. She expected him to back down, but instead he smiled back and threw the towel on the counter.

"That sounds like a challenge," he said, "Now I really want to play."

"Fine," she said and spun on her heel. Why was she getting so worked up about playing? She knew how good she was. She was a world class violinist, professional conductor, and famous composer. This guy owned a small bookstore, in a small town, and had to rent out rooms to make ends meet. She wound up thumping up the stairs harder than she wanted to. She wasn't sure if she wanted him to hear it or not.

The violin still layed there on the bed. She looked at it for a second, then changed her mind. She'd play the old violin hung on the wall. She didn't want him to think it was the instrument. Who was this guy? She spun again and headed back down the stairs.

"You start," Noah called from the kitchen, "I'll join in once these muffins are out."

"Sounds good," she said glibly as she headed to the living room. The woman was still there picking at her muffin, nose stuffed in the book.

Valerie grabbed the fiddle from the wall, there was a bow next to it. She plucked the strings quickly and was surprised to find that it was almost in tune. She nested the instrument into her shoulder and pulled the bow across. For steel strings it sounded quite good. She adjusted the pegs until it was perfect.

"Do you mind if I play?" she asked the woman.

"I'd love that," said the woman, smiling and adjusting herself on the couch.

Valerie moved to put her back to the fireplace. She hadn't played publicly for a crowd of one since she was in college. She breathed deep and closed her eyes. She allowed the air to slowly leave her body between tight lips. The first pull of the bow was divine. She allowed her sadness to pour out into the room, swamping it with sound. It was pure melancholy, filtered through the tightest of sieves. The sound was true and steady. The tip of the bow slowly rose and dropped as she allowed the weeks of pain to flow through the instrument.

She became lost in the sound. Mesmerized by the slow and steady thrum of the instrument. It startled her when she heard the words "Someone's had a long day."

She opened her eyes. The woman had stopped reading and was just staring at her. Valerie blushed at the attention. Noah had come into the room, his hands on the back of the couch as he leaned in. He had been the one who spoke. Valerie continued to play as she looked at him. There was no mockery in his eyes. He appeared to have been sincere. His eyes were so bright, she found herself not being able to look away. "It has been," she said quietly. She was composing in the moment, using previous bits she'd written and stealing liberally from some classics; but it was her song.

Noah came around the edge of the couch and she assumed he would head to the piano room. Instead he picked the banjo off the wall. Her eyes rolled heavily. Of all the instruments to join her dysphoria, the banjo was close to the worse.

"You don't have a kazoo?" she said, tilting her head at the banjo.

Noah laughed. She liked his laugh. It was a calm, genuine laugh. Almost dignified. He sat down beside the woman and slid a steel pick onto his left thumb. "I can't promise it'll be good," he said, "but it won't be bad."

He listened for a while, before joining in. Just small notes. A ping against her thrum, a sliding twang that lingered in her melancholy resonance. Valerie was shocked at how it added to the music. The banjo wasn't trying to control the song, just following along, but the addition was magical. As they continued she couldn't help but feel it was like two friends, sympathizing with each other. Two different voices, sharing different things, but with a common warmth, a known emotion. She could see the friends, sitting at a bar in Los Angeles, commiserating with each other. She realized she had begun playing faster and Noah was following along.

They played for a while, the song changing and evolving. From sadness it moved to a small sigh, it crossed a bridge and began to smile. The notes were getting shorter, the tempo increasing until it hit a crescendo of laughter. Valerie herself was smiling now. She couldn't take her eyes off Noah's. They were locked into a vibration, a zone that neither one could stop if they wanted to. Noah plucked at the strings rapidly now and she would throw in a plucked response from the violin and both would laugh.

The woman on the couch had completely forgotten both the book and the muffin. Her eyes moved from one musician to the next and her son now sat on her lap. The older couple leaned on each other at the back of the room. They smiled with memories washing over them as the song drew to a close.

The spectators all began to clap excitedly the moment the sound faded. Valerie felt everything wash over her. The pure joy, the calmness, the delight at the event, the memory that had just been created. She tore her eyes from Noah and nodded to the watchers. She didn't know why, but she felt like she was about to cry. She was overwhelmed. It wasn't from winning awards, or great success, she was overwhelmed with passion for a song that had come out of the blue and took her for a ride through every emotion she'd ever had.

She realized that in her grand pursuit of happiness and success, she'd forgotten to take a moment and just be happy.

WHO	WHEN	RATING

Notes:

☆☆☆☆☆

Notes:

☆☆☆☆☆

Notes:

☆☆☆☆☆

Notes:

☆☆☆☆☆

Notes:

☆☆☆☆☆

Notes:

☆☆☆☆☆

Notes:

☆☆☆☆☆

Notes:

☆☆☆☆☆

A Northern Lake Remembers

Matt Thurston

It's Been Far Too Long

Felix left his office later than he had hoped. In a well-rehearsed motion, he hit both the call button for the elevator and the nearby switch for the fifth floor lights. There was no need to doublecheck. He knew he was the last to leave. On the ride to underground parking, he re-examined the e-vite. There was always the chance he had imagined it.

> *You are Invited!*
> *Celebrate Labour Day weekend with the Original Six.*
> *It's been far too long.*
> *Just bring yourself and some swimmies.*
> *The Fort*
> *1138 Fire Lane #1*
> *Fort Pontiac, QC*

Please RSVP by July 15
Love, Ethan and Charly

Ethan got top billing in the complimentary close. However, Felix knew Charly authored the invite. It was 'swimmies' that gave her away.

Felix had properly sent an RSVP. It was a month and a half earlier when he scurried out of bed in a partial panic. Did 'by July 15' mean before or on July fifteenth? Ambiguous boundary condition. Inclusive or exclusive? It was the fourteenth of July, twenty-two minutes before midnight, when he sent his reply.

The elevator opened to an empty garage, save the little blue EV Felix had rented for the weekend. The car model was a Leaf. The rental company only offered it in blue and white. No green?

The Leaf was parked in one of his company's overflow spots. Felix had declined a parking spot assignment. He didn't own a car. He commuted by light rail. And anyway, the spot assignments were an anachronism. Three floors of underground parking with fewer than fifteen cars on the busiest day.

Why hadn't he just parked next to the elevator?

After the short stroll, Felix got into the *blue* Leaf and psyched himself up. He hadn't been outside the city limits since Boxing Day. The winter before the pandemic.

Road Trip

Felix was late but prepared. He had pre-packed his overnight bag (with the requested *swimmies*) and had rented the car on his lunch break. No extra stops were required.

He notified the Original Six group chat:

leaving the office now, map says 2h6m. see you soon

Felix put an earbud in his right ear. He didn't trust hooking his phone up to a rental's infotainment system. Who knew who had accessed it in the past?

Not worth getting hacked. He would listen to his audiobook: The Feynman Lectures. But with only one earbud in. Safety first.

He headed north.

Even The Artist

Twenty minutes into the drive, Felix approached a fork in the highway. The GPS guided him to the right.

This was a welcome change. He'd been fighting the low sun with a combination of the EV's flimsy visor, his sunglasses, and slouching.

That low late summer sun was putting on a show in hazy skies.

Feynman was putting on a show as well.

In the introduction section of his lecture on the Laws of Gravitation, Feynman quipped, 'even the artist appreciates sunsets and the ocean waves. And the march of the stars across the heavens.' Felix chuckled. And now that it wasn't assaulting his eyes, he took a moment to appreciate the sunset.

And his mind wandered.

Wandered right into thoughts of his dad. Felix had mentioned this cottage weekend to his dad in their weekly chat. His dad followed up the next day with a playlist link: *Cottage Roadtrip Tunes*. Felix knew this shouldn't upset him. It was his dad's way of connecting. Felix heard his therapist: 'there's little to gain in a twenty-year-old grudge.'

Still, he picked the Feynman lecture over the playlist. But Felix's thoughts fixed on that playlist.

It was all Canadian content. No surprise there. He remembered that *Bobcaygeon* and *Lake Fever* by The Tragically Hip were on it. And Blue Rodeo's *Lost Together*. There were at least three Neil Young songs. *Harvest Moon* for sure. A couple tracks by Joni Mitchell. Joni had been his mom's favourite. Somewhat oddly, his dad had included two versions of *The Wreck of Edmund Fitzgerald*. Gordon Lightfoot's original and a cover version by the Rheostatics. There were a half-dozen or so other songs he couldn't recall. He resisted the temptation to look at the list on his phone while driving. Safety first.

Felix was sure of two things.

1. Those songs were all great.

2. They were filler. It was the bookend tracks that mattered: *Decked Out* and *A Northern Lake Remembers*. Both by The Jack Pines.

The Jack Pines had been a big part of Felix's life.

A huge part of his dad's life.

The Jack Pines

Felix's dad's given name was William, but almost everyone called him Wiz. Short for Wizard, Wiz was monosyllabic inevitability. It was Wiz's music studio skills that earned him his nickname. Those, and his unkempt gnarly nest of a neckbeard.

Wiz was an audio engineer and music producer. He was semi-retired now, but always willing and able when the right call came in. He had worked, almost exclusively, at North Shore Studios. Wiz had spent endless hours at that studio. So did Felix, for a time.

North Shore Studios was unimaginatively named for its location on the north shore of Lake Ontario.

A converted turn-of-the-century (twentieth century, that is) stone farmhouse that was a half-hour drive west of Kingston. The studio was *just like a trip to the cottage* but with a reasonable commute. Assuming you were based in or around Kingston. It was further than the Muskokas for the Toronto bands.

Wiz had a long list of engineering credits but got to call himself a producer because of his work with The Jack Pines. Originally, he was hired as the in-house audio engineer for their sophomore album. During those sessions, he was promoted to producer.

The story goes that Owen, The Jack Pines' lead singer and primary songwriter, was defending a line from *Decked Out*:

> *Decked out, in the afternoon*

Me and you, and the bottles empty too soon

The record label's producer insisted they change the lyric to '*and the bottle empties too soon.*' But to Owen, the singular '*bottle*' evoked the hard stuff. He was singing about swigging cold ones out on the deck.

There was profanity and projectiles, and the presumptuous producer was sent packing. All over the singular form.

Good news for Wiz. The band loved Wiz.

A field promotion on the rock and roll battlefield.

North Shore Studios

North Shore Studios doubled as Felix's summer camp. He went with his dad whenever he got the chance. He'd smash away at the drums, learned some piano, and got quite good at guitar. There was no shortage of musicians around to learn from. They were generous with Wiz's curious kid. When serious recording was going on, Felix would make himself scarce and tear around the nearby woodlots on his BMX. On hotter days, he'd cool off in Lake Ontario.

Nights afforded Felix time to tinker. Wiz embraced cutting-edge gear. The studio was stuffed with pedals, pre-amps, synths, speakers, compressors, conditioners, microphones, mixers, and reverb racks. And so, so many cables. North Shore could also mount an exhibit on the history of digital recording. Every size, shape, colour, and generation of audio workstation was once found in the studio's control room.

Felix experimented with it all. His career in tech owed much to those summer nights, on the shore of Lake Ontario, hacking some decommissioned system to the soundtrack of the *next big thing*.

Twenty-Year Grudge

Felix hadn't been back to North Shore Studios since the summer before university. It was also the last time he wielded a musical instrument.

Early that summer, Felix's mom fell ill. After some back and forth with doctors and tests, cancer was diagnosed. The prognosis wasn't fatal and a treatment plan was set up. There was hope.

At North Shore, the Jack Pines were in session, recording their fourth album. Wiz had buried himself in the work. It left Felix to shuttle his mom to and from her appointments. As the summer plodded on, Felix grew angrier at his dad's absence. His mom, never wanting anyone to fuss over her, deflected his anger. She assured Felix that she would be fine.

She couldn't have known.

It wasn't the cancer that killed Felix's mom, but a staph infection. She was admitted to hospital with fever on the Friday of the August long weekend. She passed on Monday. Wiz did leave the recording session when she was hospitalized. He was at her bedside with Felix when she passed.

For Felix, the damage was done.

He could never bring himself to listen to The Jack Pines' album recorded that summer. Or any that followed.

You Have Arrived At Your Destination

The GPS' statement of fact pulled Felix back to the present. He eased the Leaf onto a grass field to the left of a big house that looked even older than North Shore.

The *Fort*.

Beyond the *Fort*, Felix spotted the flickering of a campfire. And beyond the fire, the waters of the Ottawa River. Wide enough here to impersonate a lake.

The sun was now below the horizon, but the sky held fast to a pastel palette. Felix stepped onto the grass. A shadow approached from the campfire. Feynman was still lecturing in Felix's ear. He pulled out the earbud.

"Felix, how are you?", asked the shadow.

Felix recognized the voice and replied, "Bobs."

Bobs approached, came in for a hug, and Felix obliged.

"So glad you made it. It's been far too long. We got a fire going. You got a bag or something? Throw it in there." Bobs pointed to a screen door on the side of the *Fort*.

They made their way to the fire.

Nicknames

After greetings and more hugs, Felix sat on one of three logs that horseshoed the campfire. Bobs put a cold one in Felix's hand and sat beside him. Charly and Ethan were seated on the log parallel to the river, and Dez and Alice across the fire from Felix and Bobs.

The Original Six.

'It's been far too long.'

Felix lost track of who had said it last.

Bobs' real name was also Ethan, but he was the second Ethan at the startup. Ethan-one (of Ethan and Charly) was co-founder with Dez. Felix joined in the startup's first month on the same day as Alice. They had never settled who was employee number three or who was four. Charly joined next. And Bobs (Ethan-two) made six.

The Original Six.

For the first couple years of the startup, addressing an Ethan was an ambiguous mess. Happily, 'Bobs' was baptized in the startup's second autumn. They had just crossed the fifty-employee mark and had spawned an HR department. Mandatory team-building was a necessity. It took the form of a fall fair. Ethan-two thoroughly dominated the apple-bobbing contest. 'Bobs' was born. A pre-pandemic pastime, to be sure. Who would share slobber water these days?

At the campfire, Felix focused on re-engaging his atrophied social skills. It was never his strong suit, and it had been *far too long*. Luckily, he genuinely liked all of these people. They had built a great company together. Sure, it had been acquired, downsized, rightsized, upsized, reintegrated, reacquired, refinanced, but it was still a shared source of pride.

The Original Six had made out well.

Charly asked it first, "So Felix, you're still working there?"

He used his canned response, "Someone has to keep the AIs in line."

Half-hearted chuckles.

Radio Free Pembroke

A hand-crank storm radio quietly played at the campfire. Charly had it next to her. She perked up excitedly on hearing the DJ's voice, "he's coming back on. Felix, you have to hear this guy. He's so good."

She turned the volume up and silently shushed with an index finger to her lips.

A built-for-radio baritone transmitted out of the radio's four-inch speaker.

They joined mid-sentence:

"...from the Skydiggers' seminal album *Restless*. This is Big Billy Buffer coming to you on 93.3 FM, C-K-I-don't-know. Radio Free Pembroke. The bots stole our jobs, so we stole back the airwaves. I got all the Can-Con, so your long weekend can rock on. The phone lines have all been ripped out, and I threw my mobile in the river, so yer gonna have to send all yer requests telepathically. But don't you worry, the Buffer is keepin' the good times rollin' straight through till Monday mornin'. Hope you've found yourself wherever you are with a cold one in hand and loved ones who understand. Tip one back for this rocking cottage number. From Kingston's finest, The Jack Pines, here is *Decked Out*."

The intro drum salvo warbled the tiny radio's speaker.

Felix chuckled to himself and wondered if Feynman would have posited the corollary, 'even the scientist appreciates serendipity, the poetry of coincidence. And the march of the stars across the heavens.'

"Ha! Felix, that's a great quote, but what's the coincidence?" asked Bobs.

Felix, flustered, looked towards Bobs, and managed to emit a "What?"

"What's the coincidence?" he asked again.

Felix looked down and glared accusingly at the citrus-noted craft cold one in his hand. Had his Feynman thought been thought out loud?

It had.

Bottles Empty Too Soon

While *Decked Out* rocked the antique storm radio, Felix managed to do something outside his comfort zone: he shared.

He had to do something to explain his Feynman outburst.

So, Felix shared the story of *Decked Out* and North Shore Studios.

Felix was careful, though. He shared how his dad was a recording engineer. How he got the nickname Wiz. How Wiz was the producer on *Decked Out*. How Wiz earned his promotion. How he produced nine Jack Pines albums. How Felix had spent summers at the studio. How it was *just like a trip to the cottage* but with a reasonable commute. How he learned to play guitar and, adding emphasis, learned tech at North Shore. But he did leave out the difficult details of his last summer there.

Their surprise: 'How did we not know any of this?' and 'Who knew you were so mysterious Felix?' and 'You can play guitar? Really? C'mon?'

And even: 'Wonders will never cease.'

Ethan asked Felix, "Would you play us something? There's a guitar up in the house."

Felix shook his head in four-four time at one-twenty beats per minute, "No, no, No, no. No, no, No, no."

The First Night Effect

The campfire wound down with less impactful conversation, and the Original Six made their way to bed just before midnight.

They entered through a screened-in porch that spanned the river-facing side of the *Fort*. Bobs had set up a day bed as a sleeping nook on the porch.

"It's going to be just like sleeping under the 'march of the stars.' But without the bugs."

There were bugs.

Bobs would sleep inside the next night.

"Difficulty sleeping in a novel environment is a common phenomenon often described as the first night effect." This was the opening sentence of a journal article that Felix often referenced to explain why he slept poorly away from home. The theory behind the first night effect is that the brain is primed for defence in novel environments. This led to shallow restless sleeping.

This was just one of the things on Felix's mind as he got ready for bed.

Had he overshared?

How bad would the first-night effect be tonight?

Would he find the bed comfortable?

Could he use lack of sleep as an early escape plan?

Did he need an escape plan?

Had he brought his noise-cancelling headphones?

Had he remembered to download his binaural beats (both delta and theta wave versions)?

Had he overshared?

Breakfast

The sounds and smells of breakfast preparations woke Felix.

His headphones were still in his bag. His binaural beats, downloaded or not, were unplayed.

He felt refreshed.

Wonders will never cease.

Felix made his way downstairs and headed toward the sounds and smells. A thick rectangular slab of a table dominated the *Fort's* kitchenette. Running alongside the kitchenette, a half-wall framed a view of the kitchen.

Alice chopped fruit. Ethan tended bacon, sausage, and a tofu scramble on the gas stove top. Tater tots were keeping warm inside. Dez kept an eye on the toaster while flipping flapjacks on an electric skillet.

Felix's stomach grumbled. Bobs placed a mug of black coffee in his hands.

Charly sat at the far end of the big table cradling a coffee of her own.

Felix took a sip. Charly launched, "Felix, I had an idea. You shared something personal last night, and the rest of us were..."; she reached for the words, "...taken aback, I guess. We didn't reciprocate. That's not fair. So, tonight, we are going to have another campfire, and everyone else gets their turn to share. You know, a cottage story. Like yours at North Shore.

"What do you think?"

"Uhm..."

Charly jumped in, "you are off the hook, you already shared."

Distracted by the arrival of flapjacks to the big table, Felix responded, "Okay, looks great. Sorry. I mean. Sounds good."

The sausage and scramble, bacon and berries, marmalade and maple syrup, toast and tater tots followed the flapjacks.

They feasted.

A Lazy Cottage Day

At breakfast, Ethan proposed a trip to town to fetch a special treat. Charly declined. She promised herself that she'd work on her crochet this weekend. Dez and Felix had eyed the chessboard in the sitting room.

Bobs and Alice agreed to join Ethan.

Charly, Dez, and Felix settled into the sitting room.

Big Billy Buffer continued his marathon weekend, but had been upgraded to Ethan's uncle's hi-fi. The DJ's baritone was now met and matched by the system's vintage tubes and ten-inch woofers. The morning's set list included Leonard Cohen, Rufus Wainwright, k.d. lang, and the Cowboy

Junkies covering *Sweet Jane*.

Dez and Felix traded wins at the chess board. Charly spent equal parts of her time consulting an introductory book on crocheting, and the craft itself.

A quiet cottage morning.

The town trippers returned at noon laden with farm-fresh produce. And Ethan had acquired his prize: semi-illicit unpasteurized Quebec cheese curds. He promised poutine with dinner: "it's not 'pooo-teeen'. It's 'puh-tin'"

Big Billy Buffer shifted gears and kicked Saturday afternoon off with Bryan Adams' *The Summer of '69*.

The energy level picked up.

Charly announced it was time to get out on the water.

Chekhov's Swimmies

"Everyone remembered their swimmies right?"

The other five, some audibly, some not, replied, "Yes, Charly."

No one was hungry for lunch, so they packed snacks for the boat. It was built for a lazy day on the water. It had big banana-yellow pontoons, a zippered canvas enclosure, and its starboard-side sported a retractable diving board.

They spent the afternoon anchored on the Ottawa river. It was sunny and hot. They took turns going in for a dip.

Bobs giggled with adolescent glee when he splashed a cannonball back towards the boat. This received a muted response. A half-eaten bag of sour cream and onion chips was the least impressed. Alice was a close second.

Alice flapped her paperback in an attempt to minimize the water damage.

Felix, also aboard at the time, asked, "Is that a novel you are reading? Like, fiction?"

Felix never read fiction. In the startup times, he and Alice often shared articles and books on cybersecurity, privacy, big data, machine learning, and cloud-native horizontally-scaling software architectures. Never fiction.

Alice answered, "I found it in town. It's Cory Doctorow. We've read his non-fiction stuff.""

Felix nodded.

She showed him the cover: *Red Team Blues*. "It is a cybersecurity story. I've been trying to read less academically these days. This might be a step?"

Felix nodded again, "Sorry, I didn't mean to..."

A rumble of thunder interrupted Felix. The sky above the boat was still a brilliant azure, but the western sky had gone indigo.

"We should get back." Ethan directed his request at the swimmers while pointing an informative finger west.

Neither artist nor scientist would get to appreciate a sunset that evening.

Mandatory Team-Building

The storm cancelled outdoor grilling, but Ethan's poutine did not disappoint. He fried hand-cut potatoes in a Dutch oven--masterfully manipulating the oil's temperature with a Fahrenheit-only relic of a thermometer. The mushroom gravy was scratch-made. And the cheese curds. Pasteurized or not (there was significant discussion on the veracity of that claim), they were ooy-gooey delicious. The poutine was no side dish. When their plates were cleared, it was bits of grilled sandwiches and glazed carrots that were left over.

After a collective cleanup, Charly clarified that the lack of a campfire did not get them out of sharing. Ethan joked to Bobs, "mandatory team-building." They both caught Charly's unimpressed glare. Ethan mouthed an apology.

The rain continued, joined by thunder. They gathered in the sitting room. Big Billy Buffer was turned down quiet on the hi-fi. But he kept the weekend going with a stormy night soundtrack that included The Grapes of Wrath, Robbie Robertson, Neil Young (in a Crosby, Stills, Nash configuration), and The Guess Who's *These Eyes*.

Sharing is Caring, Caring is Sharing

Alice went first. She fondly recounted visits to her grandparent's vacation trailer on Rice Lake near Peterborough. Her grandfather, a math professor, created scavenger hunts that involved word puzzles, ciphers, and tiny treasures he would hide around the campground. On one hunt, when she was six, she came across a full unopened 'sixty' bottle of an unidentified brown liquid that had washed ashore. Its label was lost at sea. She returned it to grandpa for identification, thinking it was part of the hunt. The adults laughed at her innocence.

"You were solving ciphers at six?" asked Bobs.

Alice succinctly said, "Yes. And it's your turn."

Bobs grew up in Toronto, his mom was a lawyer, and his dad a mechanical Engineer. They didn't have a cottage tradition, but he did recount a Great Lakes fishing trip. Bobs embraced the spirit of sharing and delivered his story with dramatic flair.

He stood to address the room, and with gusto, "we set out from Toronto, drove north and west to Tobermory. There, we boarded the Chi-Cheemaun and made the two-hour ferry to the mighty Manitoulin Island under a vast beautiful blue sky." He waved his right arm in an arc. They guessed he was drawing...the sky? He went on, "we were not satisfied with a mere ferry ride. The next day we rented a proud vessel and acquired provisions for a day of angling. My mother, still sea sick from the ferry passage, remained ashore. But father, myself, my brother, and sister set out to sea. The boat was old but not a stranger to rough waters. And rough waters we found. A storm kicked up and surprised us. We...", he lost his steam.

He continued, in his normal voice, "It really wasn't all that dramatic. There was a bad storm, but we made it back fine. I was young, though. Like five or six. I was pretty freaked out. The thing I remember most is how comforting my older sister was. She's eleven years older than me, and I was always closer to my brother. But she was so great that day."

Charly politely acknowledged Bobs' story, but jumped in quickly with hers. She recounted a trip to a hunting lodge in her university years with her dormmates. It was right after spring exams. The lodge was near Algonquin park. She hurried through some details: A grotesque collection of mounted animal heads. A 'bedroom' that was just a room packed wall-to-wall with bunk beds like an army barracks. An oversized bat that found its way indoors (they guided it back outside with wooden tennis rackets).

And then the kicker. That weekend at the lodge was also Charly's twentieth birthday. Her friends had all forgotten. Not even a cake. She looked over to Ethan. He knew this story. He was keeping his cool. She said, "when I told Ethan my hunting lodge story, he arranged a surprise birthday weekend at a similarly disgusting hunting lodge."

Alice, Bobs, Dez, and Felix shared puzzled glances. Dez asked it, "Why have we never heard that story?"

Ethan intercepted the question, "It was back when I was still *officially* Charly's boss. I guess we were pretty good at keeping our secret?"

Their nods were accompanied by a harmony of *ahhhh's*.

Dez was up. They were estranged from their parents. The Original Six all knew this. Expressing gender outside an Adam and Eve archetype was not acceptable in Dez's family. Dez graciously spared the sharing session from an uncomfortable tale of conflict. Instead, they recounted how an older cousin had taught them chess during summer visits. The game wasn't explicitly forbidden by the family's cult-adjacent religion. But the two of them enjoyed treating their games with a little clandestine excitement. Dez had a knack for finding the positive.

Finally, it was Ethan's turn.

The Poetry of Coincidence

The *Fort* was central to Ethan's childhood. He took full advantage of the current stormy night situation to set the mood. He told them of the Canada Day weekend when he was thirteen. A thunderstorm had knocked the power out at the *Fort*. Cousins, aunts, uncles, Ethan's parents, and his brother had all gathered in the sitting room to tell ghost stories by candlelight. Ethan hammed it up: "this *very* sitting room."

Before Ethan could continue. A crack of lightning. It was close. The sitting room went dark. The hi-fi silenced.

A pungent plume of ozone wafted in.

They were shaken.

Bobs tried to lighten the mood, "I guess that's the poetry of coincidence."

It didn't work.

A Northern Lake Remembers

The *Fort* itself was fine. A nearby elm, less so.

The power was off all night. They got by with flashlights and camp lanterns. The storm persisted, coming in waves. Windy at times. Heavy rains. And more lightning. No one slept well.

At dawn, the skies stayed gray, but the winds died down. Light rain fell all day.

It was mid-afternoon when the power was restored.

Felix and Dez were playing chess. Charly was crocheting. Alice was reading *Red Team Blues*. Bobs was flipping through the *Fort*'s collection of vinyl records. Ethan was studying a cookbook.

The hi-fi came back to life, interrupting their quiet activities, "This is Big Billy Buffer coming to you on Radio Free Pembroke. 93.3FM. That was one helluva storm last night. Even with the power out, Big Billy was never in doubt. God showed us Her wrath. She always gets the last laugh. So here we go, from your brainwaves straight to the Ottawa Valley airwaves. We're gonna need a sad song for this gray-scale Sunday. A fun fact about this next track: it's the singular song penned by the band's producer and honorary fifth member, William 'Wiz' Thomson. From their tenth and final album, the title track, by The Jack Pines, *A Northern Lake Remembers*."

The Original Six traded wide-eyed looks.

Bobs turned up the volume.

They listened:

> *On the shore at dusk, a down-on-one-knee request*
> *To spend forever side-by-side*

A Northern Lake Remembers

I swore that night, I'd always put you first
You hid your doubts behind a smile

A northern lake it listens
And floats our worries away
A northern lake remembers
Our love

On the shore at dawn, with your belly eight months on
I was busy arguing on the line
I swore that day, that I'd put both of you first
He kicked hard when he heard my lie

A northern lake seeks no judgement
We're innocent on its shore
A northern lake remembers
Our love

A northern lake it listens
And floats our worries away
A northern lake remembers
Our love

On the shore at dark, alone and I whisper
To the heavens for you to hear
I swear on this night, I'll get back in his life
Cause I've wasted too many years

A northern lake is my judgement
No innocence on its shores
A northern lake remembers
Our love

A northern lake it listens
And floats my worries away

A northern lake remembers
Our love

The song ended.

Bobs was the first to speak, "Okay, that's the poetry of coincidence."

This time, they agreed.

Heading Home

The Original Six planned an early escape Monday morning to beat the cottage commute. They said their goodbyes standing in the wet grass of the *Fort*'s makeshift parking lot.

'I still can't believe your dad wrote that song, Felix.'

It was Charly that said it last.

Felix kicked water off his shoes before getting into the Leaf. As the others pulled out onto the fire lane, he pulled out his phone and dialled his dad.

One ring. Picked up.

"Hey bud, everything okay?"

"Yeah, dad, everything's fine. Can I come visit next weekend?"

"Sure, sure, no problem. I can be free. It's not a problem. You sure nothing's wrong?"

"Nothing's wrong."

"Okay. Cool. How was your cottage weekend? Did you listen to that playlist I sent you?"

"Sort of." Felix gulped and asked, "You wrote, *A Northern Lake Remembers*?"

"Yeah, bud."

"It's about mom?"

"Yeah. Well...and you."

"Can you tell me about it when I visit?"

"For sure."

"Cool. See you then."

"See you next weekend, bud."

Felix started the Leaf, enabled Bluetooth on his mobile, and connected. Safety was second.

He swiped over to his dad's playlist, tapped the screen, and cranked the volume. The Jack Pines' *Decked Out* punished the Leaf's sound system.

It sounded great.

Listen to The Jack Pines' two-song soundtrack

at https://jackpines.ca/

WHO	WHEN	RATING

Notes:

☆☆☆☆☆

Notes:

☆☆☆☆☆

Notes:

☆☆☆☆☆

Notes:

☆☆☆☆☆

Notes:

☆☆☆☆☆

Notes:

☆☆☆☆☆

Notes:

☆☆☆☆☆

Notes:

☆☆☆☆☆

Camp Cross Words

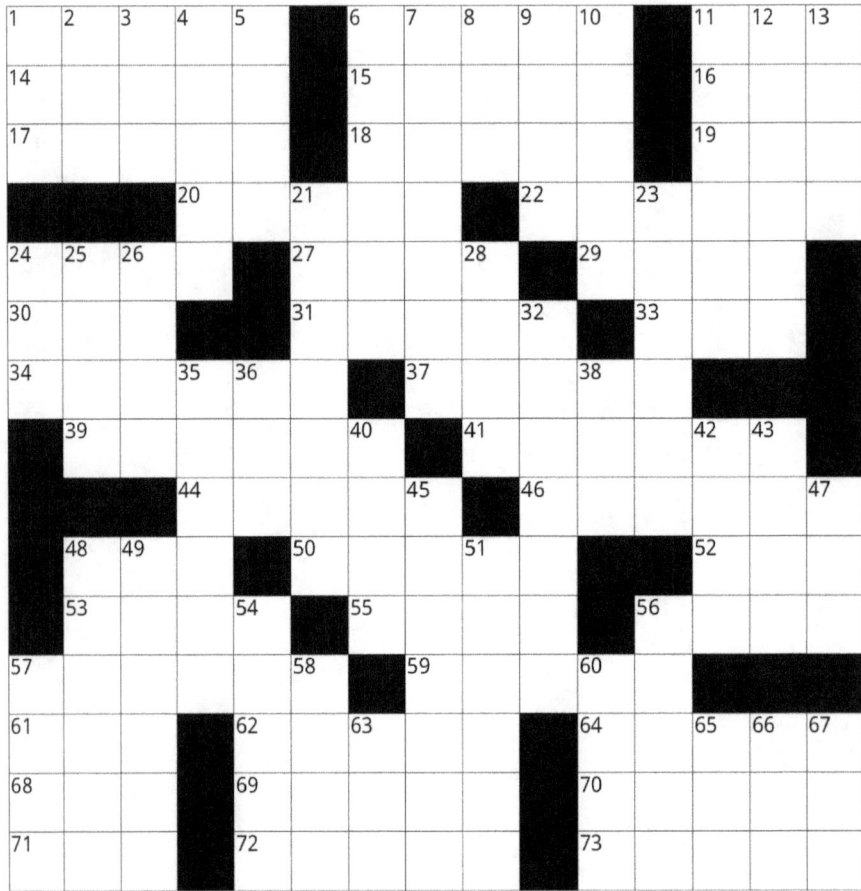

Across

1 Spends a few days in the woods
6 Yellowstone & Yosemite
11 Messi's team; familiarly
14 "Get ___ of yourself!"
15 ____ of faith
16 Portuguese greeting
17 Spanish appetizers
18 Roofing material
19 Canada's smallest prov.
20 Swear
22 Misbehave
24 Tree with needles
27 Slippery swimmers
29 Close
30 Whiz
31 Regions
33 Country N. of Kenya
34 It's often in hot water
37 Playground fixture
39 Curtains
41 Events with lightning
44 Submarine detector
46 John of "Full House"
48 Antlered animal
50 Securely fasten with rope
52 Speak softly
53 Get together
55 Actress Turner
56 Spill the beans
57 Tested the weight of
59 Allow to attack
61 Gallery display
62 '90s commerce pact
64 Cookout spot
68 Colour system on a TV screen
69 Groups of three
70 "The Devil Wears ___"
71 Poor grade
72 Long look
73 More loyal

Down

1 Purring pet
2 "Eureka!"

A Northern Lake Remembers

Try this one, it was very hard to make. Making a crossword turned out to be a tricky task. It's amazing the paper can have one every day.

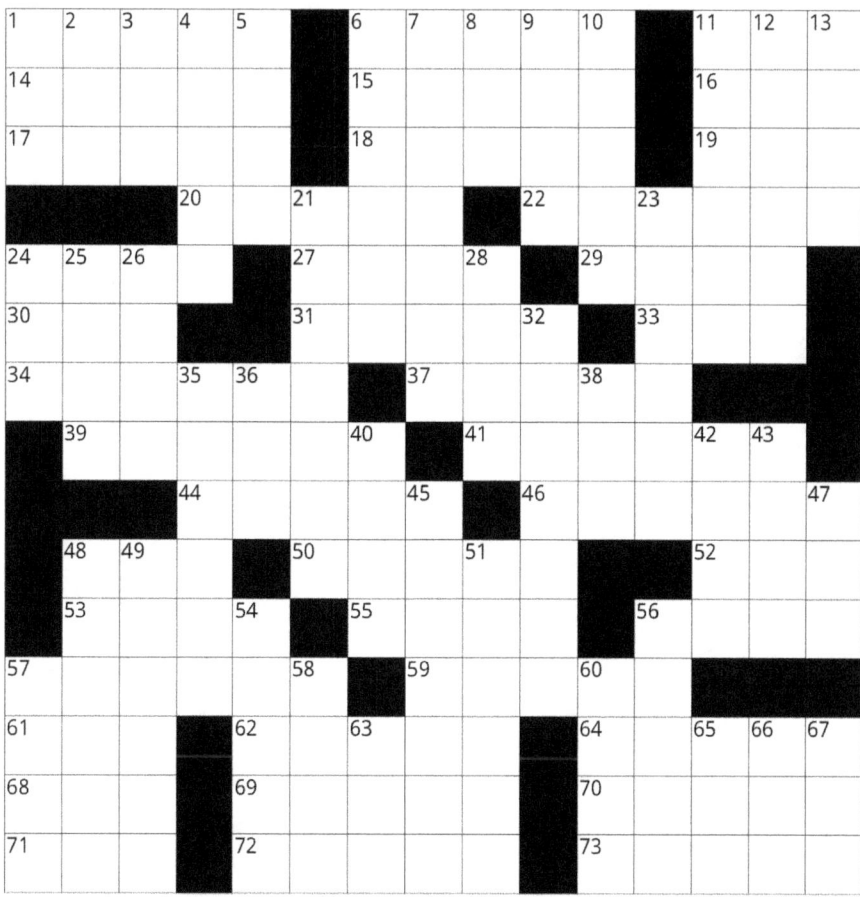

3 Unruly head of hair
4 Finish second
5 Southern California Sch.
6 Quaterback, often
7 What made Mendel's peas different
8 "V for Vendetta" actor Stephen
9 Series of martial arts exercises
10 Glasses, for short
11 Fly that's caught
12 Nancy Drew, for one
13 Trot or canter
21 Need in chemical synthesis

23 "Let us move from ___ ___ of confrontation ..." R. Nixon
24 Bit of butter
25 Covered with frosting
26 Close by
28 "Do The Right Thing" Pizzeria
32 Hangs tight
35 Hamper
36 Mil. Address
38 Speck
40 Jib or spinnaker
42 2101 in Roman days
43 Shortly
45 Open house organizer

47 Soak
48 Come into view
49 Did not disturb
51 Anxiety
54 Camping shelters
56 Ringo of the Beatles
57 Challenging
58 Pub projectile
60 Date with an M.D.
63 Fédération Internatio- nale de l'Automobile
65 Letter after sigma
66 Suffix with ox- or sulf-
67 Rower's need

Canoes & Coffee

The Stars Return

Kenneth Roland

Looking at the moon, Valero carefully twisted his large glass blowing pipe. Carefully he touched and poked at the glass, attempting to create the colour variations he was seeing in the glowing orb. He was solo blowing in his family's shop. A large picture window allowed passers by to view the glass sculptors as they worked. The street was empty now, the sun long set and only the light of the moon shining down through the window. Valero cupped the ball of glass with pumice, smoothing it into a perfect sphere. He smiled as the bubbles in the glass became clear, giving the appearance of the moon, with its craters, scars, and abrasions. For a moment his mind wandered as he stared into his own personal moon. Its pock marked surface gave it beauty and life. Scars added patina to your life, physical or otherwise. They create character. The moon wouldn't be as beauitful without its wounds and lesions. As he became mesmerized by the spinning glass, Valero thought about his own scars.

Two stories above Valero on the roof of the shop, Ava was crouched in her handmade cardboard observatory. She had carefully crafted the dome out of Amazon boxes and duct tape. Her most prized possession, a ten inch diameter Dobsonian telescope was nestled inside. She used it to hunt comets in the night sky. It took years of after-school work to save up for the instrument. The work had taken her out of the house, and she had been happy about that. Now that she was older, there were too many other responsibilities. She couldn't imagine spending her money on something as frivolous as a telescope. It meant everything to her, and she kept it in perfect condition, knowing she could never replace it.

Ava stood, stretching out through the hole in her observatory. She scanned the sky with binoculars. Tonight's target was the comet C/2021 S3 - Panstarrs. No clouds in the sky, but unfortunately a very bright moon. Ava frowned. There was still time before the comet was expected. She decided to scan the moon with her binoculars. She could just make out some of the larger features. It was a disaster. Like a post-apocalyptic world of craters and defacement. Subconsciously she reached to her cheek, to her own scar. The one her father had given her the day her mother left. It was that scar that prompted her aunt to take her in. It was like losing both parents. She sighed, chosing not to think about "the old days". Ava and her aunt lived on the third floor of an old brick building with a large chimney up one side. The Vazquez' owned the building and lived on the second floor. They ran the glass factory that consumed the first floor.

Ava's aunt had turned sickly. Ava had to work to help with the rent, along with the cleaning and caregiving. She felt it was the least she could do after her aunt had opened her home to her. The roof with her telescope had become her retreat. After her aunt would settle in for the night, Ava could escape to the quiet and darkness of the rooftop. She heard the door of the shop open and was curious who would be working this late. Stepping lightly over her cardboard creation she walked to the edge of the rooftop, leaning on the wide trim that surrounded it.

Valero Vazquez was on the street, staring up at the moon. His back was to her. She could see that he still wore his worn leather apron, his curly black hair slicked back to a ponytail where it burst into a tangle of curls. His hands were on his hips and he was completely still, head tilted up to the moon. She glanced up at it as well, wondering what he was thinking. She watched him for a while. Valero was a good guy. She didn't really know him that well, but he was always polite and kept to himself. Not too pushy, or talkative. Ava liked that. He was also tall, lean, and handsome. Ava liked that as well.

"Hey!" she shouted down. Valero looked around, spinning in a circle. Ava began to laugh. Finally he looked up at her. "You know if you stare at the moon too long, it'll start staring back at you."

Valero chuckled. "What are you doing up so late?" he yelled back.

"Comet hunting," she called. "C'mon up if you have time."

Valero looked up and down the street. No one was in sight. He glanced into the shop window, then up at her. "You know what, I do have time." He started to head around the side of the building. Ava could soon hear his footsteps on the metal of the fire escape as he climbed to the roof.

Ava suddenly felt butterflies in her stomach. She hadn't really expected him to accept. She didn't know what she would do once he got up here. How does one talk to tall, handsome, creative types. She was glancing around the roof, looking for something, anything, that could be interesting or worthwhile.

"I don't think I've been up here in ten years," Valero said as his head rose above the ledge. A metal ladder arched over the ledge, but he just pulled himself up and over without really touching it.

"You used to come up here?" Ava asked, genuinely interested. "I love it up here, it's quiet."

"Yeah," said Valero, looking intently at the cardboard observatory. "My dad used to bring me up. We'd look at the stars, and he'd point out constellations to me. I guess you'd know all about that." He pointed at the black, igloo-like craft project.

"Oh," Ava smiled. "I'm more interested in comets than stars." She looked at the cardboard as well, avoiding staring at Valero. "They have movement. A direction, you know? Like they're going someplace."

Valero smiled. "I get that." He looked from Ava up to the sky.

Neither spoke for a moment, the chirping of a cricket was the only noise on the roof.

"What is it that makes people need to move?" Valero suddenly said. "Like, what is it that motivates someone to leave the place they grew up in. Do you know what I mean?"

Ava looked at him. This was not the conversation she expected. "Do you mean why do people want more?"

"Yeah. I mean no. Maybe? You can want more and still stay in one place. You could want to make *this* a better place," he held out his arms. "I don't know. I was just looking at the moon tonight," he smiled, "as you saw." His smile made Ava giggle. "And at first I was thinking how cool it would be to travel to the moon. To live in this bright spot in the middle of night. All the room you could ever want. Then I realized, there's nothing up there for me. Maybe it's the same everywhere. If I went to America, or Australia, or Japan … Why would it be any different from here? What's there that I think is going to be so great?"

Ava was thoughtful for a moment. "Maybe it's not that you are trying to get somewhere, it's that you are just trying to get away from something?"

"Hmm." Valero bit his lip. "I know that when my dad used to bring me up, and we'd sit under the stars and just watch them, I didn't want to be anywhere else. Now he's driving me crazy, I think he wants me to leave."

Ava smiled. Sitting under the stars with Valero sounded wonderful. "Maybe that's what your dad liked about the stars. He liked that they stayed the same. They were stable and consistent. Now he worries that his life is changing so fast." She pointed at Valero, "Like his son is now a man."

Valero cocked an eyebrow and looked at her. "You're very insightful." he said. "When I think about it, you could be right." Valero started to wander the roof. "My dad was happy teaching me the trade. Showing me the *old ways* and methods of glass blowing. It was when I had my own ideas, thought of new ways to do things, that's when our relationship ... Well, here I am blowing glass in the middle of the night by myself."

"People like change when they're young," Ava shrugged. "They like the speed ... the thrill. It seems to me that as you get older, you like to soak in the past, reminiscing of the times when you were making changes, but not making changes anymore."

"Yeah, maybe," he was thoughful, "I think I'm going to go. Start my own shop, in a new town, with new people. Become the hero of my own story as they say. What about you?" Valero asked. "You seem to be an old-soul, no offense, why are you looking for comets?"

Ava looked down. She wasn't sure what she should share. The moment seemed so intimate, but tomorrow would be another day, and there'd be no one to share with. "I don't know. An escape I guess. I spend a lot of time working, or looking after my aunt." She half-heartedly pointed to the stairs," It's just nice to get out once and a while and view freedom."

"Aren't they hard to spot?"

"I guess. That's part of the fun. Like being a voyeur into the private life of a thing so free it just hurtles through space without a care in the world. No responsibilities, just crash into whatever you want."

"As long as it follows the laws of gravity," Valero smiled.

"Well, yes," Ava smiled too.

"Let's see one!" Valero said, clapping his hands together.

Ava laughed, she didn't know what else to do. She spun her makeshift observatory so the opening in the top and bottom lined up and they could move inside. It was extremely cramped with the telescope and the two of them. She felt bad for Valero. His tall frame was hunched and bent awkwardly to deal with the slope. She could smell the leather of the apron and the musk of sweat mixed with cologne.

"Sorry," she said, "It's not very big."

"That's Ok. It's pretty cool, you built this yourself?"

"I did," she stood proud. "Well, sort-of. A man I work with has a 3D printer and printed these rollers," she pointed to the plastic that allowed the top to spin, "I guess a printer seems like a better purchase than a telescope."

"Hey," Valero interjected, "We all have our things. That's what makes the world interesting. He's probably happy he could print something that someone else could use for their thing."

She laughed. What was worthwhile about a cardboard dog house on a rooftop?

"So how do we find these comets?" Valero asked.

Ava looked up. "Oh. Umm ..." She fetched her binoculars. "For Panstarrs, that's the one I'm looking for tonight, we should be able to spot it with these. Then we just ... ", she shrugged, "Point the telescope at it ..." He seemed so close. It felt far more intimate than Ava was expecting.

"Sounds simple enough. I'm guessing it's going to be up?" He pointed towards the sky.

Ava laughed, and Valero smiled, then he couldn't control himself and laughed as well.

"Yes!" she said, still laughing. "It will be 'up'." She air-quoted the word.

Valero moved to the opening and stood. Stretching before he lifted the binoculars to his eyes. "Wow! These are really good."

"Thanks," Ava replied shyly.

"You can really see the scars on the moon."

"You call them scars too?" Ava asked quietly.

"Yeah," Valero breathed. He didn't take his eyes away from the device. "It's beautiful."

There was a moment of silence.

"I don't understand," Valero said suddenly. "Do you know that song 'American Music' by the Violent Femmes?" he asked out of the blue.

Ava had to think for a bit. "Oh yes, 'Do you like American music?' You really just jump from one topic to the next."

"Right?" Valero laughed, "Just stay with me. He says in the song; 'Every time I look at that ugly moon'. What do you think he means by that?"

"Maybe it's a joke?" Ava suggested. "Or maybe it'd be better if it was shiny, and smooth, like a metal ball."

"I don't know," Valero said thoughtfully. He moved his head and began scanning the sky. "Whoa! I think I see one!" He was excited. Something Ava had never seen. He quickly handed her the binoculars and began pointing out into the night sky. "Look that way! Over there!"

Ava was all business. She took the binoculars and began scanning the sky where he was pointing. Valero looked at her, "I don't think you have it."

Suddenly she felt his hand on her shoulder. "This way!" he said excitedly. A warmth spread from her shoulder down to her arms and fingers. She wasn't sure how she was managing to hang onto the binoculars at all.

Ava was having a hard time focusing. The night sky swirled in her vision. His hand went to her hair. Pushing it into her scalp as he tried to suggest physically the way she should turn her head. Ava let out a small gasp. No one had touched her since her mother left. At least not gently. Valero's touch was like a whisper, a suggestion of touch. She couldn't focus at all. Her mind was adrift with what was happening. "Do you see it?" Valero asked from beside her ear, and she realized she had built the situation up too much in her mind.

"Umm, not yet," she said softly, trying to collect herself. Why was his hand still on her head? She didn't want him to take it away. "Where did you see it?" she asked in a husky voice. Oh God, she hoped he didn't hear the difference.

His voice seemed like a whisper as he moved behind her. With a hand on each side of her head, he gently guided her vision into space. "There."

She wanted to close her eyes and sleep there, with his hands holding her.

Then she saw it. "Oh my God!" Her brain switched gears with a jolt. Adrenaline filled her veins, pushing the sweet softness out as it went. "That's it!"

Ava handed Valero the binoculars and moved to the telescope. She bent and carefully found the area where she had seen the comet. She adjusted the settings, slowly zooming in on the space where the comet flew through the sky. Once she found it, her deft hands quickly centered it and began focusing, zooming, and tracking it through the sky. "Got it!" she squealed.

Valero moved close to the eyepiece, but he waited patiently. Eventually she moved her head away, and allowed him to view. "It's amazing!" he said.

They took turns viewing the comet until it left the sky. When it was over Valero spun the observatory and went out the opening. Ava followed, thinking he was leaving. Instead he went to the edge of the roof again.

Ava leaned on the ledge beside him, staring up into the night sky. Stars were everywhere.

"That was cool," Valero said eventually.

Ava smiled. "Success!"

"I think I get it now," he turned to face her directly. "Comets come and go. They fly across so fast, and then they are gone. Stars stay. They shine where they are. They watch the comet go by, they see the world change, but they don't need to be part of it. They're ok just watching. They see the world change, but that doesn't stop them from shining."

Ava looked at him. She knew what she wanted to say, but she wasn't sure she should say it. Shw was likely just setting herself up for embarrassment. Why was embarrassment so bad? How did you learn if you didn't embarass yourself once in a while.

"Stars are the heroes," Valero said, "Providing light for everyone equally. Then we try to out-do them, making our own light. Phasing them out until we can't even see them anymore. We think progress is best, change is constant, out with the old."

Ava wasn't sure what he was driving at.

"We need to let stars be stars, and people be people. Maybe I'm suddenly an old man, but I think we need to stop hiding the stars. It's time for the stars to return."

"I don't want you to move away," Ava blurted out. Her eyes went wide and she felt the blood rush to her head. Why would she say something like that?

Valero's eyes became very serious. He looked at her with an intensity that worried her. Nothing happened for a moment. He didn't seem to blink, he didn't look away, nothing.

"I don't want to move away," he said.

Ava blushed again.

"How did this just happen?" Valero asked, staring into her eyes.

"We're the stars," Ava breathed.

"We are," Valero took her hands, "We're back. Let's make *this* town amazing," Valero wrapped Ava in his arms and she immediately hugged him back, gripping his strong back tightly towards her. "We can shine right here, there's nothing out there we need."

Canoes & Coffee

WHO	WHEN	RATING

Notes:

☆☆☆☆☆

Notes:

☆☆☆☆☆

Notes:

☆☆☆☆☆

Notes:

☆☆☆☆☆

Notes:

☆☆☆☆☆

Notes:

☆☆☆☆☆

Notes:

☆☆☆☆☆

Notes:

☆☆☆☆☆

G-O-D Spelled Backwards

Hallie Ranta

Edison and I watch the moon rise between the branches of the surrounding pines. As soon as it hits the top of the tallest tree it will be time to call it another perfectly wasted, scorching summer day inside our rock oasis.

I note the tiny sliver missing from tonight's orb. Not only will it be full tomorrow, but according to Ernie it will pass in front of the sun, a rare annular eclipse. Instead of excitement I feel an unease building in my stomach.

"Something's coming up, isn't it?"

The only one left to hear my questions, Edison merely continues to stare out at the trees. A single swish of his tail confirms my theory.

I did indeed ask a lot of questions. Mother's responses were short, both in length and tone, as if I should have been born with all the knowledge of the world burned into my brain. My father was a taboo subject, but I couldn't help inquiring about his absence now and then.

"He's gone, Puck."

"What was his name?

"Killian. Perfectly fitting."

"What did he do?"

"Music."

"Three words to describe him?"

Mother snatched the homework assignment out of my hands and dashed off replies to the rest of the questions, then wrote a strongly-worded letter to Miss Jenkins. I didn't dare read the answers until late that night under the covers, but I learned my father was 'a foolish, air-headed dreamer' whom my mother met 'while stupidly high at the youth-destroying noise festival known as Woodstock."

I got a C-plus for not completing the assignment myself.

Grandpa on the other hand answered my questions with 'the world is your oyster' flair, and with the accompaniment of pictures, books, and real life examples. He attributed Mother's frustrations to loneliness, having never met her own mother and bearing a child without a partner.

"Be nice to your Mother, Puck, and learn from her. Don't play the game of life alone."

Maybe they shouldn't make the rules so hard, then. One snake-eyed roll of the dice shouldn't leave unasked questions coiling in your mind and empty spaces squeezing your heart…

If Mother hated Woodstock so much, why did she let me keep the plush likeness of the Peanuts bird Grandpa gave me? Why did she wrestle it from Mr. Next Door's flea-bitten mutt and sew its head back on?

If dogs were underworld demons, as Mother claimed, why did she swerve to avoid hitting one in the street?

Its eyes glowed in the headlights, white at first before flashing red like everything else.

I came to slowly, hearing the steady beeps of my heart and realizing the lady sitting next to my bed wasn't my mother.

Nurse Blunt wasted no time telling me of my mother and grandfather's ill fate before firing off a rapid series of questions. I answered to the best of my groggy ability.

Puck Walters, ten years old, born May 14, 1970 here in Fairview. No living relatives; both grandparents now dead, Mother was an only child. I don't know who my father is, or was.

"Aren't you supposed to have this information somewhere?"

The nurse left in a huff and was replaced by a social worker who asked the same questions. I was shouting in frustration by the end of the second interrogation, and Doctor Considerate came in and shooed her away. He gave me a popsicle and told me to rest, which I did for three days before they said I could go.

"Go where?"

The social worker waited patiently while I walked through the house that now felt like a ghost town. She promised I could get the rest of my things later, so I crammed Woodstock and four dresser drawers of clothes into a small suitcase.

"Where am I going?" I asked again.

"Camp." She explained throughout the long drive that before I lived in another house I had to go 'into a system,' and while normally that meant staying in an orphanage, the local orphanage residents were spending the summer at Camp Rydon in the mountains.

I stayed silent as we wove up the narrow road, chewing on my thoughts and a Big Mac (ten year old orphans don't eat Happy Meals anymore). Soon I became queasy (from the car ride, surely) and dozed the rest of the way.

Dennis the head counselor gave me a quick tour and rundown: rise at 8, team building and activities throughout the day, lights out at ten. Orphan cabins on the east side, delinquent cabins on the west.

"Delinquent?"

Dennis either ignored or didn't hear me over the bell that sounded from the mess hall.

After a dinner of wilted salad and soggy cardboard pizza, another counselor named Ernie led me and several other boys to our cabin. He seemed a lot friendlier than Dennis, calling us all 'little dudes and bros' and talking to the surrounding wildlife. Mother would have hated him.

I had missed the opening bonfire, but Ernie promised several more campfires and sleeps under the stars.

"A little fireworks display Friday night for Independence Day, and kick off the dog days of summer!"

"Dog days?"

"The days you can see Sirius, the 'Dog Star'…and when it's so doggone hot."

I shivered all night, hugging Woodstock and watching the moonlight creep slowly across the cabin floor.

I spotted the cave on our first nature hike, a small opening amongst the rocks halfway up what was known as Sunny Summit. Ernie said we would trek to the top one day this summer, but I immediately had my mind set on getting there sooner, on my own.

Our cabin spent each morning meditating, reading horoscopes, and nature watching, all in the thick of the trees. The rest of the group was eager to swim, paddle and race as far away from Ernie as they could during the physical activities of the afternoon.

"That guy's so boooring," Camper Drawl complained as we changed into swimming gear. "Who wants to talk about 'paths and signs of the universe'?"

"Some people need an explanation for everything," Camper Nosebleed agreed, rolling his eyes.

"Like people who have lost everything?" I reasoned. "Don't you think he's trying to help us...I dunno...make sense of our lives?"

"Make sense?" Camper Lefty spat. "We know it don't make sense, Puck, that's why we're here!" He gave my right shoulder a painful jab and everyone else made for the lake, shooting dark glares my way.

I didn't follow, hanging back and rubbing my aching shoulder. I looked around for Ernie and saw him shuffling a deck of cards under a tree, oblivious to what had just taken place. Hoping to set my escape plan into action, I sat down next to him.

"Puck, my man, in need of some more celestial guidance?"

I had already heard my daily horoscope so I declined, pointing instead to a small poster depicting a wheel of animals.

"What are those?"

"Twelve animals of the Chinese Zodiac. Use the lunar calendar to see what Year you were born in, and what inner traits you possess."

I scanned the wheel for 1970.

"Year of the Dog?"

"Year of the Metal Dog," Ernie nodded, flipping through a small book. "I might have known: honest, independent, and persistent, though stubborn."

"Can I independently do some exploring? Just for a bit?"

Ernie was skeptical, but I promised to be back in an hour and stay on the east side of the camp.

"You're a persistent metal dog, all right," Ernie laughed. He handed me a whistle from his pocket and I headed straight for the base rocks of Sunny Summit, hidden from view of the lake by a line of pine trees.

It didn't take long to see how Sunny Summit got its name; my shirt was drenched with sweat in minutes. The climb wasn't too difficult, but the rocks were hot underhand. I collapsed gratefully into the shady shelter ten minutes later, my neck and arms burning.

A few moments to catch my breath and I eagerly looked around the cave. About ten feet wide and deep, its walls were surprisingly smooth. The ceiling was low, however, a fact I discovered when I jumped at the shock of realizing I wasn't alone.

In the far corner sat a small dog. Through watering and popping eyes I could make out he was some kind of terrier. His beige fur stuck out at every angle, like he'd stuck his paw into an electrical socket. I immediately decided his name should be 'Edison,' but years of living next door to a monster made me wary to approach him.

"Mind if I join you for a bit?" I walked toward the entrance and sat down, taking in the view. Camp Rydon was almost completely hidden, and for a brief moment I forgot why I was an attendee.

The dog had moved next to me. He peered intently into my eyes, and I saw my fragile reflection in his. Suddenly the pain returned in my head, shoulder, and heart. I remembered I was alone in the world, even in a camp full of boys in the same situation. My awkwardness would likely follow me to the orphanage where I would not have free range, and despite the desire to make sense of it all, the others were probably right in their belief that life had no rhyme or reason. It simply sucked.

Edison sat, still as a statue, alternating his gaze from me to the trees. His presence provided a sense of security; it was okay to feel like roadkill, to curse the world, and to cry.

So I did.

I spent all of dinner negotiating my daily allotted free time with Ernie. I got him all the way up to three hours, providing I participated in morning rituals and one team physical activity, and reported back to camp by five.

"Deal?"

"Deal, dog."

Morning activities were a breeze, but by lunchtime the yearning to decamp camp would start to build. While I pitched, ran, and swam with the boys my mind was already up the cave, often resulting in painful returns to the physical playing field.

"Earth to Puck, head in the game!" Camper Sucker Punch called, beaning me with a fastball.

I shook off their laughs and took my base. An hour later I iced my arm and breathed rhythmic insults that slightly echoed in my cool stone confines. The meditation practice definitely had its perks.

Edison waited for me each day, though he didn't eat any of the table scraps I brought him or engage in any kind of activity. He simply sat at my side, and when I voiced my questions to him he answered with a throat growl, head tilt, or tail wag.

I learned to tell time by the position of the sun, and if I dozed off I would awake to a reverberating bark that prevented me from missing my curfew.

My absences did not go unnoticed. Despite Ernie's claim that I was attending grief counseling, some of the boys did not buy it and followed me one afternoon. Not wanting to give away my hiding spot, I stalled at the edge of the pines and pretended to tie my shoes.

"Hey Puck, crybaby building is that way," Camper Acne sneered. "Where are you going?"

"What do you care?"

"You're skipping too many physical activities, you've got to stay in shape," Camper Muscles said. Hoisting me up by the armpits, he carried me squirming all the way to the end of the dock.

"The Puck drops here." They howled with laughter as I splashed into the lake.

Had Grandpa not taught me how to swim I may have met my watery demise that day. As I made my way back to the dock, Acne picked up my backpack.

"Going on vacation or something?" he asked, dumping its contents. Out spilled snacks, books, and Woodstock.

I gave a strangled cry as I pulled myself out of the water and lunged for him, but he tossed the bird to Muscles and a game of keepaway ensued.

"What, can't sleep without your little baby toy?" Muscles laughed. "Okay, you can have him back." As I grabbed Woodstock's body, Muscles kept hold of his head and pulled.

RIP.

The two parts came apart completely, and the air exploded with white confetti. I couldn't hold back; I slumped to the ground and let the angry sobs escape.

"What's this, Puck?" Muscles wheezed. "Your mother was too poor to stuff your toys right?"

I wiped my eyes and looked around. Instead of fluff, I was surrounded by crumpled paper. I also saw Ernie making his way around the lake. While the other two were distracted by 'the fuzz' I threw everything into my bag, gathering as much scattered paper as I could. Ignoring Ernie's calls I hightailed it to the Summit and didn't stop until I was facedown in the cave crying a new wave of tears and screaming every curse word I knew.

I paid no attention to the setting sun, making a meal of the provisions in my bag and curling up to sleep in the corner.

Edison kept watch at the cave entrance the entire time, a silent sentinel.

Dark slowly turned back into light. I awoke with every muscle stiff and sore, and the previous day's events came back with a jolt when I pulled

Woodstock's head from my bag.

Groaning, I dumped him and the paper stuffing onto the floor. Though I was tempted to hurl each piece down the hill, I picked up the nearest one and began uncrumpling it.

It was a newspaper page, dated August 18, 1969. Across the top read the headline WOODSTOCK ROCKS. Beneath were several dozen pictures of crowds with captions such as *Music Lovers Unite in Front of Stage* and *Creedence Clearwater Revival Delights Thousands*.

Along the last row was a close-up picture of two people. I immediately recognized the first. My mouth fell open as I studied Mother's younger face. She was happy. The man next to her had long hair pulled back into a ponytail, one arm raised with a guitar in the air and the other wrapped around Mother. The caption read: Lunar Phazes' Killian Michaels embraces fan.

"Father?!"

I eagerly read other articles, though their tone became steadily grimmer: LUNAR PHAZES ENDS LONG TOUR, BAND TAKES RECESS WHILE MEMBERS TACKLE PERSONAL OBSTACLES, BAND CUTS REUNION TOUR SHORT…

One page was a flyer for a Lunar Phazes concert: May 14, 1977 at the Armstrong Arena, just outside Fairview.

I thought back to my seventh birthday…Mother had insisted we go to Disneyland for the weekend to celebrate, even though I had never asked to and we could scarcely afford it.

I smoothed out the last page with a sense of foreboding. The headline dated November 12, 1979 indeed made my stomach drop: LUNAR PHAZES' MICHAELS DIES FROM OVERDOSE. The accompanying picture of my father showed a lot more than ten years of wear on his face, his eyes no longer full of passion and hair cut short, yet still unruly in an oddly familiar way.

"WHY?"

All the time asking who my father was, and now that I knew it didn't do me a lick of good. I was still alone. Mother could have told me the whole truth and ended my curiosity. She could have told Killian he had a son, and maybe his fate - our fate - could have been different.

I curled into another fit of angry sobs until Dennis showed up late that afternoon. I didn't care how he found me or how severe my punishment would be; I felt nothing as we started down the Summit. I looked back for Edison and saw only the darkness of the cave.

Over the next few days I really did spend time at grief counseling, though Doctor Feelings wasn't as good as Edison. I refused to participate in any sports, and our morning rituals were put on hold because Ernie had taken leave. I read most of the time, and Dennis showed me the basics of sewing. Woodstock got his head reattached after I stuffed him with Muscles' pillow contents.

I have permission to spend one last day in the cave. To my relief, Edison is back and we spend the entire time watching clouds drift by and the moon creep upwards.

Edison confirms my ominous feelings, and I reluctantly make my way back to camp, wondering if tomorrow's eclipse will change how the world looks.

"Whoa." Even Muscles is tripped out by the midday darkness making its way slowly across the grounds. I chance a quick glance up at the 'ring of fire.'

Kinda cool.

Then, as quick the sunlight left, it returns and we all resume our activities. For me that means reading up on Taurus personalities under the shade of a tree.

"Missed it, didn't I?"

I look up as Ernie sits down. Yes, you missed a lot.

"Where'd you go?"

"I had some important things to take care of." He doesn't elaborate, but reaches into his shirt pocket and hands me a creased newspaper article.

"You dropped this."

I unfold it and stare once again at my father's face. The article is an obituary, headlined KILLIAN MICHAELS: MAY 11, 1946 - NOVEMBER 11, 1979. I skim through it, looking for any hints of myself. 'Persistent.' Well, that's one thing.

"You know, May 1946 is a Taurus and a Dog, like you."

"Really?"

"Yep. You read the end?"

I find the last sentence: Killian is survived by his parents Frank and Emily and his sister Jillian.

"Survived by means…?" I think I know, but I'm afraid to say it.

"You have family, Puck. And they want to meet you. Soon."

I reread the last line until it's too dark to see.

August 11, the final dog day of summer. I want a good look at Sirius, so I make the familiar trek under the cover of darkness. I sit at the cave entrance and watch the small twinkling light move slowly toward the horizon of the coming dawn.

"You still here, Father?"

Edison is gone, but a quiet bark echoes off the cave walls and into my heart.

Canoes & Coffee

WHO	WHEN	RATING

Notes:

☆☆☆☆☆

Notes:

☆☆☆☆☆

Notes:

☆☆☆☆☆

Notes:

☆☆☆☆☆

Notes:

☆☆☆☆☆

Notes:

☆☆☆☆☆

Notes:

☆☆☆☆☆

Notes:

☆☆☆☆☆

The Last Hike

Kenneth Roland

Brad put his foot on the bench in front of the Monson Visitor Center in Maine. He leaned over and pulled his boot laces tight, deftly weaving them into a bow. The lavender colored building loomed over him. He hadn't been on the Appalachian Trail in years. Purposely avoided it. Hiking was his joy, and he went three or four times a month, all year. Never on this trail. As he stood up and stretched, he thought about how much of Maine he had seen in the last few years. Every nook and cranny now carried his footprints.

The full Appalachian Trail starts far away in Georgia. Crossing briefly into South Carolina before riding the border of North Carolina and Tennessee. There's a long stint across Virginia and Pennsylvania before rapidly slicing through New Jersey, New York, Connecticut, Massachusetts and Vermont. Then it's just New Hampshire and the end of the trail here in Maine.

People spend up to six months attempting to walk the entire thing straight through. Brad had attempted it. With Christine. After four and a half months, they had entered Maine. Brad had never left again. Christine had flown home in a box. She'd never be back.

Today, Brad planned to hike five miles in from the trail head and back. He would slowly walk the remaining portion of the trail that he and Christine didn't get to finish in small chunks. Once he had stepped on every piece of the trail, he hoped for closure. The end of the trail would be the beginning of his new life. One where Christine no longer haunted him.

It was almost two miles to the trail head, and he considered driving to it, but decided he'd rather walk. He picked up his trekking poles as he watched a silver-gray truck turn on to Pleasant St. and head toward the trail head. Maybe he should have hitch-hiked, he thought for a moment, then crossed the road and followed the truck.

Pleasant St. was narrow and tree-lined. If not for the wires and telephone poles, you could almost believe you were already on the trail. Houses were few and far between and once the pavement ended, there were even less. Brad had come to appreciate the beauty of Maine. He knew no one, and no one knew him. He was good with that for a long time, but he needed to get back to life.

The gravel crunched under his boots as he strode along the edge of the road. His mind wandered of its own accord, slipping back to the last time he was on the trail. It had rained pretty heavily the day before. He and Christine had spent that day tented up. They had played cribbage, twenty-six games of cribbage. She laughed every time he said "One for his knob." Then she would correct him graciously "It's His Nobs," and she would laugh again. God, he missed that laugh.

They had made it to the Kennebec river just after dawn the next day. Fording across the wide river was frowned upon since the 1990s. There was a canoe ferry that would come at 9:00 but Brad didn't want to wait. He pushed Christine. "Taking the boat is cheating. You have to walk the whole thing." Someone had left inner tubes, and they used these to float their packs. The rocks were slippery and Brad cautioned Christine to watch her footing. God that was the last thing he had said, "Be careful."

It's the survivor's guilt, he consoled himself. Repeating what every therapist had told him. He blinked away tears as he reached the trail head.

It's been years now. It was time to let it go. Not be haunted by it anymore. He jabbed his trekking poles into the earth to get water from his pack. The violence with which he stabbed them into the soil surprised him. He began the breathing exercises he had practiced.

Brad felt better as he got into the woods proper. His mind became focused on the roots, rocks and other treacherous obstacles he needed to avoid. Focusing where to put each foot and pole began to take all his concentration. He could hear the wildlife out in the forest. Chirps, scratches, and the rustle of leaves kept a constant conversation with him. Christine had never seemed to run out of things to talk about. She didn't talk all the time, but when she did speak it was always some new observation or insight into the world that Brad would add to, or question. Then the conversation would run through the day. Sometimes quietly, each in their own heads, mulling over their own thoughts. Other times loudly, shouting across streams and valleys some new idea that had just come to them. Brad smiled, thinking about it.

He lost his focus on the ground in front of him. He could see Christine stepping across rocks, her trek poles hanging loosely from slim wrists. Brad had always marvelled at the way she hiked the trails with such grace. Her hiking boots barely seemed to touch the ground as she moved. She would dodge branches and leap from rocks like she was in a ballet. The prima ballerina on nature's stage and an audience of one.

As Brad neared the five-mile mark, the forest began to thin, revealing a rocky outcropping overlooking a valley awash in fiery autumn colors. He paused at the edge, his breath catching at the view. Christine would have loved this. She'd have taken out her sketchbook, crouched on a flat rock, drawing the play of light on the hills. Brad would be rummaging their sacks, planning a meal. He could almost hear her voice in his head, narrating the scene for him. She would describe the clouds as though he had never seen one before. By the time she was done, he would feel like he knew each tree personally and could name their children. He would think to himself that all he had to do was look up and he could just see the real thing for himself. Somehow he enjoyed it more the way she described it.

He sat down and pulled out the small tin he'd been carrying in his pack.

It was stainless steel with an inscription on the lid, "Nature gives more than it takes". He hated that quote. Christine's parents had chosen it. Brad couldn't believe they still believed it. Nature had taken Christine. Nature had taken everything. Nature could never give back enough to make up for what it had taken.

Inside the tin was a handful of Christine's ashes. They'd been with him on every hike he'd taken since she passed. He was supposed to scatter them into nature, but he'd never been able to do it. It was like giving up on her. He felt like it would be letting her go and never being able to get her back.

This trip was about stopping the haunting though. About closure, and moving forward. This would be where Christine wanted to be. He wiped his eyes with his sleeve and stared at "nature", wishing it to give something back to him. Anything he could use as a sign that it was time.

Brad opened the tin and the breeze immediately carried her ashes into the valley below. At first he was alarmed and almost slammed the lid back on, then a sense of peace overtook him. He could feel the world grow larger. For the first time in years, he didn't feel a weight pressing on his chest. He felt lighter, as if Christine's spirit was now part of the world she loved so much.

He watched the ashes slowly drift out, their weight carrying them downwards towards the water. Sometimes they would sparkle in the sun, or at least he thought they did. He emptied the rest of the container then sat back leaning his hands behind him. Staring at nothing and everything at the same time.

He stayed there until the sun dipped low. Sitting on the same rock watching the sun paint the sky in shades of orange and pink. He packed up, carefully making sure he left nothing behind. It was going to be dark by the time he got back to the trail head. He went into his bag and fetched his flashlight, flicking it on to ensure the batteries were working. As he did, something lit up on the ground by the trail. It twinkled in the light. Brad went over to look, bending down to pick up a small, heart-shaped rock. It was smooth, worn by years of water and wind. He flipped the smooth stone over and over in his hand, then looked back out at the sunset. For a moment he thought of throwing it out into the void, his heart, sailing after Christine's ashes. He had his hand raised and back, then suddenly changed his mind. He fetched the stainless steel tin out of his pack. He re-opened tit and slipped the rock inside. Nature gives more than it takes, it thought.

On his way back to the trailhead, Brad felt something he hadn't in a long time — peace. He didn't need to finish the whole trail anymore. He'd already found what he'd been looking for: not closure, but connection. Brad realized he didn't need to get rid of Christine. Being haunted by her was a problem to be solved. It was a special link. She wasn't gone, she was everywhere — in the trees, the streams, the rocks. And in his heart, always.

Canoes & Coffee

WHO	WHEN	RATING

Notes:

☆☆☆☆☆

Notes:

☆☆☆☆☆

Notes:

☆☆☆☆☆

Notes:

☆☆☆☆☆

Notes:

☆☆☆☆☆

Notes:

☆☆☆☆☆

Notes:

☆☆☆☆☆

Notes:

☆☆☆☆☆

Lost and Found

Kyle Rogers

Roses are red
Violets are blue
Camping with Gary
Is worse than eating dog poo

I scribble the words in my notebook.

"What are you writing?" Gary asks. He's breaking down tree branches into campfire kindling.

"A poem," I say.

"Oh yeah? Read it for me."

I avoid his gaze and let the silence settle in. He doesn't try again. Maybe he's finally catching on.

Gary was persistent when Mom started dating him a year ago. Movies, the arcade, mini golf, baseball games. I could usually come up with an excuse, but Mom wouldn't let me back out this time. Maybe if I'd said "yes" once or twice to a movie I wouldn't be stuck here — a week of island hopping on the Turtle-Flambeau Flowage, living out of a canoe, and Gary's incessant attempts to bond.

My last time camping had been with Dad, not long before he got sick. I fiddle with the pocketknife he gave me on that trip, the same one that had belonged to his father. "This knife is magic," Dad had said. "When you're in a jam — any jam — it'll give you exactly what you need."

Magic might've been an overstatement, but it was a good knife and did its job. And if nothing else, the rhythm of snapping the knife in and out of place always calmed me. But if there was any real magic in it, now would be a great time for it. Maybe it could conjure up a monsoon or something to end this trip early.

"Want to build this fire?" Gary asks.

"I'm going for a walk," I say.

I circle the island's perimeter. As I near the campsite on my return, I hear a gun shot. Then a second one, and a third. I find Gary armed with a shotgun, scanning the shoreline.

"What happened?" I say.

"I saw … a bear," Gary says.

We go down to the shoreline. All we find is our canoe, its canvas exterior shredded with bullet holes, water pouring in, submerging the boat into the shallows.

Gary of course doesn't have a patch kit.

"We'll call your mother in the morning," Gary says later while sitting in the glow of the campfire.

I stick a hand in my right pocket, searching for the pocketknife, my favorite distraction. It's not there. Left pocket neither. When did I last for sure have it? I can't remember. Panic sets in, and a knot emerges in my chest. One of the few possessions of Dad's I had kept and now it's gone forever. Just like that. Just like him. I close my eyes tight, tears leaking out the corners.

"It'll be okay," Gary says. "Don't worry. Like I said, we'll call your mother in the morning. Someone will come help us."

I don't say anything, stand up and crawl into the tent. The tears flow freely now. I hear Gary's footsteps outside the tent and worry that he's coming to check on me. Always checking on me. But that's all it is. Footsteps. I eventually drift off to sleep.

The kid hates me. It's obvious. Or is that just the normal expression of a pre-teen? That's what Sharon keeps telling me.

I snap a tree branch over my knee to add to the firewood supply. The kid, Dylan, is focused on his notebook.

"What are you writing?" I ask.

"A poem," Dylan mumbles.

"Oh yeah? Read it for me."

Nothing.

I don't push it further. Sharon says to be patient, but it's been a year. I've tried so many different times. All the things 12-year-olds are supposed to like. If a little progress can't be made on this camping trip, I don't know what else to do. I thought camping would be sort of a grand gesture. I know Dylan used to do a lot of camping with his dad. What better way to show him that I'm serious about his mom. And him too. Everything. But maybe I've overthought this whole thing.

"Want to build this fire?" Might as well keep trying.

"I'm going for a walk," Dylan says.

I go back to organizing firewood. Ten minutes later, a crunching sound in the direction of the shoreline catches my attention. I turn and it's huge. Big, black. Instinct takes over. I grab the shotgun resting on a nearby stump and fire. Once, then again and again. A squirrel scurries away. The big, black menace remains. I squint through the darkening haze of dusk and realize it's … the hammock I strung up earlier. It sways, occasionally ballooning to a gargantuan size when the breeze catches it just right.

I hear Dylan's voice behind me. "What happened?"

"I saw …" I hesitate. I can't admit that I just got spooked by a hammock. "… a bear."

A knot forms in my chest when we go down to the shoreline and I see our canoe bobbing in the water, less and less of it remaining above the surface as water gradually filters through the bullet holes.

"We'll call your mother in the morning," I tell Dylan later by the campfire.

Per usual, he says nothing. Suddenly he looks frantic. Then tears. Great, I've made the kid cry.

"It'll be okay," I say. "Don't worry. Like I said, we'll call your mother in the morning. Someone will come help us."

Dylan doesn't say a word, stands up and crawls into the tent. For a moment I think about going to check on him, but then I remember what Sharon said: "Give him his space. It's complicated. He'll come around eventually."

I walk around the fire, kicking at the dirt, then decide to walk around the island. Give Dylan that space Sharon keeps talking about.

It's a clear night and the moon is bright. So bright I don't even need my headlamp. I pull it off and shove it in a pocket. I pause a moment to stand along the shoreline and look out toward the water. My mind wanders to thoughts of my father. Or the imagined ideal of him I'd been creating since childhood, the one who'd take me on a camping trip like this.

The reality was he'd arrive in town every so often, a bundle of energy, taking me to the movies or a ball game, and we'd have a great time. Mom would try to temper my expectations, but I fell for it every time, the wave of disappointment stinging harder each time that he'd disappear again for six months. I vowed I'd never be the same way if I had the opportunity to be a dad. I really think I could be that for Dylan, if only I could find an opening.

Suddenly the glint of something in the moonlight catches my eye. I walk toward it, reach down, and pick it up. It's a pocketknife, I think the same one I've seen Dylan playing around with. I stick it in my pocket and return to the campsite.

"You packing up camp by chance? No worries if you aren't, but this is our favorite site."

I open my eyes at the sound of unfamiliar voices and stare at the ceiling of the tent. I hear Gary respond.

"Soon hopefully," he says. "We're kind of stranded at the moment. Got a problem with our canoe."

I listen to the rest of the conversation. Seems we've been saved. I start to rise, then notice it sitting on the tent floor beside me — my lost pocketknife. Maybe it is magic after all. I crawl out of the tent.

"Hey, you're awake," Gary says. "Good news. These guys can help us out. They have supplies for patching the canoe."

He looks down at my right hand flipping the pocketknife around in my palm.

"That pocketknife is yours, right?" he asks. "I walked around the island last night and happened to find it along the shoreline."

So not magic. Just Gary. Is he really that bad? Maybe not. Mom's been bugging me to give him a chance. A real chance.

"Yeah," I say. "Thanks."

We return to the boat landing without incident. After strapping the canoe to the roof of the car, Gary slides into the driver's seat. I sit in the passenger's seat, doodling in my notebook.

"Sorry," Gary says. "We don't have to do that ever again. Dumb idea."

I glance at him. He looks sad, and for the first time I feel bad about it rather than being annoyed. I turn to a fresh page in my notebook and put pen to paper. I tear the sheet out when I'm finished and give it to Gary. I attempt a smile.

Roses are red
Violets are blue
I'm not calling you Dad
But I guess you will do

Lost and Found

WHO	WHEN	RATING

Notes:

☆☆☆☆☆

Notes:

☆☆☆☆☆

Notes:

☆☆☆☆☆

Notes:

☆☆☆☆☆

Notes:

☆☆☆☆☆

Notes:

☆☆☆☆☆

Notes:

☆☆☆☆☆

Notes:

☆☆☆☆☆

Warm Days

Never Trust a Sandwich

Kenneth Roland

Never trust a sandwich. That's something I learned as a child. My father believed that anything edible was a viable filling for a sandwich. It didn't matter if it was canned, jarred, refrigerated, or raw; it could be crammed between slices of bread and called 'Lunch'. Mixing things together was completely acceptable, as long as the total height of the sandwich was equal to four times the height of a slice of bread. The offering of "Would you like a sandwich?" was not a question you could answer in our house. Did you want a sandwich? Yes. Would you like the sandwich you got? Unlikely. There were successes, which led to my enjoyment of a peanut butter, mayonnaise, and lettuce sandwich, but there were more failures. Many more failures. The peanut butter, that surprisingly brought out the tang of the mayonnaise, did not do as well with tuna, or sauerkraut. Now as I stood in the trendy luncheonette housed in an old milking parlor on a converted farm in the town of St. Jacobs, I was again being offered a sandwich and these memories awoke.

I was meeting another writer, who shall remain nameless, but for the sake of the story, called Jonathan Grisham. I looked at the chalked up menu, spying a cranberry, brie, and goat cheese panini. Hmm, that sounded exactly like the type of thing my father would concoct. I opted for a spinach salad. Jonathan put his faith in the panini. Jonathan also went for a breakfast tea, but I felt it was too late in the day for anything designated breakfast, and opted for water. The server, behind their reclaimed wood counter, judged us each appropriately, handed us a small, numbered stand for our table, and sent us into the dining area. A large thirteen was chalked onto the stand in a serif font. It was apparently our order number. I felt that the unlucky number thirteen was not a great sign for Jonathan's sandwich and only affirmed my choice of leafy greens.

There was no wait staff in the brightly lit, rustic, dining area. You filled your own water from a jug that stood on an old wine barrel. Personally, I would have used a milk can to stay on theme. I really felt like they missed out on that one. Now we just had to wait for them to shout from the front when our order was ready. It was quite trendy to remove the wait staff and instead make the customer wait themselves as you screamed random numbers at them.

The dining room itself was beautiful. Slate floors shifting from moldy green to muddy red. Original chunky oak timbers were exposed from the ceiling with hand-made, reclaimed barn lumber chandeliers hanging from them. It churned out quite well, if you get my meaning. The wood trimmed windows were likely added for the cafe. I don't remember milking parlors having many windows, just two raised stages where the ladies of the bovine world came in twice a day for therapeutic release.

While Jonathan fetched his tea, I took the time to study the other persons in attendance. Writers are often found staring at people, making mental notes for future characters. It may appear rude, and likely is, but it's critical to the craft. Had I not noticed the small mole below the ear spacers of the bearded gentleman sitting across the parlor, I wouldn't have been able to include it in this story. I can almost feel your disappointment if it had been missed. He was at an angle to me, and I could only see the right side of his face as it poked out from his laptop cover. His gaze, behind the thick glasses, was intense. His beard slowly faded in length as it approached his ears until there was practically only skin. This semi-skin encircled his head until it bloomed into a thick, shiny, tightly styled lid of hair on the top.

There was a woman in a yellow summer dress, also seated on her own. She was thumbing through her phone as she sipped from a delicate tea cup. It was hard to tell what was in the cup, but it steamed, and I guessed that she had somehow got a refill despite the lack of wait staff. Her plate was pushed aside, some crumbs and a small crust left on it. I could understand that. Eating a sandwich is exhausting, and upon reaching the far crust, it's just not worth the effort to push on.

Jonathan had sat me strategically facing out of the room so that he could face into it. The only other table I could see had two people who were eating and talking at the same time. One was a woman, who would use her pinky, in an effort to be dainty, to push salad back into her mouth as words tumbled out around it. Her partner was wearing gray slacks, a black billowing blouse and was chewing sincerely as they nodded repeatedly. Their wind swept, crop cut hair shifted only slightly in comparison to their apparent agreement.

I was disturbed by a chair leg scraping across the stonework as Jonathan sat down. "I need this," he stated, sipping his tea before his body was settled into the seat. "Have you been writing at all?"

Of course I'd been writing. Jonathan's questions had the specific intention of luring you into asking him the same thing. You knew he had something amazing to tell you because he would ask how your day was. If he was struggling with life, he would immediately ask "Are you getting by Ok?".

I decided to play along, "Little bits, here and there. I've been seeking inspiration, a muse if you will. In the meantime I've been busying myself with research. Yourself?"

"Oh, I'm deep into one now. You would love it." Jonathan began laying out the current book he was working on. It was a murder mystery. Or just a mystery, as they are called now. Murder has been dropped since there are times the victim is found to still be alive. In some books, it's a mystery why no one was murdered, as you would have liked to kill off half the characters yourself. After almost fifteen minutes of non-stop chatter, I discovered Jonathan was having the opposite problem.

"You see, the murderer is then murdered. The detective believes, of course, that they now have a serial killer on their hands. Then that murderer is murdered. I'm seventeen chapters in, and I've killed everyone except the final murderer and the detective. I think my only option is to have the detective poisoned," he took a sip of tea, then held it up, "by his tea, in chapter one. He then slowly dies throughout the book and shoots the last character before his own demise."

"Interesting," I said. "Do you think readers will appreciate that you've killed the entire cast of the story?"

"I'm pretty sure they'll be overjoyed. Happy to be rid of the lot of them. I know I will be happy when they are gone. There isn't a redeeming quality among them. I think I need to work in a false appendage."

"Interesting. Why?"

"I need a space to hide the murder weapon."

"Which murder weapon?'

'The third. It comes off as awkward that a Nun is just carrying a weapon out in the open."

"What if there was a sword, where the hilt was hollow and the Nun hid a knife in it?"

"I'm thinking more of a false leg, where the thigh opens to reveal a pistol," Jonthan said thoughtfully.

"What about a pistol sandwich?" I asked.

"THIRTEEN!" An ominous shout came across the quiet cafe.

"I'll get it," said Jonathan, pushing his chair back, scraping the stone floor and sending shivers down my spine.

The couple were still chatting gregariously. The woman in the summer dress had left at some point. The man was now rubbing his temples in slow circles. Apparently the relationship between himself and his laptop had grown tumultuous.

Jonathan returned and placed a plate of dry spinach leaves with feta and hard cranberries in front of me. It felt like the chef had served me the sandwich, just without any bread. I eyed it suspiciously. Jonathan's panini, however, smelled really good. I was beginning to question my choice, when his words shocked me in a way I can honestly say, I've never been shocked before.

"There's a dead body at the counter that wasn't there before." His words went through me like a shot of whiskey. I tingled from my head to toes, and a warmth grew from my stomach.

"What?"

"Yes, exactly. Laying in the entry, is a dead body. Big knife sticking out of its back. Definitely wasn't there when we came in."

"Well no! That's the type of thing one notices as they are making their lunch choices."

I rose hurriedly from the table and began to stride to the front entrance. Jonathan rose as well, grabbing half his sandwich before following. "Wait for me," he whined, "if there's a story I'm calling dibs, I saw it first."

The staff was quietly wiping the counter, completely ignoring the man laying just on the other side. The body itself was large, but not obese, just hefty. It appeared to a man around the age of forty based on the lines of the face. The dark stained wooden handle of a butcher knife protruded from the suit coat that wrapped the body. The man was clean shaven with a thick head of black curly hair. One arm was trapped beneath him, and the other leaned against the counter. Crimson stains were seeping out onto the stone floor turning it black.

"Do you not see this?" I asked incredulously of the staff.

They looked at me, then peered over the counter, balancing on their toes to see the man laying in front of them. "Yeah, that's Addison Miller, the theater actor."

"And HE'S DEAD!" I shouted with vexation.

"No he's not."

Jonathan nudged the body with his foot and the arm flopped onto the floor. "Oh, I'm pretty sure he is," he said around a mouthful of panini.

"He does this once a month," the server stated, "comes in all dying and flailing, then asks for a free sandwich for the show. The chef gives him one, I wouldn't personally, I don't think he's that good." They carelessly returned to wiping the counter.

I crouched and looked at Mr. Miller. He certainly appeared dead. I rolled his head to the side and it moved without resistance. I used my fingers to prop open one eyelid and looked into his amber coloured orb. There was certainly no life in it. The eyelid slowly closed as I took my hand away.

"Mr. Miller!" I shouted. "Are you dead?"

No answer. Well that settles it. I stood and put a hard look on the staffer. "Mr. Miller is dead," I stated.

"How do you know?" they replied. "He never answered."

"He is currently leaking out onto your floors and I imagine it's going to take a good deal of scrubbing to get him out."

The staffer eyed me suspiciously and finally came around the end of the counter. Jonathan was chewing absent mindedly. He watched as the server dropped their cloth on the counter and bent down to poke at Mr. Miller. "Addison?" they queried. Shortly they came to the same conclusion as myself, Mr. Addison Miller, the theater actor, was quite dead.

Jonathan and I finished our lunch while we waited for the police. They had asked that no one leave, so we got to chat briefly with the couple and the trendy man with the laptop. Nice people, but when the detective arrived, Jonathan and I were first in line to talk to him.

We were immediately disappointed. He didn't look like a detective. No trench coat, no fedora, no obvious flask of alcohol. He was distinctly lacking the three days growth expected of a detective. His eyes seemed bright and alert, and his demeanor almost seemed engaged. This was not the weary eyed, seen the world at its worst, hardened man that Jonathan and I expected.

"Are you sure you're a detective?" Jonathan asked outright, eyeing the man in his police services jacket and uniform pants. Authors were good at getting to the point. Unless they weren't, as you are likely realizing.

"I'll ask the questions, thank you."

Jonathan spun on his heel, "Oh! He's a detective alright." We both swarmed the poor man.

"I'm a writer," we said at the same time.

"Interesting," was his only reply. "Did you witness the death?"

"Not really," Jonathan started, "I saw the body when I came to pick up our lunch. I believe I missed witnessing it by less than five minutes."

"Although," I interjected, pointing at Jonathan, "he may have killed Mr. Miller when he kicked him. It sounds like before that, he may have only been acting."

Jonathan looked shocked, "I most certainly did not! I told you when I came back with your salad that there was a dead body. I didn't say there was something acting like a dead body, did I?"

The detective blocked my answer with a hand movement. "Gentlemen, we're going to need to interview you separately." He pointed at Jonathan, "You, head back to the dining area." He turned and suddenly pointed at me, "You, come with me outside."

I could see Jonathan was hurt. He felt like he had discovered the body, and should get to go first. I was excited, and quietly raised a fist behind the detective's back. If ever, there was story fodder, it was here. A real police detective, investigating a real case. He led me out the wood door to the gravel parking lot. The lot was built around the old milking parlor and surrounded a barn that housed a reclaimed lumber studio as well. Railway ties separated the cars from each other, except for the police car which was pulled up quite close to the door.

As we walked to the front of the squad car, I decided to make my move. "You know," I drew a line down the hood of the squad car with my finger, "detectives and writers usually work together. Solving cases and exchanging witty banter. It's a special bond."

"Is that so?" said the detective. "Sounds more like a trope than a bond." I was shocked. Why wasn't he jumping at my obvious offer of friendship and confidence? Instead, he decided to question me about the woman in the summer dress. The one that had left. "Did you see this woman?" He held up a black and white headshot, about the size of a business card, with the woman's serious face staring out at me.

"I did indeed," I replied, "I can tell you all about her. She was wearing a yellow dress, and looking at her phone. She had dancers' calves, the muscle high on the leg if you know what I mean. She appeared somber but not sad. I believe the day was on autopilot for her, her thoughts far away. If you asked me, she had planned on more, what with the bright yellow dress and open toed shoes. Something had put her off in the morning, and now she was reflecting on her life."

"So you saw her," he noted. I was put out that he didn't take in my full analysis. He didn't even have a little notepad to flip the page and jot down some intriguing bit of information culled from my description.

"Are you sure you are a detective?" I asked him.

"Are you sure you are a writer?" he quipped.

I paused. That was uncalled for. I chewed my lip for a moment as he handed the picture to a constable nearby. I placed my hand on the hood of the patrol car and tried to look nonchalant. "Quite a mystery here. Like one of those locked room capers."

"How so?" The detective was looking at me again. He crossed his arms in front of him. His body language said he was about to reject anything I had to say.

"Well we were all in the dining room," I said sheepishly. "The windows were all closed and the only doors out were to the washrooms, the kitchen, and to the order area."

"Right, so a locked room with multiple open exits. Look Mr. Roland, I don't have time to help you create a story. Did you see this woman?" The detective held up a different photo.

I'd never seen this woman before. Was he testing me? "No," I said cautiously, watching his face, "I don't think I've seen that woman before."

"Um hm", he grunted. I couldn't tell if I was supposed to have seen her or not. He continued, "Ok, the constable will take your information and you can go."

I felt I was losing my chance for a great source of real-world information. "First," I held up a single finger, "we'll need to find the murder weapon."

The detective somehow glared and squinted at me simultaneously. "There's a ten inch butcher knife sticking out of his back," he said.

"Ahh," I tried to sound contemplative, "but perhaps his back is uniquely suited to hold a ten inch butcher knife." The look on the detective's face was starting to make me feel awkward. I continued my conjecture just to delay the silence. "Perhaps, through surgical or other means, Mr. Miller has a sleeve-like fold of skin that could support a knife," I folded my hands in front of me, "like a sandwich.. You have to admit it would be perfect for acting."

At this point Jonathan broke through the front door, "I demand to be seen! I have solved the case!" The constable attempted to hold him back, but the detective, if that's who he really was, waved him forward. Jonathan straightened himself out and walked to the front of the car.

"I believe Mr. Miller was coming to a clandestine meeting at the cafe when he was confronted by his current lover. He was then killed by a poisoned panini," he rushed to get the words out. "The chef, insulted that someone would go to the trouble of dying from one of his meals, stabbed the man in the back. We will find his secret love arriving at any moment!" He pointed out into the parking lot with a flourish, and for some reason, we all turned to look. In the quiet of the moment I could hear a shrill bird warble out a short tune.

"What? The cardinal?" Asked the constable.

Jonathan didn't let it deter him. "They may have hit traffic, but hear me out, the knife is a red-herring!"

"I knew it!" I gloated, attempting to give the detective a mirror to the glare he had given me previously.

"The knife is a knife," said the detective. He seemed right perturbed now. "Did you know a red-herring is just a smoked, cured, herring? How is that relevant? It's been half an hour since Mr. Miller was killed. If he was having a clandestine meeting, the other party would have already been here."

"Ah hah!" I shouted. "Perhaps the fold in Mr. Miller's back could accommodate a smoked herring!"

"We have Mr. Miller's phone. He was texting," the detective held out his hand and the constable handed him the photo, "this woman!" He shoved the headshot into Jonathan's face so fast I thought he would break his nose. "Her name is Ruth Harvey. She's a ballroom dancer. She and Mr. Miller were partners, and were recently invited to appear on Dancing With The Stars."

"Oh!" I exclaimed. "And who were they to be dancing with? I've always felt like George Hamilton deserves a second shot, he was quite good."

"An actor that can also dance," Jonathan mused, "surely he was in high demand! Imagine if there was a writer that could also act?"

"They aren't going to be dancing with anyone, because he's dead. I believe she did it!" The detective seemed quite angry now. "Mr. Addison Miller was coming to tell Ms. Harvey that the show only wanted him, and she was being left behind. However, secretly, he was messaging", he hand shot out again, and the constable handed him the other photo, "this woman, who he was actually going to take to the show."

"Oh, a bit of an Addison Miller sandwich issue," I said.

The detective ignored me, "When Ms. Harvey learned of the other woman, she killed Mr. Miller. End of case."

"Well that's bland," stated Jonathan, crossing his arms. "Seems a bit on the nose, doesn't it?"

I was aghast. "If that's true, this is certainly the worst caper I have personally been a part of." I placed my shoulder against Jonathans and crossed my arms as well. "I'd appreciate it, if you could keep my name out of the news media with regards to this."

"As would I," Jonathan nodded sternly.

The detective's face seemed to redden. I could only imagine how embarrassed he was by his own involvement. His one eyebrow was twitching awkwardly.

"I believe our detective here is wishing his own tea had been poisoned this morning," I joked to Jonathan.

"I'm still not sure about that," mused Jonathan. "I do like this ballroom dancer angle though. I would still need to work in a false appendage that could conceal the murder weapon."

The constable was leading us further out into the parking lot. I imagined the detective wanted some alone time to deal with his shame.

"Now that's a hook," I said. Jonathan laughed, and it took me a while to get it. "Oh my, yes a hook. Like on an amputated hand. Oh brilliant."

"Yes, a knife hidden in a revolver, hidden in a hook. A weapon sandwich!" said Jonathan. "This mess," he waved his hand back at the cafe, "is certainly not how we would have written it. The ending is stale and dry. It's missing the mustard." Jonathan turned back and shouted at the Constable "You need mustard!"

"Agreed," I said. "I'd never write this drivel. What an embarrassment."

WHO	WHEN	RATING

Notes:

☆☆☆☆☆

Notes:

☆☆☆☆☆

Notes:

☆☆☆☆☆

Notes:

☆☆☆☆☆

Notes:

☆☆☆☆☆

Notes:

☆☆☆☆☆

Notes:

☆☆☆☆☆

Notes:

☆☆☆☆☆

Tour Muskoka

Kenneth Roland

This morning Marjorie's dream was about to come true. Her cruise boat, which is much different than a cruise ship, was about to take on its maximum capacity of eight passengers. The boat had a little cut out bow where she could stand and an extra seat sunk low in the stern for the Captain. She wasn't sure the man she hired really qualified as a captain, but maybe a skipper? The rest of the pirates off the coast of Peru called him Captain though and he demanded that he keep that title. There was a roof over the passenger section in the middle, held up by poles along the gunwale. Marjorie loved it. It was red to just above the waterline than gleaming white for the rest of the hull. The seats were a bright red fabric and the roof was blue. It was beautiful. She stood there in the morning just taking it all in. The skies were an azure blue and the water was still. She was daydreaming of the tour around the lakes of Muskoka to view the cottages of the rich and famous.

"Marjorie's Major Muskoka Meander" was the name of her tour. She didn't really know who lived in the cottages, but figured, neither would any of her passengers. You rarely saw actual people as you cruised by their docks, stunning yards, and triangles of glass and wood. It would be easy to say it was the cottage of Ashton and Mila, or Goldie and Kurt. She might even throw in a Wayne and Janet for some Canadian content. The people would ooh and ahh and they'd be at the next cottage. She had prepped a map of the lakes and scoped out the best cottages ahead of time so she could get the patrons excited as they would round an outcrop and view the gorgeous windows of somebody's vacation home. She made a copy of the map and had taped it to the boat right in front of the captain's seat. Everything would be perfect.

Marjorie was deciding if she should include Ozzy and Sharon's cottage on the tour when the first passengers arrived. She was excited to see the pair arm in arm strolling down the dock. "Is this the launch of Majorie's Major Muskoka Meander?" they asked together.

"It is!" she shouted back, waving her arms. This was going to be great. They looked like a perfect couple to have on the tour. "Where are you two beautiful people from?" she asked.

"We're from Toronto," said the woman, "almost locals."

"Amazing!" returned Marjorie.

"We own one of the cottages that we'll be boating past," the woman added.

"We've always wanted to see what it looks like from the water, but we're not big boaters," added the man.

"Plus we'll get to see who our neighbours are," whispered the woman, and the pair laughed.

"Amazing!" Marjorie managed to get out as her jaw dropped. How would she know which cottage was theirs as she claimed it was owned by a current A-list actor. She would need to figure out a way to get them to tell her. She decided to call this couple "The Residents". Before she could think about it anymore another couple was coming down the dock. Where was the Captain?

"Welcome, welcome," she called out, but the new couple stopped. They appeared to be egging each other on to continue. Both were already wearing life preservers and the woman carried a life saving ring in bright red. Marjorie looked at her own red rings hanging from the side of the boat. "Majorie's Major Musk" was painted on them. That's all she could fit in the font size she had used. It had worked out, since she ran out of paint and the last one just said "Marjor". She had hung it off the side of the boat that faced the lake so no one would notice.

The couple had stopped completely now, talking to each other in whispers. Marjorie yelled out to them, "We have our own life preservers, you don't need to bring your own. Plenty for everyone."

The man turned and looked at her, then turned back to the woman and began whispering again. Finally they turned towards her and the woman dropped her red ring. From out of nowhere she suddenly had a paddle in her hands. Marjorie's eyes went wide. Where had she been keeping that? "Yes!" she shouted, figuring out the pantomimed question, "We have paddles as well." She waved them towards her. "Are you here for the tour?"

The couple finally began to advance further. They went in single file along the middle of the dock, both holding their hands out as though walking a tightrope.

"Yes," said the man, who was in the lead. "Please excuse us, we've never been on a boat ride before. Or on a lake," he added.

"That's OK!" said Majorie with more confidence than she was feeling. "This is the safest boat in the Muskoka's. Built by a shipwright from England. And it's only a three hour tour," she added at the last second out of pure rascality. The woman instantly stopped. "I kid!" she said, "I'm sorry, that wasn't necessary." She helped both of them over the gunwale, a process that took almost ten minutes. They each took a seat in the aisle, even though each of the four rows held two.

"You're not going to sit together?" she asked, glancing at the Residents who appeared to be deep in their own conversation pointing at things on the dock.

"We read it's safest to be near the aisle," said the man. "People on the edges may fall out into the water. Thinking of which, do you have fifteen meters of rope?"

"What?" asked Marjorie. She wasn't paying attention and instead was trying to see what the Residents may be pointing at.

"Every sail and power boat from six meters to nine meters is required to have at least fifteen meters of rope, chain, or cord in some combination," said the woman from her seat behind the man. Marjorie decided to call this couple The Girl Guides.

"Of course we do!" she said, wondering if she had anything like that. Where the hell was the Captain? She turned back to the dock and was shocked to find a bearded man standing right at the edge of the boat. "Oh Gawd!" she shouted, clutching her chest. "You scared the crap out of me."

"I am ready," said the man calmly. He held up a large coil of rope. "I brought rope."

"Amazing," said Marjorie, "thanks Captain." She bowed and moved out of the way to allow him aboard. He immediately set out for the back of the boat and began inspecting the engine.

Marjorie checked her watch. Ten minutes until departure time. She looked up at the dock and saw another couple approaching. Perfect, just two more passengers and they'd be full.

"Ahoy!," called the woman from the dock, waving her arm at Marjorie.

"Hello!" Marjorie called back, "Welcome to the tour!"

"We're ornithologists," said the man.

"Birders," said the woman covering one side of her mouth with her hand, like it was a secret.

"We're hoping to spot an Olive-sided Flycatcher on this trip," finished the man.

Marjorie noticed the binoculars hanging from their necks now. "Interesting," she said, "Is it rare?"

"It's no Hudsonian Godwit," said the woman.

"But we haven't collected it this year," the man finished her sentence.

"Fascinating," Marjorie replied, even though she had no interest in birds and wouldn't be able to tell a Godwit from a Flycatcher if they were standing right in front of her with name tags on. She felt a tap at her shoulder and looked to see a white blotch that was slowly moving down her top. "Can you do something about the seagulls?" she asked the birders.

They both laughed, then the man leaned in and sniffed the white goo. "That's actually a Chipping Sparrow guano," he said seriously.

Majorie caught herself leaning her head to smell her shirt, then stopped herself. "Interesting," she said, "feel free to take your seats, we're just waiting for two more and we'll be on our way."

The woman looked over Marjorie's shoulder. "It looks like we're the last."

Marjorie spun and discovered the front seats were taken now. Occupied by two human shaped creatures in wet suits and snorkel masks. Their flippers stuck straight out towards the bow. She jumped again, "Oh my goodness!" She quickly apologized, "I'm sorry, I must be jumpy today. I didn't even see you get on board." The frog people just nodded.

The Birders didn't mind taking the outer seats left by the Girl Guides. They took a bit to squish their way past the overdressed pair, but made it to their seats.

Marjorie went back and told the captain to get the boat ready for launch. She returned to her notch in the bow and flicked on a large karaoke speaker. She grabbed the microphone and spun with a flourish, "Welcome everyone to the maiden voyage of Marjorie's Major Muskoka Meander!"

The Residents clapped from the back and the Birders joined them politely. The Frogs just stared straight ahead. One of the Girl Guides had their hand up. The engine roared to life, then settled into a rhythmic rumble as she pointed to the Guide. "Yes?"

"Will there be a safety presentation?" the woman asked.

"Umm, yes," Marjorie murmured. "If the boat catches fire, exit the boat. If the boat is sinking, exit the boat. Once you exit the boat, return to shore," she pointed with both hands at the shore, "Please refrain from setting the boat on fire, or causing it to sink. Thank you."

The captain was leaning over the gunwale, untying the boat from the dock. He pushed off and the boat drifted out into the water. He glanced at the frog people and shrugged on his way back to the stern.

Marjorie put a foot out in front of her to steady herself as the boat began to move forward. She lifted the microphone again. "First you are going to see the amazing Ferndale boat house," she began reciting. "Built in the early two thousands, it's a feast for the eyes."

The boat cruised through the water smoothly. "Is your cottage on this side of the lake?" Majorie asked the Residents.

"No, we've never been in Ferndale Bay before," the man smiled back.

"Oh!" Marjorie returned, "We'll be in Ferndale Bay and Lake Rousseau for most of the tour." Internally she gave herself a high five.

"Oh yes, our cottage is on Lake Rousseau. Sorry, I thought you were asking about the bay."

Majorie's internal high five missed and smacked her in the face. "And is it on this side of Lake Rousseau?" she asked again.

"Oh, I'm not sure. We usually drive. What do you call the sides of the lake, like port and starboard or something? I think we're on the starboard side. Near the bow."

Majorie just stared at the man. Was he pulling her leg? She noticed the Captain, sitting right behind the man. He was spinning his finger around his ear in the sign of "Crazy." She couldn't help but agree.

"Well, be sure to point it out to me when we're close," she said.

The passengers were thrilled as the Ferndale house came into view. The residents took some pictures with their phone. Maybe she didn't need to worry. That was when she noticed the Frogs were gone. Two empty seats at the front of the boat. No one else seemed to notice. She glanced back at the captain. He had obviously noticed them exit, but he just shrugged. Ok, thought Marjorie, so maybe they went for a swim or something. What was she supposed to do? If she didn't see them by the time they got back and they weren't on the dock, she'd have to call the police. She wasn't sure what she'd say when the other passengers eventually asked about them.

They were on the coast of Lake Rousseau now and would soon slide between the mainland and Fairview Island.

"The beautiful cottage you see towering on the mainland once belonged to Beatles legend George Harrison," she began to recite. "It's known for its grand architecture and the staircase to the boathouse that plays 'Got My Mind Set On You' as you descend. Each stair playing the next note." She smiled. This is why she got into this business. "I've had a few nights there where I just walked up and down the stairs. Unfortunately going up, it plays backwards and it's not the same effect."

The passengers again took out their phones to photograph the cottage on the hill. Marjorie posed and pointed at the cottage. She noted Fairview Island coming up on the other side with a beautiful home right on the water. She began to point towards it when she felt something land in her hair. She reached up to touch it gently. It was sticky. The Birders were instantly there.

"That was an Ivory Gull!" The woman screamed. The man was smelling her hair. "This is the best trip ever!"

Marjorie took her hand away from her head and the man's nose.

"An Ivory Gull?" she asked, wiping her hand on her jacket.

"Yes!" said the man, clapping his hands and jumping from foot to foot. "So amazing!"

Marjorie smiled and pointed the two back to their seats. She hoped they wouldn't notice the empty chairs at the front. "I was just about to say, if you look towards beautiful Fairview Island ..." she stopped. Pulling up alongside the starboard was a smaller boat with a large decal "Police" on the hull. "Uhh ..." she murmured and trailed off.

"Are you Marjor?" a man yelled from the boat. He was dressed in a police uniform under a life preserver. Marjorie just stared at him for a minute, refusing to believe that she was somehow being pulled over by the police with two missing passengers.

"Marjorie," she corrected.

"Oh, it says 'Marjor' on your life preserver, I just assumed," the man continued.

"Oh! Yes," she said, "I ran out of paint. This is Marjorie's Major Muskoka Meander, we're a tour boat," she explained.

"Interesting," said the police officer, who appeared completely not interested. "Do you have fifteen meters of rope?" he asked.

"I do!" said Marjorie, excited. She looked back to see the captain carefully taking stuffed bags from the engine compartment and dropping them off the back of the boat. Her eyes went wide and she immediately turned back to the police officer. "Is that why you stopped us?" she asked, trying to draw his eyes to her.

"No," the officer said. He had started to look towards the back of the boat following her gaze, but his eyes came back to her. "There has been a series of thefts along Lake Rousseau. We believe the thieves are coming from boats and breaking into cottages, then leaving again on the water."

Marjorie instantly thought of the Frogs. Oh no. "Well we're a pleasure cruise, certainly not robbing any cottages or anything like that," she said with more belief than she felt.

"If you come across a boat without any occupants, we'd appreciate it if you called the O.P.P.," the officer said.

"Absolutely!" said Marjorie.

The Girl Guides burst in, "Did you feel this boat was up to code?"

"We noticed that you didn't board, is that because you were concerned?" said the other.

"No, no," said the officer, attempting to placate them. "I'm sure you're fine with Major here."

"Marjorie," Marjorie interjected.

"Right," said the officer. "You all have a great day on the water, and be safe." He pushed the small craft away and they heard its engine fire to life.

Marjorie's Major Muskoka Meander began to follow the shore line again. Marjorie pointed out Nicholas Cage's summer home, a cabin that had belonged to the late Walt Disney and was starting to think she needed to pull out a rock star when it began.

"There's a boat out there with nobody in it!" It was one of the birders, their binoculars trained on a small cabin boat in the middle of the lake. Majorie put her hand up to her brow and looked at the boat. It was rocking side to side with the waves, but it was also rocking from bow to stern.

"Oh, I'm pretty sure there are at least two people in that boat," she commented.

"We need to signal the police!" shouted Mrs. Girl Guide. She suddenly had a large orange flare gun in her hand.

"Where did you get that!" Marjorie shouted. The woman wasn't paying any attention to her. She closed her eyes, turned her head away from the flare gun and fired with a loud thunk. The flare drove straight into her husband's life jacket, bouncing roughly into his seat and then falling onto the floor. Mr. Girl Guide stepped back before his knees hit the gunwale and he fell legs kicking out of the boat. Mrs. Girl Guide opened her eyes to discover what she had done. She screamed loudly.

"I got this!" yelled Marjorie grabbing the lifesaving hook and pole from the side of the boat.

The flare rolled on the wet deck of the boat and fell into the hole where the captain sat. He screamed as his bags began to quickly catch fire.

Marjorie was attempting to get the large shepherd's crook through the poles that held up the roof and managed to jam the hook right through the cloth roof. The hook twisting was now nested on the top of the cloth. She yanked at it and a large portion of the roof tore down with it.

"For f...reedom's sake," she moaned, attempting to turn the large pole to get the hook near the splashing Mr. Girl Guide. Mrs. Girl Guide was now holding the other end of the pole and couldn't seem to figure out that it was not helping.

"Oh my!" shouted Mr. Birder. "I think that's an American Avocet!" He was jumping up and down and pointing, smoke beginning to wrap around him from the fire in the stern.

The captain grabbed the burning flare and threw it back onto the deck. He began to pat furiously on his bags of narcotics. "No, no, no," was all he kept repeating.

The flare rolled up to the torn roof and began to shower it with red light.

"Your little fire," said Mrs. Birder, "is causing too much smoke. We can't see the Avocet." She bent down and began to throw the flaming bags out into the lake.

"Noooo!" yelled the Captain, "that's all I have left!" He lept into the lake after his contraband. His foot caught the rutter as he dove and caused the boat to go into a sharp turn.

Mr. Birder immediately tumbled over one side while his wife fell off the other.

Marjorie was brought to her knees as she attempted to stay in the craft. Luckily the long lifesaving pole gave her more balance. However as she yanked it to center herself it pulled Mrs. Girl Guide with it. She stumbled across the deck, giving Marjorie what she would later call a "look of utter disgust and vileness", before grabbing the gunwale and flipping over into the water.

The boat spun in a few ever widening circles before crashing into a rocky outcrop and coming to a sudden stop. Marjorie found herself suddenly on her bottom. She could see water swelling up from the stern. At least that will put out the fire, she thought.

She lifted herself to her feet. There were rocks from here to the shore. Her beautiful boat was sinking in a three feet of water. She sighed. Looking back at the boat, she noted the last tatters of the roof blow out onto the lake, burning until they hit the water.

"That was amazing!" came a voice.

She had forgotten all about The Residents.

They came forward and stepped out onto the rocks. "We will highly recommend this tour."

Marjorie looked at them with a blank stare.

"This is our cottage," said one. "We're home!"

Marjorie felt a drop on her hair, and a shout from the water "The American Avocet! We *have* to take this tour again!"

WHO	WHEN	RATING

Notes:

☆☆☆☆☆

Notes:

☆☆☆☆☆

Notes:

☆☆☆☆☆

Notes:

☆☆☆☆☆

Notes:

☆☆☆☆☆

Notes:

☆☆☆☆☆

Notes:

☆☆☆☆☆

Notes:

☆☆☆☆☆

The Cabin Commute

There's only one way to enjoy that four hour road trip up to the cottage. Once you find all the words, the first set of remaining letters will spell it out for you. All of the following are cottage related words have been hidden in the grid below. They may be forwards, backwards, vertical, horizontal or diagonal. Some letters may be used more than once. Try to find them all.

```
F H R T S I L Y A L P P O L E
A I O R R P O T S T S E R A Y
E K A E B A R B E Q U E E E E
L E D T E R U T N E V D A S S
E H T A E R B L I G K C O D P
L S R W F L A S H R A O E M Y
A N I X L U U I S I M E U I W
K O P A H M N N N L R J R R O
E I F A M I L Y U L O V E G O
K T O E H X G M S O M T V P D
U C R K N U B H C I T D I E S
M E E X H A L E W I P C R R O
A R S G O L A S R A N I B A C
P I T T E N T C L I Y E E L K
L D S T R E A M C H O T D O G
```

ADVENTURE	FUN	POLE
BARBEQUE	GRILL	RAIN
BREATHE	HIGHWAY	RESTSTOP
BUNK	HIKE	RIVER
CABIN	HOTDOG	ROADTRIP
CRITTER	JUMP	SEAL
DEER	LAKE	STREAM
DIRECTIONS	LEAF	SUMMER
DOCK	LOGS	SUNSHINE
ELK	LOVE	SWIM
EXHALE	MAP	TENT
EYESPY	MOOSE	WATER
FALL	OCEAN	WOODS
FAMILY	PICNIC	
FOREST	PLAYLIST	

Lake Funshine

Kenneth Roland

Harry had never actually been water-skiing before. But how hard can it be? He'd been skiing, and he'd been swimming. This was just swim-skiing. Nothing about water-skiing looked very hard. You leaned back, and you held on. Those were basically the only rules to the entire thing.

The invitation to Ryan and Anita's cottage had been a welcome break to the summer. When they had mentioned the water-skiing originally, Harry had still been daydreaming about having a Scotch on the dock at sunset. He'd simply nodded his head as they went on about "how much fun it would be", and how he was going "love it".

Harry had enjoyed riding in the boat while Anita showed off her skills on the water. Sliding the skis back and forth behind the boat, launching into the air as she crested the wake. It looked like fun. For somebody else. When it came to his turn, he had tried to use the old "bad knee", then the "upset stomach", finally the "lost my grandmother in a water-ski accident", but they were having nothing of it. Now they had left him on the dock, the comfort of the boat only seventy-five feet away.

He squished his feet into the skis rubber booties. Gross. Clinging to the tow rope, he jumped off the dock. His life jacket causing him to bob in the water. He was feeling better about this already. He looked at the boat and saw Ryan and his wife Anita waving at him. He took his hand off the tow bar for a moment to give them a thumbs up. Ryan returned the thumbs up and turned back to the controls. Anita just continued to wave.

Harry saw the water turn white behind the boat before he felt the pull. The front of the boat lifted into the air and Ryan began to adjust the trim. The rope quickly went taut and Harry felt the pull as the tow bar began to lunge forward. He shoved his legs in front of him in the water. He was surprised how fast his body began to lift itself. His head had been the only thing exposed, but suddenly he was above the water from the waist up. He tried to stay calm as he noticed the number of people on the beach watching him.

Harry's skis came out of the water and began to skim along the surface. As they bounced and shook he quickly realized he had to adjust his footing to keep them more level with the water, not digging into it. As he watched the skis he realized he was starting to lean forward and shifted his weight. One hand left the tow bar and cart wheeled broadly as he attempted to keep his balance. When he returned his hand to the bar, he could hear cheers from the beach. Looking over, he noticed about half the people on the beach seemed to be watching him. Didn't they have anything better to do.

Suddenly his skis launched over the wake of the boat and he was airborne. Harry's head instantly swiveled back to the water in front of him. Ryan had apparently put the boat into a wide turn. The boat was headed across the lake perpendicular to the way Harry was heading. Knuckles tightening he began to bend his knees and adjust the skis to deal with the turn.

Harry watched as the boat lazily turned to head back up the lake. He felt confident that he would be able to adjust to such a light curve. He was stunned as his speed began to pick up. The skis began to skip across the water rapidly, bouncing him around as the tow rope suddenly snapped towards the boat. He lifted his right leg in an attempt to keep his balance and was stunned to see the wooden ski keep going down the lake away from him. He was now heading in a wide circle at a blistering speed with one foot held awkwardly out beside him. He shifted his weight over to the other ski.

Harry couldn't believe the force of his turn. His eyes wide, he gripped the tow bar tightly as he was flung around the apex. His one ski was skipping across the water and he could see the next wave of the wake of the boat coming towards him. He flew into the air as he hit the wave. The remaining ski took off on its own towards the beach on the far side of the lake. Harry did a full spin in the air, legs flying over his head and back down. The tow bar twisted in his hands and came back in front of him. Harry's head was spinning as he landed on his feet and was surprised to find that they didn't immediately drop into the water. His heels began to skip along the top of the water, following the boat. Harry didn't have time to think about the pain. He could hear people cheering from the beach, but he ignored that too. His only thoughts were on staying upright. His back wriggled as he adjusted to his new situation, flip-flopping from straight to hunched as he struggled to keep himself upright.

He looked up long enough to see Anita giving him a thumbs up from the boat. Harry just glared at her, not willing to take a hand off the tow rope to show a thumbs down, signaling to stop the boat. Ryan glanced behind him and gave a wave. Harry just shook his head. Ryan pointed to the crowd on the beach. There were a lot of them now. Sun bathers and swimmers standing along the edge, clapping and cheering for him. His pride began to swell. Maybe he was doing awesome. He should stop being afraid and enjoy his ability. Carefully letting go of the bar with one hand he waved at the crowd. He would look back on that as a horrible idea.

Harry's body began to twist as the tow rope pulled him forward. He launched into the air, completely horizontal for a moment. "I'm flying!" he thought briefly, his one arm stretched out in front of him, the other still attempting to wave at the crowd. He quickly brought it back to the tow bar as his stomach hit the water. He skipped like a stone across the waves, his stomach absorbing the impact each time. The crowd on the shore began to cheer so loud Harry could hear them, but he was more concerned about keeping his head up. He attempted to flip himself, like he was tossing in bed. As his body skipped off the water he quickly twisted and managed to rotate himself to his back.

The next time he hit the water, his bathing suit was yanked down to his ankles. He managed to catch it on one foot, lifting it into the air. It flapped like a flag from his upraised leg. The crowd on the shore cheered loudly as they watched Harry go past, flag raised, naked body bouncing across the water.

Harry's body continued skipping across the lake, the roar of the cheering crowd mixing with the sound of water slapping his back. His bathing suit, still flapping proudly from his ankle, seemed to be the pinnacle of entertainment for the beachgoers.

"Harry!" Anita shouted from the boat, finally realizing something was wrong. "Should we stop?"

Ryan turned to watch his buddy bounce once more into the air.

Harry's face was plastered with equal parts terror and disbelief as he was dragged along like an unwilling Olympic flag bearer. He flailed his free leg and managed to fling the bathing suit into the air. It landed with a squish on the head of a pair of teenagers following on a Sea-doo. They screamed and turned sharply, dropping them both into the water.

Ryan finally eased off the throttle, but the sudden deceleration of the boat did nothing for Harry. He skipped twice more, his final impact launching him like a human torpedo into the shallows near the beach.

Harry stood up, covered in seaweed, water dripping off every part of him. The crowd erupted into thunderous applause. A kid running up to thrust a half-eaten popsicle into his hand like a trophy.

"Legend!" someone shouted.

"Encore!" yelled another.

Harry, clutching the popsicle in one hand and attempting to cover himself with the other, looked back at the boat where Anita was laughing so hard she was doubled over, and Ryan gave him a sheepish thumbs up. He took a deep breath, raised the popsicle high, and gave the crowd a bow.

As the applause grew louder, Harry muttered under his breath, "Maybe next time, I'll stick to paddleboarding."

Lake Funshine

WHO	WHEN	RATING

Notes:

☆☆☆☆☆

Notes:

☆☆☆☆☆

Notes:

☆☆☆☆☆

Notes:

☆☆☆☆☆

Notes:

☆☆☆☆☆

Notes:

☆☆☆☆☆

Notes:

☆☆☆☆☆

Notes:

☆☆☆☆☆

Tiles and Tiles of Smiles

Unscramble the tiles to create a phrase. You may be smiling now, but this puzzle may drive you crazy.

Each tile is only used once. Use the spacing, punctuation and common words to find adjacent tiles. Some words may be split onto two lines.

U T		O N	S E		T O		S U	C A U	I S		L O P
T H E	T U R	P	F		Y O	L E		D O N	G	A	F L I
I S	N ,	N D	U Z Z	N I N	P U T	N D		T H E			
S	A	E R		W E	U R	H E A	D	O	S	P	T H I
A T H	E										

Till We Meet Again

Stephen Young

Till sat cross-legged on his cot, patiently waiting for the gaoler to make his rounds. To pass the time, he plucked straw from the mattress and tied it into little people. By the time his cell was checked on, Till had managed to create a small village's worth of little straw people. They were gathered around him on the cell floor in a little semi-circle, as if waiting for an announcement. Did that make him their mayor? So caught up in his creation was Till, that he was quite startled at the rapping of a baton on the bars of his cell door.

"Oi! What're you doin' in there?" The gaoler's voice was both higher-pitched and younger than Till had imagined. In his mind's eye, all gaolers were grizzled and gruff, and this lad with the keys to his cell was unfortunately not living up to his expectations. Till looked at the gaoler, who watched him through the bars.

"I was about to give my inaugural speech." Till smiled and waved a hand to gesture at his arranged villagers, waiting as patiently for his speech as Till had waited for the guard. The gaoler's reply was a look of stupid confusion; it appeared well-practiced.

"What? Who are you? What're you doing in this cell?" At the gaoler's questions, Till did his best to reply with the same look of stupid confusion but found it difficult to look quite that stupid or confused.

"I'm your prisoner. This is my cell."

"No, you ain't. How'd you get in here?"

Till answered with his most winning smile.

"Since I'm not your prisoner, will you let me out?"

The guard's eyes narrowed in suspicion.

"I never said that... What're you in here for?"

"Ah, it was worth a shot." Till scratched his chin and thought about his answer.

"Breaking and entering, I suppose." Till plucked some more straw from his cot and started making another villager. The gaoler watched him quietly for a minute, then walked away, muttering at Till to stay where he was.

Till didn't like being told what to do. Once the gaoler's footsteps had faded away, Till abandoned making a straw villager. Instead, he unwound his work and then started shaping and tying the straw into the shape of a key. Once his key was finished, Till got off his cot. Then, careful not to step on any villagers, he made his way to the cell door and slipped his key into the matching hole. Before turning the key, Till looked over his shoulder at the assembled villagers.

"Terribly sorry, instead of an inauguration, you're getting an abdication. May whoever follows in my wake be twice as kind and half as handsome." Then with a twist and a click, Till was out of his cell.

Till wandered the halls of the dungeon, peeking into the various cells to see who lived within; avoiding the occasional patrol by ducking into the shadows. It wasn't long before an alarm was raised. A bell was ringing vigorously, and shouts of 'escape' echoed down the halls. An escaped prisoner sounded like a dangerous prospect, so Till let himself into the nearest cell and locked the door behind him. As Till watched through the bars of the cell, hoping to catch a glimpse of the escapee, there was a polite cough from behind him. Till spun on his heel in surprise and was met with the sight of an equally surprised old man standing in the corner of the cell. The man was thin, with a white beard that hung low on his chest. His clothes were threadbare, his shoes nonexistent.

"Terribly sorry," said Till, "I didn't realize this room was taken." And he turned to leave. As Till did, the old man held up a hand.

"Oh! Please wait a moment. I don't get many guests."

Till stopped, cocked his head in thought, and put one finger to his pursed lips. "Is it visiting hours? I'd hate to get you in any trouble by breaking the rules."

The old man appeared to mull over his choice of words for a moment. "I don't believe there to be any rules governing visiting hours here. I've simply never had anybody care to visit me."

Till considered the old man's answer, then smiled and gave a nod. "I accept your offer of hospitality!"

The old man smiled and clapped his hands, then hurried over to a small wooden table near the cot. On the table was a jug and a single fired clay cup. The old man filled the cup from the jug, then offered the cup to Till.

"Watered wine. All I have to offer, I'm afraid."

Till received the cup in both hands graciously, dipped his head in thanks, and sipped the offering. "It's the finest wine I've drunk since I've been here, thank you."

At this, the corner of the old man's mouth quirked into a half-smile. "Have you had much wine since you've been here?"

"This is the first."

"So it's also the worst wine you've drunk since you've been here?"

"Well, yes, but that didn't seem as polite to say." Till took another sip of the wine. "I've yet to learn my host's name, which is uncommon."

The old man hesitated. "I am Albus."

Till swirled the wine in his cup. "Just Albus?"

"Is more than Albus safe?"

"While I am bound by the laws of hospitality? Of course!"

"Would you share your full name in turn?"

Till grinned at the wily old man. "Of course not! I don't plan on staying here. I've decided that prison is boring. I spent most of the day just sitting around. Just Albus is perfectly fine." Till stuck out his hand. "I am Till."

The old man took the offered hand and shook it. "Pleasure to meet you, Till. Welcome to my cell."

There were no chairs in the cell, so they sat cross-legged on the floor and talked. Till emptied the cup of wine, and Albus refilled it. Till insisted that Albus drink, and when it was empty, the cup was refilled and passed back to Till. They talked and drank. Albus did most of the talking. Till had endless questions for the old man about the life he'd led and the things he'd seen. Albus, for his part, had lived a lot of life and seen a lot of things. At one point, as the old man filled his cup again, he commented that he swore he'd only had one or two cups worth left in the jug, but somehow they'd been drinking for what felt like hours. Till raised his hands in a "who knows?" gesture and gave a wink.

Till and Albus were interrupted by a young man's voice shouting. "He's here!"

When Till turned his head to see who it was, the room kept spinning for a moment. Even the thinnest of wines will get to the most practiced of drinkers, given enough volume. Squinting to help focus his eyes in the same direction, Till recognized the face of the young gaoler he'd spoken with earlier. The young man appeared to be fumbling with some keys. Looking back at Albus, and gesturing towards the guard, Till asked, "Is he invited?"

Albus laughed. "No, he most certainly is not."

The gaoler found the key he was looking for, and the cell door clicked and swung open.

Albus made a shooing gesture with one hand.

"Please leave, you're spoiling our good time." The gaoler ignored the old man, stepped forward, and raised a baton to strike Till. With a speed that defied Albus' apparent age, emaciation, and drunkenness, the old man jumped to his feet and put himself between Till and the gaoler. The young guard didn't hesitate; he struck the old man on the side of the head, and Albus fell to the ground, limp and still. Till looked at Albus, then up at the gaoler.

"Oh, that won't do at all." The gaoler raised his baton to strike again, and as he did so, Till raised an open hand towards the young man.

"Sleep," he commanded.

The gaoler slumped to the floor, his baton rattling against the stone. Till then turned his attention to his host. He gently placed one hand on the old man's shoulder. Till gave a little shake, then called out softly.

"Albus." Another gentle shake. "Albus, wake up." The old man woke with a start and a sharp inhale of breath. He sat up slowly, looked at the sleeping guard, then at Till, who sat cross-legged next to him, unmoved from his spot. With a shaking hand, Albus touched his head where he'd been struck with the baton, and it came back wet with blood, but there was no pain of injury. There was a question in Albus' eyes, so Till answered it, in his own way.

"I can't have you put me in your debt like that, then go and die so I can't repay you. That just won't do at all."

Albus blinked and shook his head in an attempt to clear it of the alcohol and recent head trauma.

"Is there a boon that you desire, Albus? If it's within my power to grant, it's yours."

The two of them locked eyes for a moment; it did not take long for the old man to decide.

"I want to go home. I wish to be free of this cell and to go home. And I'd like for you to visit me again, so we can share stories and drink wine."

Till gave Albus his most winning smile. "It shall be done. Until we meet again."

Albus didn't remember leaving the dungeon. He had only the fuzziest notion of returning home. His cottage was just as he'd left it, which was a pleasant surprise. The months he'd spent imprisoned had not been long enough for father time to do his terrible work. Albus set about tidying up. Even if the place hadn't gotten run down, he hadn't planned on being away for so long.

By the time Albus was satisfied with the state of his cottage, the hour was late. Albus slept in his own bed for the first time in months and dreamt of Till. Albus dreamt of boys playing pranks, wives telling their husbands jokes, girls tricking their friends, and of men drinking and telling stories with exaggerated details. His dreams shifted and moved from scene to scene, but in each one, Till was there. Not as a person, but as a feeling, as a thing Albus knew, as one does in dreams.

Albus did not remember his dream upon waking. He didn't remember getting released from prison. He told himself that he must have been released and never questioned the gaps in his memory. Albus went back to his life as he'd been living it before, hunting, trapping, foraging, and selling the fur to the nearby town. Life kept the old man occupied, and he spent little time reflecting on his time locked in the dungeon. Though he was far more cautious about not placing his traps on the lord's property.

Seasons passed, winter came. One evening Albus sat by the light of a candle reading a book of fairy tales. During his last trip into town there'd been a travelling merchant and among his various wares, he'd had this book. Typically, Albus could not have afforded such a luxury, but the merchant was willing to part with the book for a single fox fur.

One of the stories told of a trickster spirit, one that revelled in pranks and rejected authority. It was a story his mother had told him as a child. The telling was slightly different in the book, but it was familiar nonetheless. As he read the story again, there was a knock at his door. Albus startled at the sound, nobody came to visit him. A voice with a hint of song called out to him.

"Albus! Open up! I've brought wine!"

WHO	WHEN	RATING

Notes:

☆☆☆☆☆

Notes:

☆☆☆☆☆

Notes:

☆☆☆☆☆

Notes:

☆☆☆☆☆

Notes:

☆☆☆☆☆

Notes:

☆☆☆☆☆

Notes:

☆☆☆☆☆

Notes:

☆☆☆☆☆

What do you want to do?

Unscamble each of the words, then use the circled letters to unscramble the final phrase. Good luck!

OAGLON

FMCEAPIR

ANTSHU

CIBAN

NSMLOA

OESTFR

WDSOO

GFRO

LNDASI

Under Plants

Kenneth Roland

The doctor looked directly into David's eyes. He was afraid to look anywhere else. David was covered in plants. From head to toe: ferns, ficus, and fungi.

"Lots of people talk to their plants, Doc. It's not that unusual." David had agreed to this counseling only for his wife.

She sat on the couch next to him. Her face; a combination of dismay, disbelief, and disgust. She pulled the bottom of her lavender skirt down and crossed her legs. "Nobody believes their plants talk back to them, David." She spit out his name.

"We don't know that, Karen." He tried to put the same disdain into her name, but failed.

The doctor interrupted. "Taking the idea of the plants talking back to you offline for a moment, what made you decide you needed to start … wearing them?"

David looked down. It was as though he just realized he was wearing plants and was shocked to find them wrapped around him. "I don't know," he stuttered. "I was talking to Fernando — that's my Boston Fern."

"I guessed that," said the Doctor, "I actually named mine the same thing."

"Right!" David confirmed. "So I gave Fernando his water. It was summer, so I watered him Tuesdays and Saturdays."

"Great, great," the Doctor encouraged him.

"I turned to Lilly — that's my Peace Lily."

"Oh, you're a creative genius," Karen mocked.

"I don't see you coming up with any of the names!" David turned to her.

"You named your Philodendron 'Phil' and your Pothos 'Porthos,'" she said exasperatedly, her hands flying up towards the doctor in a gesture of disbelief.

"Porthos was one of the three musketeers!" David said defiantly.

"And you named your Aloe Vera 'Athos', and your Anthurium 'Aramis'. You got stuck on a theme! I was very surprised when you didn't call your snake plant D'Artagnan!" Karen cried out.

"My snake plant was already named Snakey." He turned back to the doctor, "Snakey was my first."

"You told me I was your first," Karen muttered under her breath, arms now crossed.

"To get back to the story," the Doctor interjected, "You turned to Lilly …" He eyed Karen, daring her to break in again.

"Yes, I turned to Lilly, and from behind me I heard, 'Take me with you.'" David began again. "It was faint and like a whistling kind of speech, but it was very clear. Take me with you."

"And you believe the plant said this?" The doctor asked.

"Yes, not just any plant, I believe that Fernando said it."

"Right, Fernando."

"I ignored it at first. I mean it's crazy to think plants can talk."

"Exactly!" Karen broke in and the doctor snapped his eyes to hers with a glare.

David saw the look and decided to ignore his wife. It was nice to have the attention of someone willing to listen to his story. "Thank you doctor," he said. He continued, "I was telling Lilly how beautiful she looked that day." He ignored a moan from beside him on the couch. "And how she was doing great. I had been worried that she was root bound. I really felt like she was doing better."

"That sounds like good news," said the Doctor.

"It was. I was really proud. So I was moving on to Snakey and the Succulents, it's like a band," David chuckled. No one else did.

"I wasn't going to water them, they don't need that much, but I heard it again. Take me with you. It was still a quiet whistle of a voice, but higher. I just knew it had to be Lilly."

"Interesting," the doctor nodded.

"At first I didn't do anything. Every day I kept hearing, 'Take me with you.' It began to keep me awake at night. I needed a solution. My plants obviously needed help."

"The plants needed help?" The doctor questioned.

"Exactly." David looked down at the plants now wrapped around him. He lifted an arm that dripped philodendron and gazed at the leaves. "They needed my help," he said quietly.

For a moment there was a pause in the room. The doctor and his wife waited for him to continue. Both of their faces were skeptical, and the doctor's mouth twitched a bit.

David's head bobbed up and he looked around. "So that's when I invented the dirt boots."

"The dirt boots?" questioned the doctor.

"Yeah," replied David, "they are basically boots, but they have an outer liner that holds dirt. That way the plants can still be safely rooted while they travel with me."

The doctor looked down at the boots David was wearing. They looked like oversized garden shoes. Bright white foamy rubber, with a fold just above the sole where the stalks of the plants rose from. "Aren't they hard to drive in?"

"Oh! I don't drive anymore. The plants don't like it. You know, the environment," he explained, "they like the light rail or just walking."

"Interesting," said the doctor. "At what point did you decide to stop wearing regular clothing underneath the plants?"

Karen's eyes rolled back in her head. "You're not wearing any clothes under those plants?" She exclaimed.

"You'd know that if you looked at me once in a while!" David shouted back. "At least the doctor realized."

"Yes," sighed the doctor. "I did notice."

"It didn't make sense to have clothes on, not when the plants completely covered me!"

"It's not hygienic!" Karen shouted. "There's nothing between you and the couch except a few African Violets?!" She shifted away from him.

"I change my underplants every day!" David shouted. He shifted his own posterior causing a squeaky sound to emanate from the couch.

The doctor was staring blankly at the couple on the couch in front of him. His eyes were blank and his mouth was just a thin line across his face.

After realizing what he was doing, he shifted in his own chair. He pulled his notebook up a little and pretended to write in it.

"The plants needed me!" David said. "They were stuck in that house, barely getting any light most of the time. They wanted out! They wanted to feel the rain on their appendages."

"Then take them outside!" Karen retorted. "You don't need to wrap them around your body. They were in pots. You can just take them outside, show them the world, give them their freedom."

"They wanted to come with me," David said frustrated. "You aren't getting this. It's a symbiotic relationship. My plants help me and I help my plants."

The doctor sat up, suddenly interested. "Symbiotic? In what way? You're giving your plants a free ride, what do they give back to you?"

"Joy!" David said, getting excited again. "I don't just give them a free ride, I nourish them, and they nourish me."

"They nourish you?" Karen asked.

David reached into an Asparagaceae pocket, and pulled out a pea pod. Deftly he split the pod with his thumb and scooped the contents into his mouth. As he chewed he looked from doctor to wife. Proud, defiant eyes daring them to comment.

"And how exactly do you nourish them?" Questioned the doctor slowly.

"OH MY GOD! You poop your plants!" Karen jumped off the couch and backed away.

"It's not the same!" David spat. "I told you I change my underplants every day! They channel the fertilizer down into the boots."

"Those peas you just ate … they grew in your own …" Karen shuddered and turned away. She couldn't look at him anymore.

"Doc, you get this right?" David exclaimed standing up from the couch. His plants dangled and shifted around him. "Some people have implants, I'm literally in plants! It's all organic! Why can't people understand!"

The doctor was back to staring. He could see the hair around David's belly button in front of him. He watched as a vine slowly passed over the region and tightened against the skin. He blinked a few times. David and Karen were yelling now in a storm of insults and issues that had taken years to build up and were finally exploding, here in his office.

"I … I don't think I can help you," he stammered. Neither spouse heard him as they lashed back and forth. "I'm going to give you two some time!" He said loudly, standing up.

The pair stopped, and turned to him. "I need to go water Fernando, you two take some time to calm down. And David … "

David stopped gesticulating to look at the doctor.

The doctor pointed to David's posterior where a white pod was pushing itself out from the foliage into the light. "I think you're blooming."

WHO	WHEN	RATING

Notes:

☆☆☆☆☆

Notes:

☆☆☆☆☆

Notes:

☆☆☆☆☆

Notes:

☆☆☆☆☆

Notes:

☆☆☆☆☆

Notes:

☆☆☆☆☆

Notes:

☆☆☆☆☆

Notes:

☆☆☆☆☆

Half of a Triangle

Kenneth Roland

I reached back around the bar stool and checked if my smokes were in my jacket. Don't know why, I was just going to check again after I put my jacket on. Maybe it was some of that obsessive compulsive personality disorder that people were talking about. I slipped a twenty onto the bar and put my empty pint glass on top of it, nodding at Christine. A full pint will have magically appeared by the time I got back from my fresh air break.

I spun and slid, shoveling my jacket on as I got off the bar stool. I tapped the buffalo plaid coat in the modern sign of the cross; smokes, phone, wallet, keys. All good to head out onto the chilly wood deck that surrounded two sides of the pub. Smoking was bad for you. You knew it, because they made you go outside. "Be sure to close that door when you go!" Christine shouted, placing a sweating new pint on a cardboard coaster and swiping away the cash and empty. I pulled my toque out of my back pocket and nodded as I pulled it on. The pub was just about empty. It was still early. The Denton brothers, Paul and

Chip were holding down the gleaming bar with their elbows. They were quiet boys, unless the drink got into them. At that moment, they appeared to be deep in a debate between themselves. They had a lobster license. If I had a lobster license I wouldn't have to do the world tour tickets on the ocean freighters.

The weather wasn't great, but it was certainly better here than out on the water. I cupped my hand to protect the flame of the lighter as I pulled on my smoke. I should've waited and brought my beer with me, but it was nice to lean on the deck rail and think. The pub had a dirt drive off a paved road. People liked to call it the highway, 'cause the speed limit was 80 km/h and it was the only road in town that had any lines painted on it. Jerry Pinnacle had spent three large on a paint sprayer and was paid a third of that to paint the lines. The sprayer was in his shed now.

There wasn't much to see beyond the road except pine trees. Gave you time to think, when you had nothing to look at. Staring at trees or staring at the waves, it was all the same to me. I know there's people that don't like being in their head all the time. I prefer it. Thinking about nothing, maybe I just meditated naturally, I don't know.

A raccoon sat across the road at the edge of the woods. He was chewing on something. Maybe it was a her? I don't know much about raccoons. It eyed me the same way I was eyeing it. Just leave me alone and we're fine.

The coughing sputter and rattle of a car on its last tank of gas made me look down the road. An old Buick Skylark, that should've been a metal cube 20 years ago rolled onto the gravel. I thought Junior would've pushed that car into the bay by now, but here he was, the one working headlight shining on my face as he slid to a stop on the gravel.

"Now, look who's back," he shouted as he jumped out of a door that screeched in protest. Junior had never heard of the word subtle. He was still wearing his high visibility gear from head to toe. His voice was so loud I wouldn't be surprised if my neighbours knew I was back now. I hadn't been to the house yet, a gym bag of clothes sat next to my bar stool inside. "You are not going to believe this one bud," he said too loudly, stomping up onto the deck. "You're not leaving are ya? Got time for a beer, eh?"

I nodded and stuck out my hand, which he ignored and wrapped me in his big arms. The man was a giant, likely the offspring of Paul Bunyon and Big Joe Mufferaw. Junior gave the type of hugs that were genuine and life threatening. Squeezing you so tight you came out of the experience a different shape. He had barely let me go before he started, "So you know Jerry? Not Jerry Pinnacle, but Jerry - that's the girl?" I nodded and tried to get a puff in, hoping my lungs still worked in their new location. I noticed the raccoon had left. Wish I could do that.

"Well I got an eyeful of her the other day, walking back from the lighthouse. She was walking, I mean, not me!" He let out a guffaw so loud the Denton brothers turned to look out the window to see what had caused the noise. I continued to nod. I'm known in town as a good listener, so people seem to tell me stories. It helps that I don't talk that much, so they feel they can tell me the real story without everyone else hearing it too. "Gawd, she's a beautiful girl, ain't she?" He wasn't looking for an answer and kept right on going. "It wasn't warm out, so I'm thinking I should pick her up. You know, the gentleman thing right?" I continued to nod and smoke, nod and smoke. I could see my beer through the window. Next time, I would definitely bring it out with me. My cigarette was down to the filter and he was still going. I walked over to the paint can filled with sand that was used as an ashtray. Junior managed to figure out the signal and finished off, "So Debbie is now all in a tizz about the whole thing," Debbie was Junior's wife. The woman had the patience of a saint. " I told her, 'Don't listen to the muck around town, I'd tell ya if there was somethin' goin' on with Jerry.' And that's where it's at. Deb's in a mood I'll tell ya. Anyway, just keep it to yourself eh, bud?"

I nodded bluntly and pulled the door open, waiting for him to go ahead.

"Oh, I gotta smoke first," Junior interjected, "I didn't have any in the car. You got one on ya?" I fished out the pack and made sure he had a light before heading in.

I left my mind alone while I enjoyed my pint. The old brain likes it that way. It can do whatever it wants while I'm busy having a few. At work, it's all mine, I need it sharp and focused. At home it gets to wander. Scurry around the dark expanse of my memories, yanking out odd nostalgia and holding it up, before moving on to something else. Junior eventually came in and headed to a booth. "Boys!" he yelled out loudly waving at the Dentons. He caught Christine's attention as he walked holding up two fingers. Junior was a big man in a small world. It's a world I came back to whenever I got the chance. Some characters were meant to dominate the scene, others were comedic relief, and some were just in the background, living their lives.

When Christine got back from taking a couple pints to Junior, she checked on the Denton boys and came down to me, "You got room for another, bud?" she asked, "There's still change on your tab."

I nodded and winked and slid off my stool. Throwing on my coat, I checked my pockets and then remembered my last outing. I turned and waited. "You can't leave the deck with this eh?" Christine said as she put the full glass on the bar. I nodded and winked again, heading outside. Coming in through the door was Jerry (Not Jerry Pinnacle, Jerry - that's the girl). I winced involuntarily as she ran up and threw her arms around me, carefully holding my pint up and out of the way.

"You goin' for a butt? I'll go with you! I didn't even know you were back." She spun on her boot heel and was out the door before it even closed.

I put my beer on the rail and brought out my pack. She didn't want one, so I lit my own. She seemed anxious, and didn't say a word until I was leaning on the rail, smoke blowing out of my nose. She got lost for a bit staring at Junior inside, then turned back to me. "So you know how I like to walk out to the lighthouse?" I nodded, but I had no idea. I'd only seen Jerry at the pub, and that wasn't anywhere near the lighthouse. I didn't even know what she did for a living, let alone what she enjoyed in her spare time.

"The other day I was out there … with a friend." She had hesitated. I turned an eye towards her. "I know, I know, all in good fun though, nothing crazy." She waved at the smoke, shooing it away. "Well, when I was walking back for a drink, who pulls up, but Junior." I raised my eyebrows appropriately for the amount of shock I was to display, as though I hadn't heard this already. "He's driving that piece of crap he calls a car, and pulls right up beside me." I felt like I knew this part, so I took a sip of my beer. Placing it back, I noted how the grain of the wood was really poppin' on the old rail. The maroon coloured stain was coming off in flakes. I poked one flake and it drifted off the edge and down to the gravel. The raccoon was back across the street. It was dragging a garbage bag with a hole in it through the ditch. That's the life. Just dragging your garbage bag full of treasure around. Something eventually twigged in my brain that the story was slowing, so I looked up at Jerry.

"So as I'm leaving the hair appointment, feeling great and looking the same," she paused to strike a pose, "I hear Jerry Pinnacle yell out his window, 'Shame, shame, everybody knows your name.' Obviously that gets me worried, you know? The dink has the same name as me anyway!" I nodded, I think everyone in town had already twigged to the fact that Jerry and Jerry had the same name. "Once they hear something at the hairdressers, the whole town is going to be talking about it, putting their own spin on what happened," she continued. I twitched my mouth and held up my half-full beer.

"Yeah, let's get inside, thanks for listening though, I appreciate it." With that she wrapped me up in a hug and with a knock, the half beer I had left shot straight up out of my cup. I tried to catch it in the glass, looking over her shoulder, but it was gone. It splattered against the rough wood of the deck. Oddly that spot now looked cleaner than the rest of the deck. I sighed, it was too early for the poor soul. "Pour soul", I smiled at my own wit. We went inside and I casually ignored her heading straight for the booth where Junior sat holding his head over a pint, an empty one sitting beside it.

I put my beer down on the coaster and tossed my coat over the stool back. The Boston game was starting on the TV hung behind the bar. Looked like they were playing Arizona. No idea what a city in the desert was doing with a hockey team. As I watched, I realized that Jerry was the perfect catalyst. She caused reactions, but somehow remained unchanged. She didn't mean to be the center of attention. In fact, actively avoid it. But if anyone came in contact with her, drama was instantly created and that person would never be the same again. I wondered briefly if good looks were a curse. You could never have a normal interaction with someone. Luckily I didn't have to worry about that. Maybe that's why raccoons wear the mask the whole time, no one can tell what they really look like.

By the end of the first period Boston was up, two-nothing, thanks to

Brad Marchand. Now that boy put the hooligan in Haligonian. I chuckled to myself. I could be pretty funny when my brain wasn't going. I wanted to pop out for a quick dart so I could be back to hear Ron McLean and his team during the break. I was already on my way to the door before I finished the sign of the cross.

Smoke hanging from my mouth, elbows on the rail, I watched the silhouette of the trees moving in the wind. The sun was behind them now, the day ending. I lost myself for a bit until an ash from the end of my cigarette landed on the back of my hand. Like a bee sting, I swatted my hand and waved it around.

"You waving at me?" It was a husky, female voice.

I grabbed the smoke out of my mouth and turned. Debbie, Junior's wife, was coming up onto the deck. I smiled as she came up, showing her my smoke like it explained everything. "Oh gawd, they're both in there!" she hissed. I followed her gaze through the window to the booth where Junior and Jerry sat (Not Jerry Pinnacle … well you know.) I shrugged and made a face. I hoped it said "What are you going to do?" I really wish I had one of those masks like the raccoon. I could probably get through a whole smoke without someone deciding they needed to share.

"I was talking to Margie at the post office, and she gave me a right earful about Junior's day." Again, I raised my eyebrows, but I felt my acting skills were failing me. I'll stick to amusing myself in the future. I still liked that 'pour soul' one. "Have you heard what he's been up to? Probably not, since you must've just got home!" She suddenly smiled and lifted her arms, "I'm sorry, I can't believe I didn't welcome you back before I started laying my troubles on your doorstep." She enveloped me in a hug that probably lasted longer than it should have ethically speaking.

She let go and looked in the window again. Suddenly she turned on me, causing me to jump. "I'm going to get this straightened out right now." She flung open the bar door. The twine that held the bell to let Christine know someone had entered snapped and the heavy bronze chime flung out onto the deck, bouncing to a stop by my boot. Well, this wasn't going to go well. Debbie was the type of character that forced herself into a situation. She didn't even need to even be in the scene to take control of it. I flicked my butt out into the parking lot and followed her in. I would've rather went over to see what the raccoon got from the garbage.

No one was looking at me thanks to Debbie's scene. I slid into my stool and pushed my coat off onto the back. Grabbing my glass I looked up at the TV. The closed captioning was talking about Marchand's second goal. Without any warning Christine's face loomed large right in front of me. The two Denton brothers had moved to the stools on either side of me. They leaned in close, eager to learn what I had heard outside.

"Hey," Christine whispered, "You got any insights into the triangle over in the corner?" She pointed towards the booth where Junior, (girl) Jerry, and Debbie sat. She covered her pointing hand behind the other, as though the three would have no idea we were about to discuss them. The fact that the only other people in the bar had suddenly gathered around my stool might have been a hint. I glanced over at the three. They were deep into something, and certainly not worried about us.

I realized that in every story, there had to be someone to consume it. These three at the bar were the consumers. They didn't have a part in the love triangle that the other three were dealing with. They didn't have any skin in the game as they say. They just wanted a good story. "I think I've got half of it," I said.

Christine, Paul, and Chip all leaned in closer, "Oh yeah? What's going on?" asked Paul.

"I need to quit smoking," I said.

Canoes & Coffee

WHO	WHEN	RATING

Notes:

☆☆☆☆☆

Notes:

☆☆☆☆☆

Notes:

☆☆☆☆☆

Notes:

☆☆☆☆☆

Notes:

☆☆☆☆☆

Notes:

☆☆☆☆☆

Notes:

☆☆☆☆☆

Notes:

☆☆☆☆☆

About the Authors

Kenneth Roland

Kenneth Roland grew up in St. Catharines, Ontario, Canada. He attended Westdale Primary School, West Park Secondary School and Niagara College Tertiary School. He has worked at a newspaper, pre-press shop, real estate office and ran his own tech company for 7 years. He now works in Waterloo, Ontario for tech startups, caring for and helping to create the culture of the tech world. He lives in Kitchener with his wife.

Dorian Blackwood

Dorian Blackwood is an aspiring author who grew up devouring books of all genres. Over time they were particularly drawn to darker tales, gothic novels and weird fiction. These stories introduced them to beings out of space and time, haunted houses, haunted people, and paintings that could capture the soul. When not reading, they love to sit down and tell stories with friends through table-top roleplay games. If they're not doing that, they can be found sewing up a storm in their craft room!

Matt Thurston

Matt, a recovering computer programmer, is spending his semi-retired years attempting to author more words than lines of code.

Kyle Rogers

Kyle Rogers resides in Wisconsin's Northwoods, where he spends as much time as possible outdoors — kayaking, camping and trail running in the spring, summer and fall; skiing and snowshoeing in the winter. But writing makes for a good indoor activity. To counter his day job as editor of trade magazines in the B2B publishing world, Kyle enjoys participating in various fiction writing competitions.

Stephen Young

Stephen Young is a Canadian writer and judo instructor whose speculative fiction explores the quiet tensions between the ordinary and the uncanny. His short stories "Till We Meet Again" and "Flytrap" appear in this collection. When not writing or teaching, he works as a 911 operator and occasionally remembers to sleep.

Hallie Ranta

Hallie lives in Cleveland, Ohio. Enjoys writing short stories and microfiction, often based on quirky prompts.

Steve Boose

Steve Boose has been telling stories his entire life; over almost thirty years of a preaching ministry and longer, he has connected with congregations and other audiences by analogizing the scriptural text with personal experiences, historical events, and characters and situations from fiction. He loves camping, especially with his wife, as his "happy place" is sitting by a fire, either reading, playing games on his phone, or just watching the flames dance. The father of three grown children, he is a new grandfather and cannot wait to share camping experiences with the next generation.